NEWLY WED

"I did not marry you to acquire a nurse," Simon said gruffly. He took her into his arms and his lips began plying small, disturbing kisses against the skin of her neck.

Miranda sat captive, able only to offer token protest. "A wife must worry after her husband's health. . . ."

"Does that mean satifying his every need?" His breath was warm on her ear as he spoke.

Miranda tried to keep her mind on the conversation to stop the strength from sapping from her limbs. "Now that I am your wife, Simon, I must see to your comfort, your hunger—" She grasped the straw of hope that came to her. "Are you hungry? Should we stop for the basket of delicacies that Cook prepared?"

He laughed low in his throat, and she could feel the vibration to her toes. "We agreed not to stop, except for fresh horses, but to press on so that we could reach home tonight. But I am hungry, wife." His arms seemed to tighten around her infinitesimally.

"Should I unpack the basket here, then?" Miranda pulled away to reach for the wicker container stored under the seat.

Simon pulled her back into his arms. His hands were gentle and warm on her hips as he settled her in his lap. She looked up into his eyes and recognized the passion glowing there. Her own senses ignited.

Feeling as if she was so warm she must burn him wherever she touched, she smiled and held herself still. Was it seemly to remember so vividly what had happened once, by mistake? To want it to happen again? She fought the urge to lean forward and press her lips to his. "If you are hungry, Simon, I must feed you."

Her heart beat harder when he leaned toward her to whisper, "Then kiss me, Miranda, for I am hungry for your touch."

Dear Romance Reader,

In July, we launched the Ballad line with four new series, and each month we'll present both new and continuing stories set everywhere from medieval England to the American West—the kind of passionate, romantic stories you love best, written by the most gifted authors. At the back of each book, we'll tell you when you can find subsequent books in the series that has captured your heart.

Beloved author Jo Ann Ferguson continues her *Shadow of the Bastille* series with **A Brother's Honor**, as a French privateer and the spirited daughter of an American ship captain brave Napoleon's blockade and discover the legacy that will shape their passionate destiny. Next, rising star Cynthia Sterling invites us back to the dusty Texas Panhandle as the second of her *Titled Texans* learns the ropes of ranching from an independent—and irresistibly attractive—woman who wants to become a lady in **Last Chance Ranch**.

Beginning this month is newcomer Tammy Hilz's breathtaking *Jewels of the Sea* series, a trilogy of three sisters who take their futures in their own hands—as pirates! In the first installment, a stubborn earl wonders if the fearless woman who was **Once A Pirate** will decide to become his bride. Finally, fresh talent Kelly McClymer introduces the unconquerably romantic Fenster family in her *Once Upon A Wedding* series, starting with a woman whose faith in happy endings is challenged as a man who refuses to believe in love asks her to become **The Fairy Tale Bride**. Enjoy!

Kate Duffy
Editorial Director

Once Upon a Wedding

THE FAIRY TALE BRIDE

Kelly McClymer

ZEBRA BOOKS
KENSINGTON PUBLISHING CORP.
http://www.zebrabooks.com

ZEBRA BOOKS are published by

Kensington Publishing Corp.
850 Third Avenue
New York, NY 10022

First Printing: October, 2000
10 9 8 7 6 5 4 3 2 1

Printed in the United States of America

Prologue

London, 1832

His damned boots were too tight.

Simon Watterly tried, discreetly, to move his tightly bound toes. Nothing. Tomorrow the boots would have to go back to the boot maker. One more delay he didn't want, didn't need. But a soldier needed a well-fitted pair of boots, and as of today, despite the Duke of Kerstone's vehement objections, Simon was an officer in His Majesty's service, bound for India. Too bad there was no good war on presently. He could only hope to find one soon.

He glanced around the crowded ballroom, his teeth clenched with the effort it took to project a bored yet pleasant facade. He had been raised to know his duty to the family name and would not dishonor it by making a scene. He had promised the duke. And Simon Watterly had been bred to make certain he always kept his promises and did his duty. Wouldn't want to tarnish the hallowed reputation of the former Dukes and Duchesses of Kerstone.

What a farce! It was truly bitter solace to realize that tonight was the last time he need pretend to be what these people thought him . . . what he had thought himself, until last night, when he had over-heard his mother's words to his dying father—no, to the Duke of Kerstone, no relation to himself—and his life had shattered in an instant.

If the dying man had not extracted a promise from him not to destroy the family reputation . . . but that was irrelevant. The duke had been frail and pitiful as he begged, pale blue eyes flowing with tears, his fingers a faint yet bony pressure on Simon's wrist. Simon could not withhold his promise to the man he had called father—but he would find a way to get around it—if a thugee or a blood-soaked battlefield didn't see to it for him, as it had for the older brother Simon had never known. His *legitimate* older brother, blown up by cannon blast in France while Simon was still a babe in arms.

An overly friendly blow to his arm made him spit out the bitter truth, "Bastard." He turned to glare at the offender.

"Take it easy there, Cousin, I merely wanted your attention." Giles Grimthorpe discreetly cocked his head in the direction of the crush of dancing figures. "I wondered if you would care to engage in a small wager to add piquancy to this dull evening?"

"What kind of wager?"

"A matter of a successful seduction, Cousin."

Simon grimaced at his cousin's expectant grin. No doubt the cad waited for a lecture. But today he would be surprised. An hour before, Simon had adjusted his cravat in the curved looking glass in the foyer of his parents' town house and promised himself that he would do everything in his power to destroy the image of fairness and propriety that had given those who knew him cause to call him saintly. And a good start to accomplish this aim would be to wager with his cousin. For Grimthorpe was a worse gossip than any of the bored dowagers seated about the room.

He lifted his shoulders as if mildly intrigued with the idea, as he said, "My ring if you succeed."

Grimthorpe's eyes narrowed in shock; then he eyed the large ruby and silver ring on Simon's left little finger. "Good thing you're to be the next Duke of Kerstone—and wealthy, as well, if you are to suddenly take up gambling on that scale."

Nettled, Simon lifted his hand so that the ruby glinted in the lights. He knew how much it irritated Grimthorpe that his branch of the family had fallen in society as Simon's had risen. For a moment he considered confiding the truth, but dismissed the idea. His cousin wouldn't appreciate the irony, but he would indeed cause a scandal. "Perhaps I don't expect to lose it."

A confident sneer appeared on Grimthorpe's fox-ish face. "The girl is odd—and plain besides. I have been showering her with attention these past weeks and now that she is ripe, I intend for her to fall into my arms."

"Indeed? And who is the lucky young woman, or are you keeping that secret to yourself?" He truly did not care. Any female who let Grimthorpe within two feet of her deserved any trouble that she might receive.

"The young miss who cannot seem to stop spouting fairy tales, of course. Miss Miranda Fenster."

For a moment, Simon thought he would not manage to master the rage and pain that twisted inside him. His cousin had no reason to know how his words struck at Simon's heart. In supreme irony, Grimthorpe had chosen to seduce the very woman Simon had planned to offer for—if he had not learned the truth of his birth. Rather than an engagement present, he had purchased a commission.

Seeing Grimthorpe waiting, Simon fought not to bring up his fists to erase the man's leer. If he were to be a devil, he must learn not to care. "I believe she has too much sense for that. But if not, no doubt her brother Valentine will protect her."

Grimthorpe merely smiled, a repellently salacious glint in his pale blue eyes. "Puppy's wet behind the ears—why his own twin sister has more sense than he, and you know she has proven herself capable of finding a fairy tale to illuminate every facet of Christendom."

"Valentine may be young, but as you say, she is his twin and there is a strong bond between them." Simon himself had noted the way the girl and her twin seemed to finish each other's sentences, read each other's thoughts, and mimic each other's gestures. He had found it disconcerting at first, and then somehow charming.

For a moment he allowed himself to wonder if she would have accepted his proposal because he was destined to be Duke of Kerstone or because she liked him. He did not doubt her acceptance. If anything about this sorry mess could be considered fortunate, it was that he had found out about his bastardy before he had become betrothed. She, of all the people in this ballroom, deserved a happy ending.

Grimthorpe wagged his brows. "I'll not attempt anything she doesn't permit."

Simon found himself relaxing as he considered the Miranda Fenster he knew. Grimthorpe had chosen his victim poorly. "Then I suspect you will lose your wager." A sudden flash of doubt nearly caused him to shudder. Who was he to judge what a woman would or would not permit?

Last night came back to Simon so vividly that he could not breathe for a moment. His father, weak, blue with the effort to breathe. His mother, calm, beautiful, full of poisonous words.

Simon had entered his father's sickroom to give him the news that his only son would soon be settling down to beget an heir and was on the verge of offering for Miss Miranda Fenster, a woman of impoverished status, impeccable lineage, and amusing imagination.

Instead, he had overheard his beloved mother speak the bitter words that made his life a lie. "I hope you are satisfied that my bastard son will soon be the Duke of Kerstone."

The words had held a sibilant hiss in the silence of his father's sickroom. Simon, reeling with shock, had stood in the doorway of the darkened room and vowed that he would never carry on a bastard line.

The remembered smell of his father's imminent death pressed upon him, and he pushed the memory of his mother's ashen face and his father's wheezed pleas aside.

"You would be surprised what a female will get up to, Saint Simon." Grimthorpe's jeering words cleared the last fog of memory from Simon's mind. "I expect a miss who believes in fairy tales and happy endings will be good for more than a kiss with little protest."

Simon could not allow Grimthorpe's predatory remarks to pass unanswered, although he tempered his rage until his words sounded almost amused. "She seems well able to speak her mind."

"Indeed." Grimthorpe winced with exaggerated motion. "I have a plan that shall keep her quiet." The music ceased and he moved toward the crowd.

Simon watched Grimthorpe's determined pace and fought his chivalrous impulses. Hadn't he just embarked upon his new career as an unrepentant soldier? He searched the crowd until he found her. Plain, his cousin had called her. He saw why, though he did not agree. She stood out like a peahen among the colorful peacocks. Her gown was modest and soberly colored, her hair unadorned—not even a feather.

He knew from experience that her jewels were her lively eyes and quick smile. He watched, torn between the old and the new Simon as she smiled politely at the man intent on seducing her. For a moment he thought she might refuse a dance, but then she lifted her hand to Grimthorpe.

He well remembered the first time he had seen her, walking through the ballroom without the coy shyness of a girl new to the marriage mart. When they had been introduced, she had looked directly at him and surprised him by asking if he had read Mary Wallstonecraft's *A Vindication of the Rights of Women*. She had seemed more amused than chagrined that he had not, offering him the opportunity to borrow her own copy.

He had, although he had not yet read it. And now he would not. He made a mental note to have Travers return the book to her on the morrow, even as he decided to protect her from Grimthorpe. She was much too fine to be tarnished by his libertine cousin. Some other man would see the potential for a fine wife in her. It was obvious to anyone who cared to take the time to look.

As he watched her smile into his cousin's eyes with painful innocence, he made his way toward them, remembering how he had been struck that first time much more by her attitude than her looks—though her chestnut hair gleamed with copper highlights in the light of the ballroom, and her eyes had the warmth of fine brandy.

What had caught his interest about her was the way she didn't melt away from him like the other young women. She had presence. He had been surprised to speechlessness the first time he had heard her offer an opinion. She spoke as if she thought her words were worth being heard. He had decided his duchess should behave so, although some of the things she said were foolish—women managing their own properties? Absurd. Almost as absurd as the realization that the next ruler of England was likely to be Princess Victoria.

As Grimthorpe led her into a waltz, Simon battled his rising anger. He could not break into the dance without causing embarrassment to them all. Watching her gracefully navigate the crowded ballroom with her partner, he was struck by the singular notion that she would not be one to shun him if he stood now and publicly announced his bastardy, renouncing all titles and lands to be given him at his father's—at the *Duke's* death.

The sense of loss was acute. But despite his vow to become the devil himself and obliterate his saintly image, he could not abandon her. Exasperated with himself, he determined to warn Valentine of the threat to his sister's reputation. Puppy or not, it was a brother's duty to protect his sister.

Unfortunately, the lad was nowhere about. And worse, when he scanned the dancers, he saw that his cousin and Miss Fenster were no longer among them.

As he entered a fortunately empty hallway, wondering if they had passed this way, he heard the shriek and the blow from behind one of the closed doors ahead. With a sigh, he hurried toward the sound, reaching the doorway just in time to prevent scandal from erupting around the woman he might have married.

Miranda Fenster flung herself through the doorway, her hair atumble, her mouth swollen from a crude kiss. The lace of her bodice trailed in the air. But her eyes burned with pride and anger—and sudden shame as she ran into Simon himself.

"My lord, please excuse me," she said distractedly, as she attempted to flee past him. But Simon stopped her with a hand to her shoulder. The shocking warmth of her flesh under his gloves almost made him remove his hand, but the sure knowledge of the scandal that would be caused were he to let her escape made him hold firm. He pushed her back into the room and closed the door.

She raised her chin a notch. "I don't believe this is any of your business, sir."

He wasted no time on her feelings, though. Instead he caught his cousin's gaze. "I think we both see Miss Fenster is no willing miss. Matters would best be served if you left and spoke of this to no one. Do you argue?"

His dashed cousin merely cast him an unrepentant grin. "And if I do?"

"Then you will wed her."

Simon heard a gasp behind him, followed quickly by a sharp protest, but he ignored her. He could not very well reassure her that Grimthorpe would sooner wed a cabbage than a meagerly dowered young miss.

His cousin's eyes widened, but he quickly conceded, "As you see fit, Cousin." With a sour glance toward the ring he had lost, he bowed and left the room.

Turning to the shocked-silent Miss Fenster, Simon said curtly, "Wait here. I will fetch your mother." Within scant minutes Simon found Valentine and sent him to collect his mother from the ballroom with a minimum of fuss. Returning to Miranda, he saw that she had made herself as presentable as possible without the help of a lady's maid. She was much calmer than she should have been as she bowed her head to him and said, "Thank you, Your Grace. I am grateful for your assistance, although I little doubt I could have handled the matter on my own."

"Indeed?" Her lack of gratitude stung him somewhat. "Have you any idea what disarray you are in, Miss Fenster? Have you any idea of the scandal your appearance would have created?"

She blushed and put up a hand to tuck back a stray curl. "I would have retired to the lady's dressing room, naturally."

"And no one there would have remarked upon your state, I suppose?"

There was a dawning horror in her dark eyes, but still a defiant set to her shoulders as she opened her mouth to reply. He was never to know her answer, however, because her mother arrived at that moment. With the bustle of a desperate woman, Miranda's mother threw her own lace shawl over her daughter's exposed bosom, clucking softly in dismay.

When her eyes found him, he could see the fear in them. She thought her daughter ruined. Without having consciously made a decision, he stepped in front of Miranda's scandalized mother, halting her flight from the room. The older woman looked up at him, her face nearly the same lavender as her gown. He heard Miranda's swift intake of breath as he said calmly, "I certainly hope that Miss Fenster's headache is gone on the morrow. May I see you to your carriage, ladies?"

He watched as realization dawned that he had no intention of noising the scandal about, and Lady Fenster's face regained its normal color and expression. With dignity, she released her frantic grasp on her daughter's cloaked shoulders and nodded. "Thank you for your kindness, my lord."

"It is nothing." They drew no comment from the few people they met on their way, and Simon relinquished the ladies into Valentine's care once they reached the hastily called carriage.

Waiting for his own carriage, he could not help giving one rueful laugh. He still had a long way to go to get this devil thing down.

Chapter One

Kent, 1837

Miranda slipped deeper into her hiding place as the duke appeared over a small rise with the setting sun at his shoulder. The hooves of his chestnut stallion flashed through the few remaining wildflowers. The last rays of the sun gleamed onto his fair head, giving him a halo that Miranda had always thought he well deserved—until yesterday.

Was she a fool to hope she could persuade him to help her brother? After all, army life changed men. It had made Valentine laugh less and shout more. It destroyed the equality between them when even her father's pompous speeches about woman's inferiority and his harsh punishments for her childhood transgressions had not.

What battle scars might the duke possess if he could quash her brother's elopement with heartless efficiency? A warning uneasiness curled in the pit of her stomach, but Miranda forced it away with a memory of Valentine as she had left him—sitting forlorn and broken in the darkness of Anderlin's drape-drawn study.

She shifted to ease the stiffness of her knees and the prickling of the yew branches that concealed her, as she watched the duke dismount near the hunter's cottage, tether his horse, and disappear inside. She refused to surrender to the doubt that made her limbs heavy and gave her heart a wild beat as she left her shelter and headed for the cottage.

The roughly hewn wooden door swung open easily at her touch, revealing the familiar room and its occupant. His back was turned away from her as he sat at the rickety old table that served the cottage for furnishing. As she entered, Miranda did the best she could to soften the forwardness of her own behavior. She smiled demurely, dropped a perfect curtsy and said, "Good evening, Your Grace." To her surprise, her throat went dry just as she began to speak. Her voice came out in a broken croak just as the door swung closed behind her on noiseless rope hinges. The room fell into darkness save for the single candle the duke had lit.

She realized her error when his shadowy figure rose abruptly and whipped around to face her. His voice rang out harshly, "What the devil?" Miranda had only the briefest glimpse of a worn leather pouch before it was hidden within his jacket.

Aware of the precarious balance of the table, Miranda warned, "Do be careful. That table . . ." The table rocked sideways, and the candle fell. They were plunged into darkness.

"Who the devil are you? What do you want?" His voice was no better than a snarl.

"I apologize for startling you." Miranda eased her

way across the floor toward the spot she had last seen the candle. "Don't move, and I will soon have your candle lit."

His breath hissed inward, as though he were outraged by her suggestion, and he was silent for a moment before answering abruptly, "I assure you that I do not wish my candle lit."

Miranda halted in confusion for the barest second and then continued her search. "Here, I have it. The candle has come loose, I'm afraid. Let me just find—" Her foot touched the loose candle. "I do so hate the dark, don't you?"

She rose from the dusty floor, intending to light the candle now reset in the holder. Her skirts brushed against something unyielding and she could feel him, only inches from her. Startled, she froze, trying to gauge how far away he stood. Only a rustle in the darkness forewarned her before the candlestick was abruptly pulled from her hand.

"I have no quarrel with the dark, only with young women who consider me easy prey." She felt the heat that radiated from his body, so close they almost touched. Belatedly, she realized that his anger was greater than she had first thought.

Instinctively, seeking to soothe him as she might an ill child, when the child was in the throes of a temper, Miranda stroked his upper arm gently. "I am sorry, Your Grace. I truly did not mean to startle you as if you were a hare to be hunted."

"I am no hare." The muscles of his arm tensed under her fingers as he spoke, sending a flush of warmth through her as she realized that he was no child and she had no business touching him so intimately. "You would be wise to consider yourself fortunate that I have not seen your face, young woman, or you and your mother both would feel the sharp side of my wrath."

"My mother is dead." Miranda whispered, pulling her hand away, as the flash of familiar guilt spilled through her.

"Go out to your aunt, then, or your guardian, and tell her your plan failed. You are dealing with me, and I will not be caught like a baited hare."

"But . . . I am alone—" Perhaps she should not have come. Perhaps he had become unbalanced as well as hardened? Nervously, Miranda reached for the candlestick and met the warmth of strong fingers. A shock passed through her, and she pulled the candlestick sharply from his grip.

He bent toward her in the dark, so close that she could feel his breath on her cheek. As she backed away, only to find the table blocking her path, he said, "Has she left you here and driven away? Does she not know the danger in that? Do you not?" She struggled to make out his face, but it was only a deeper shadow in the darkness of the room.

"I trust you, Your Grace. I know your reputation after all." She struck a feeble spark and the candlewick began to glow.

His voice was grim. "That reputation fits me no longer."

Miranda lifted the light of the flame until it banished the shadows that held the duke. His mouth hung open in astonishment; then his scowl turned to stern surprise.

"Dash it all. I would never have believed this of you, Miss Fenster."

The words Miranda had carefully rehearsed flew from her mind. She blushed and her heart hammered painfully at the disappointment that sped across his face and disappeared into a chilling indifference as she pled her case. "I wish to speak to you on a matter of grave importance, Your Grace."

His brow lifted, and a smile curved the left side of his mouth. "I trust, then, this is your brother's idea of revenge?"

His amusement discomposed her. "Valentine knows nothing of this."

He smiled so widely that a dimple graced his left cheek, but his green eyes were wintry. "I'm afraid, Miss Fenster, that even for someone with your . . . notoriety . . . I am sadly unable to oblige you by being the prince in your fairy tale."

Miranda was momentarily distracted by his smile, so that it took a moment for her to register the insult. Indignation seared her. How dare he? "You are certainly not acting like any fairy-tale prince."

He held up one hand. "Don't be offended. I have been stalked by the best and I rank your efforts highly. You simply should have chosen someone other than me."

"You are the only one who can help!"

The smile died on his face. "That is unfortunate, then. For I will certainly do nothing. Good day." He turned and left the cottage without further word.

The heartlessness of his action stunned Miranda. He had been so certain Valentine only wanted Emily's money. A moment's worth of listening to the pair would have shown him the truth of their love. Knowing that she could not give up until he had all the facts, she followed him outside into the rapidly deepening twilight where he was untethering his stallion. As she approached, the stallion whinnied and shied away nervously.

His glance held a pity that chilled her, but she put her pride aside to plead with him. "Please, you haven't heard me out."

"Nothing you can say could change my mind, Miss Fenster. Have the courage to face the fact that you have failed."

Failed. All her life she had failed at the most crucial times. But not today. His words sent a spark of anger through her, so that instead of appealing to him once more, she slapped the skittish stallion sharply on the rump. Her only intent was to move the horse farther away and give herself some time to plead with the duke. The chestnut, however, tore the reins from the duke's hand and bolted. In dismay, Miranda watched the mount gallop off. Then relief flooded her—now she had his full attention.

"I'm sorry, I didn't mean . . ." Her apology cut off as she turned and saw his fingers lift to his mouth. Her advantage had been illusory. The stallion was trained to come at his whistle.

"No!" she whispered. One of the tricks she and Valentine had employed as children surfaced in her memory, and she launched herself at his waist like a maddened bull until he overbalanced, unable to whistle. Unfortunately, as he fell, she followed, landing atop him like an ungainly goose.

When she lifted her head from his chest to look him in the face, her stomach gave a lurch. His green eyes held no more amusement, no more pity—only fury. Certain that she was crushing him, she tried to rise, but he held her tightly. She could not tell if it was anger or fear that made her limbs tremble, but whatever it was lent heat to her words. "Do you not understand what it is to love? How can you walk away without helping me?"

"I will not be compromised by anyone, Miss Fenster. I would have expected you, of all people, to understand." To his credit, he sounded calm as his hands held her hips still.

The combination of being crushed against him by his grip and the shock of his words brought a hot flush to Miranda's cheeks. "Compromise you?"

His eyes bored into her, and his brow lifted.

Miranda realized the picture they would present to any casual passerby—she lying tumbled casually atop him. She struggled once again to rise, but he bent his legs and used them to pin her hips, as he brought his arms up to pull her closer, until she was pressed so tightly against him that she could feel the frantic beat of her own heart against his unyielding chest. This was not the man she remembered from five years ago. That man would have listened to her long enough not to jump to such ridiculous conclusions.

Defeated, Miranda dropped her face into the crook of his neck. The exotic scent of sandalwood took her breath away for a moment, and her heart ached for the loss of the one man during her foreshortened Season who had treated her as if what she thought actually mattered. "I should have known I would make a hash of this. I merely came to beg you to set right what you've ruined for Valentine," she mumbled against the warmth of his neck. "I have no intention of compromising you."

"Indeed?" His arms tightened around her briefly; then he sat up abruptly, putting her aside. "I'm afraid in that matter, as well, you waste your time with me. You would do better to speak to your brother."

"I cannot speak to him. He has locked himself in the study and refuses to answer to anyone at all." As if she had not spoken, he rose to his feet and whistled sharply three times. She would not have been surprised had his stallion come galloping back. But it did not, even after another long string of whistles. Miranda watched his long, elegant fingers brush at the dust on the knees of his breeches as he waited in vain for the return of his horse. She remembered with a shiver the feel of those fingers as they held her tight against him a moment ago. She gasped as her gaze continued downward. "I've ruined your boots! I'm so sorry."

He ceased his brushing to stare at her for a long moment. "You are apologizing to me for ruining my boots, Miss Fenster?"

She recognized the absurdity. "I know how important it is to a military man to keep a good shine on his boots," she explained, as she rose from her undignified sprawl on the ground.

He gave her a level look. "Do you?"

She resolutely ignored the insult that was certainly buried in his question. "My brother was an officer in His Majesty's service, just as you were, Your Grace." She hastily added, "Though he served in a much less distinguished way than you, Your Grace."

He said nothing, but a flicker of annoyance crossed his face.

"I've brought some refreshment for us, if you'd like," she said, remembering her mission. "I have a basket with cheese and apples, fresh-baked bread"— the last from the kitchen and who knew what Valentine would eat in the morning, if he ate at all—"and some very fine ale."

He looked her over pointedly from head to toe until she was uncomfortably warm. His gaze was deliberate and thorough. Blushing, Miranda indicated the copse. "The basket is hidden in there."

"Admirable," he said. "Your planning seems to be on a par with our great generals. It is unfortunate that you are of the fair sex and so England is denied your campaigning genius—except on the battlefield of love."

His sarcasm cut deeply. "Perhaps I would have

made a good soldier, Your Grace—even if I am *only* a woman." Seeing his frown, she sighed. This was not the time for that battle. "You must admit it is much too far to the Camberley's estate for you to walk, as it will soon be dark." The clouds foretold rain, and soon, as well, but she decided it was wiser not to mention that fact.

"So you think you have won your battle?" His anger was daunting. "I told you I have no intention of being compromised."

Miranda flushed. He must hold the incident five years ago against her, despite his kindness then. "I only wish to convince you to intercede with the Earl of Connaught to win Emily back for Valentine. They are meant for each other."

"So you said. I can only wonder how far you are inclined to go to convince me." His gaze traveled her length again. Miranda recognized the look she had endured in her short sojourn on the marriage mart. But never once from Simon Watterly. A painful twist in her chest made her short of breath.

"I will do anything—" His expression darkened and she broke off in confusion.

He smiled his wonderful smile again, and Miranda did not hear his words for the rush of her heartbeat in her ears. "I beg your pardon?" she asked.

"I said," he repeated slowly, as if for a daft child, "though the idea of spending the night with the notorious Miss Fenster intrigues me, I must decline." Without further word, he turned and started across the field. It seemed to be a habit of his.

"I would suggest that you stop following me, Miss Fenster, or you will find yourself in the awkward position of being forced to explain yourself to the Camberleys. I hardly think you'd like a scandal attached to your name after all this time."

A light rain had begun to fall, a gentle misting. Miranda scrambled to keep up with his long stride as she stared angrily at his broad-shouldered back. "I care very little what those shallow, hypocritical—" Miranda broke off, surprised by the painful wave of hurt that engulfed her at the injustice that she would be ruined because some man had tried—unsuccesfully—to take advantage of her friendship. All because she was a woman—held to a higher standard, yet not believed competent to defend herself.

He turned toward her so abruptly that she nearly ran into him. In the half darkness, she could feel his fury radiating toward her. "I would not have expected this of you, Miss Fenster. I suppose it is to your credit that you are naively loyal to your brother. I believe I can find it in myself to forget this lapse if you take yourself home immediately."

Miranda found a tendril of comfort in his words. He had thought her actions honorable—perhaps even justified? No. He had labeled her naive. Her hand itched to slap the smugness from him. With difficulty, she held herself in check. As much as she longed for him to look at her and see that she was as competent—and as flawed—as any man, Miranda knew that his respect for her was not her current battle.

It was Valentine's future she needed to fight for now. And here, with the light rain pattering onto her face, and the darkness soft around them, was her only chance.

Her tightly reined anger made her bold. She took his hands in her own and stepped close enough to look up into his eyes. "I told you I don't give a fig for my own reputation. But you have crushed Valentine—he and Emily were to marry and you have torn them apart. Do you realize what your actions mean to my brother? To my whole family?" He merely stared down at her as she spoke, and Miranda blurted out, "Valentine and I are grown, but we have five sisters to bring out."

His voice was hard as he removed his hands from her grip and stepped back to bring distance between them. "Your brother knew the risk when he attempted to elope with the Earl of Connaught's daughter. If he wanted a dowry so badly, he should have offered for one of the merchant's daughters. They are always glad of a man with a title, even the title of baron."

Miranda did not want to admit that such had been Valentine's intent when he had first gone looking for a bride—to find one with a large, liquid dowry. "Emily is the only woman for him. He has known it since he first spied her on the dance floor—just as Prince Charming recognized Cinder Ella as his one true love."

"He'd best get over it. Her father has set his sights on a marquess or better for a son-in-law, and a false prince, charming or not, will not do." A smile played at his lips. "And if your brother has five more like you to bring out, he'll need all the ready he can marry."

Miranda stiffened in protest. "My sisters are nothing like me. And Valentine is no false prince." Blindly, she turned and walked away from him. Tears burned in her eyes and she let them fall. He was some distance away and it was dark. Another failure to add to her long list. It was her fault her sisters might never marry well, her fault that the investments she had made in Valentine's absence had nearly beggared them. Though she had hopes, they had not yet paid out enough to make Valentine a "catch" on the marriage market. Given her luck, they might never do so.

The tears obscured the rabbit hole until she was upon it and Miranda fell with a pained cry. Another failure. Her insides twisted in utter humiliation at the sound of boots approaching over the wet grass. He was beside her in moments, kneeling down, his fingers quick and sure as he examined her twisted ankle.

"You were heading in the wrong direction, Miss Fenster," he said. His gaze seemed focused on her as if able to penetrate the cover of darkness and rain. For a moment she feared he saw her tears.

Thankfully, the rain came down harder at that moment. She wiped at the drops on her face. "Don't allow your pride to force you to walk in this rain. Stay at the cottage, where it is warm and dry. I will trouble you no further."

What she would do about Valentine's broken heart was another matter altogether. Miranda rose, holding back a gasp at the pain in her ankle. It wasn't broken; it would get her back home. "I'm sorry, Your Grace, I cannot offer you shelter at Anderlin ... Valentine ..."

He smiled grimly. "You will take a chill." He whipped his short cloak from his shoulders and slung it around hers before she could protest. As he reached for her again, she realized that he meant to lift her into his arms.

She warded him away with her hands, stumbling only a little at the sharp pain in her ankle. "I can manage."

"No doubt," he answered, sweeping her up so that her cheek was pressed against his shoulder. She realized that she had been chilled before, only because she was now warmly nestled against his chest.

"You have no need to do this, Your Grace," she protested, a needle of humiliation plying through her. He ignored her and began walking purposefully toward the cottage.

She settled back, surprised at how easy she found it to relax against him, wrapped in the cloak that smelled of sandalwood—of him. She was aware that he did not share her comfort, his every movement indicated a great deal of tension. Hope sprang anew that this twist of fate might allow her to reach the Simon Watterly of old and convince him to help Valentine. But first, she must lay his primary concern at rest. "I will not risk compromising you, I promise. Anderlin is not far. I have walked it in the rain before, I will again." He did not answer.

The rain grew heavy and Miranda admired how little note he took of the water that gathered in his thick honey-colored eyebrows and ran in rivulets down his lean cheeks. The rain had darkened his blond hair and curls had sprung out on the back of his neck. She twisted in his arms until she brought her head level with his and drew the cloak so that it would protect him from the worst of the rain.

Though she did not feel in the least penitent, she knew he would expect an apology. In her experience, men did not give apologies, they demanded them, deserved or not. Best to give it now, and wait until they were dry and warm again before she renewed the campaign to get Valentine and Emily wed. "I'm sorry that I did not accept your refusal at the first. I'm afraid one of my many faults is an inability to understand when a battle is lost. I would not blame you if you chose to scold me."

He stopped, and turned his head until their eyes met. His grip tightened. "Is that all you think I should do? Scold you?" His voice was soft and strained.

Miranda became abruptly aware that his fingers were touching the edge of her breast. She was grateful for the darkness that hid the scarlet of her blush, and shadowed the expression in his eyes as he stared down at her.

After he resumed walking once more, there was a long silence between them. Miranda silently contemplated what his words meant. She could not dredge up within herself any mistrust of this man. He had behaved too well in the past and his reputation was impeccable, though his years away had obviously hardened his heart against lovers. And he had secrets dark enough that he would ride to a ramshackle hunting cottage before he dared pull certain items from his leather pouch and examine them.

She would not chide him for the tightness of his grip. Really, how could he support her otherwise? And if she had mended her stays weeks ago, she would likely have been completely unaware that two of his fingers pressed against the far side of her breast.

"I suppose I should be grateful that no one shall ever know of this. My sisters do not need for me to create a scandal before they come out. And it certainly could not help Valentine's cause." She thought of Valentine, sitting listless and mute in their father's chair before the fire. She had had to climb through the study window to see him, for all the good it had done her.

Miranda closed her eyes as sadness swept over her. "He said that you were right, and he should never have overreached himself with Emily in the first place."

"Perhaps he is not as foolish as I had thought. I will speak to him—"

His words dispelled Miranda's growing sense of hope. Knowing her impertinence, but anxious that he heed her, she put her hand to his cheek. The rasp of stubble against her fingers startled her. "He has been badly hurt. Do not humiliate him further by speaking to him as if he were an errant lad in need of guidance."

He turned his head so that his lips brushed her fingers as he spoke. "I take your point, Miss Fenster."

Miranda let her hand drop away from his face. But the intimacy of being in his arms and jolting comfortably against him at every step could not be prevented. "Valentine must never know that I tried to intercede on his behalf."

"It does not speak well of you that you would deceive him."

Stung by the censure in his words, she said, "Perhaps someday, when Emily joins our family, I shall tell them both."

"Then you believe your brother will not give up his hopes so easily?"

"Wouldn't you search for your Cinder Ella, Your Grace, if you had once met her at a ball and wanted no one else to be your wife?" He stumbled slightly, and her arms tightened around his neck in alarm. After a silence so long that she realized he would not answer her, she said, "No. Valentine will not give up so easily." Remembering her brother's slumped figure, Miranda wondered if she spoke the truth. "I do understand that you only did what you thought was best for Emily. I will be happy to act as though this meeting between us never occurred."

They reached the cottage as she spoke. He stooped slightly to enter the doorway, and his arms tightened around Miranda. His breath against her damp neck made her shiver. "And what if I am not?"

Chapter Two

Simon stirred the fire, his back to Miranda. It amazed him that he had not yet wrung her slender neck. So she thought he could dismiss this gross invasion of his privacy? If she had intruded any later, the damning papers in his pouch would have been laid out on the table. She could not know how he had changed if she thought he would not seek compensation for the way she had turned his life upside down this night.

He had believed his infatuation with her long dead, until today. Holding her in his arms, the feel of the rounded underside of her breast against his fingers, and hearing her innocently questioning whether he would play Prince Charming and pursue his Cinder Ella had done more than rekindle those feelings. He was ablaze with a desire so strong it was driving him mad. Why else would he be considering seducing her?

Suddenly, all he could think of was the fact that,

in other circumstances, she would now be his wife. If that were so, he would not have to play with the fire and keep his eyes turned away from her or risk exposing the heat of his desire to hold her, to kiss her, to make love to her. For a moment he regretted that he had never managed to turn himself into a devil, despite his efforts. For a devil would have no qualms in seducing Miss Fenster. But the old duke's training was too firmly branded into his heart, despite its falsity.

He sighed into the fire, bringing it further to life. But he, Simon-the-no-longer-saintly, had more than qualms. He had good reason not to marry and he'd not risk getting Miranda with child and bringing a new bastard into the world. Somehow though, tonight, the good reasons didn't seem good enough. Fate had dropped this woman literally into his arms. And he was damned tired of the cruel jokes Fate had been playing on him.

How many of his men had died in India, fighting the barbaric practices of suttee and the cruel murderous thugees who struck without warning? But not Simon. He had shrugged at danger, had thrown himself into the midst of any situation without a thought to watching his back. And still, he survived. But he intended to cheat Fate of any satisfaction for leaving the bastard duke alive. And he would do so without breaking the promise he had made his father—no, the old duke. The newest duke would soon be dead, replaced by a true-blooded heir. And Simon Watterly would exist no more. He would take another name, another life—and never would he take a wife.

Of a sudden the wind whipped up, wailing past the cottage. Simon shivered at the sound, remembering how he had stood motionless, surrounded by murderous thugees, daring Fate to take him then and there.

The thunder of gunfire and the screams of the dying men had sounded very much like the laughter of the gods for a moment, and he had not died.

And now he was here, in a one-room cottage with Miranda only a few feet away. She had been in his arms, had touched his cheek with her gentle hand. He wanted to believe that she was truthful when she assured him she was not trying to compromise him into marriage. He had thought her entirely honest five years ago.

But of course, that was before he had learned that Fate was not done playing with him. Since he had been home, acting as the Duke of Kerstone, at least a dozen or so young "innocents" had thrown themselves at his head in some most ingenious schemes, no doubt configured by their ambitious families. He had found them in his bed, in his carriage, half dressed in the garden, and fully nude in the library.

He had extracted himself from all the situations cleanly—even the miss in his bed. She had been the most innocent-looking of all of them, and he'd paid off her papa before she had even finished dressing.

Was Miranda like them? Unable to resist, he glanced over his shoulder. If he had any doubt at all that this innocent-seeming young woman was wearing no stays, the sight of her cheerfully slicing fruit and cheese in the lamplight in her damp dress answered definitively that she was not.

With a hope of dimming the smile on her face that drew the tension in his belly to a sharp point, Simon said, "Your brother would not approve of your being alone with me."

Her answer was calm, but her smile actually widened. "Valentine does sometimes worry overmuch about my judgment, but I assure you it is sound enough to know that I am safe with you."

He checked his impulse to pivot and face her, instead turning his gaze back to the flames. "If you believe so, you are a fool."

There was a momentary silence, and he pictured her imagining herself seduced and abandoned, until she dispelled that notion, her voice ripe with amusement. "I felt certain that I could trust a man who risked his life to pull one of the men in his command away from a suttee fire in which he had been thrown—or who saved a wounded man from death at the hands of thuggees, using his own body as a shield"—her voice softened, all traces of amusement gone—"or who dared scandal by helping a foolish young lady escape misfortune with her reputation intact."

Simon was taken aback. How on earth had this sheltered miss heard such tales, true as they were? Valentine's judgment must be as sorely lacking as his sister's. "A man can be brave in battle and craven in"—he searched for a delicate way to state his meaning and then decided that Miss Fenster could use a little shock—"lust."

"Not you, Your Grace," she demurred, forcing him to turn away from the dancing flames to stare at her.

Was the girl completely daft or supremely crafty? Was it possible she didn't understand what could happen to her, even after Grimthorpe's assault? "Let me make it quite clear to you that, even if it were public knowledge about our ill-spent evening, I could walk away from you with only a blot that would quickly fade. Your reputation, however, would be ruined forever."

"You needn't tell me." Her hands stilled for a moment. The tight line of her lips softened suddenly as she smiled with a shyness that was absurd given their present situation. "I was never able to thank you for seconding Valentine in the duel."

The look in her eyes was even more dangerous than that of a young woman determined to make herself his wife. He had seen such a gaze before, in the eyes of his youngest, most untried men. Dear God, the woman had a case of the hero-worships for him.

He half rose from his crouch at the fire to protest, but she lifted the paring knife from the cheese wedge she was slicing and waved him to silence. "Valentine told me all about it, you know, even though Mama strictly forbade him."

She lowered her eyes and sliced into the cheese. "It was to be my punishment—to hear nothing more of London. As if I cared." She said nothing more as she took an apple and began slicing it, wielding the knife with a stroke that cleaved the fruit cleanly into halves, then quarters, then eighths.

He was shocked. "Surely you had another chance at a Season? Your reputation remained unmarked. Your parents must have known you'd grow sensible enough for a second try?"

"I don't know. They never said any such thing before they died." With a quick shake of her head she added, "Then, of course, there was no possibility of a Season. I had my sisters to see to, and Valentine was too far away to be of use."

"Surely you were not left to yourself to provide for the family? Had you no uncle to step in?" Once again, Simon wondered at Valentine's lack of responsibility, to leave a young woman in charge of a badly out-of-pocket household.

Her chin lifted and her gaze met his, although her face was flushed with color. "I am quite capable, Your

Grace. Valentine never doubted my abilities to attend to things while he was away."

"I'm surprised you didn't set your cap for a wealthy spouse, as he did."

She shuddered. "Quite honestly, I was determined to never marry."

He nearly laughed aloud at the candor he remembered so well from five years ago, but the subdued panic on her face reminded him suddenly of the expressions of young soldiers who had not yet gone into battle as they listened to their more experienced comrades trade stories. "Indeed?"

"Husbands are as bad as fathers—they believe they have the right to decide how a woman will live her life—and to beat her if she will not comply."

There was scorn in her voice. For the first time, Simon was certain that she had not set out to compromise him. His curiosity rose. "Perhaps you should have conveyed that thought to Emily. She might not have consented to elope with your brother, then."

Her chin lifted. "Valentine is different. He is in love."

"With a well-dowered woman, conveniently."

"With Emily. And he would love her, dowry or no."

"Then he will need to adjust his expectations, and love her from afar, for he will never have her."

Her gaze met his directly. "Can you not intercede? Convince your uncle of what a fine man Valentine is? He is, you know."

Simon admired her loyalty, though he wished she didn't have the tenacity of a dog with a meaty bone. And how had she turned their conversation from her own danger to her brother's broken heart? "I doubt my uncle would much care. Once he makes up his mind, he never unmakes it."

She sighed. "Yes. That's what Emily said when she convinced Valentine to run for the border."

Simon laughed softly. "The little minx. And I always thought her so responsible—for a woman."

Her eyes flashed with momentary indignation, quickly controlled. "She wanted to help Valentine realize his dreams. They talked of what use they would have for her inheritance—Anderlin is in sore need of repair, and they wanted to invest in the West Indies trade . . ."

"Well, if he wants such dreams to come true, I'd say it is clearly Valentine's duty to find an heiress whose parents are not so particular. As a beginning, he could bestir himself from his misery, and not rely on his sister to cure his troubles."

She stared at him for a moment, her wine-colored eyes wide. And then, to his surprise, she bent her head as if in defeat. Her voice was a mere whisper. "I have done it again, haven't I? I only wanted to make things right for him, and now I've convinced you that he is truly the heartless fortune hunter you thought him." She raised her gaze to his. "It isn't true, Your Grace, I came of my own accord. Valentine would have stopped me, if he'd known."

"I don't doubt that, Miss Fenster. Still, he shared a womb with you. I would expect him to know you well enough by now. If he can't handle you, he should find you a husband who will."

Her chin lifted. "Valentine is not fool enough to marry me to a man who seeks to control me. And I would not want him to marry but for love."

Hearts and hero-worship, he should have known. "Then you are both fools, for love is a temporary aberration, and marriage requires a sharp business acumen—to ally oneself with an inferior partner will bring you nothing but disaster for your lifetime." He watched her eyes flash with fire and wondered how she might ever find a husband who was not inferior to her magnificence. The thought of her as another man's wife bred fury in him.

"Valentine is not an 'inferior' partner. He would have—he *will* make Emily a fine husband. And certainly you should not speak so cynically. You have had your choice of alliances and yet you have not married. Surely, you are waiting for the one who touches your heart as well as adds to your pocketbook? Perhaps someone from whom you would not need to hide the contents of that leather pouch of yours."

Her words were a blow to him, but he hid his pain with a quick smile. "I'll have you know, Miss Fenster, that I once, quite foolishly, nearly offered for a young woman based on the color of her eyes and the quickness of her smile. Only Fate intervened in time to save us both from an unhappy union." Fate, and the burden he carried next to his heart every waking moment.

He saw her curiosity pique, but she asked nothing of who, as many a woman might. "Nonsense. That is not love—liking a woman's eyes and smile. That is physical attraction. I am talking of a meeting of the souls and minds of two individuals who are meant for each other—like Cinder Ella and her prince, or Rapunzel and the man brave enough to climb her hair to reach her tower."

As she stared at him, fully expecting him to agree with her romantic drivel, Simon suddenly had no doubt that hero-worship was an even more dangerous emotion than the avarice felt by the army of young women angling to marry him by fair method or foul.

She was so serene, so certain that he posed no danger to her reputation that he suddenly wanted to discompose her as badly as she had unsettled him.

"Can you be so sure? What do you know of the power of physical attraction?"

Her smile faltered and she quickly turned her attention back to the apple in her hand. "I had a few suitors at first when Mama and Papa died."

Knowing the kind of men who would have offered for a young woman without parental guidance, Simon's stomach clenched in anger. "And you found none of them acceptable?"

She shook her head. "That burst of physical attraction you spoke of seems to bring most men to behave in completely unacceptable ways." She sighed. "But you yourself have risen above such physical cravings, Your Grace, so you must recognize that there is something finer, and more satisfying in a higher meeting of souls."

For a moment, Simon considered revealing how much he had been enjoying the view of her slender figure that her soaked muslin gown put on display. He imagined the way her mouth would open slightly in shock. But then she would cover herself, no doubt regaining that formidable composure of hers within minutes. No, he needed something more . . . shocking . . . to bring Miss Fenster to her senses. And he did not want to forgo the pleasure the sight of her curves gave him. It was like probing a sore tooth with his tongue: looking at her, knowing the danger—to them both—in seducing her.

His own clothes were as soaked through as hers, which gave him the idea for which he sought. He had already stripped his sodden jacket off and thrown it over a stool near the fire. Casually, as if he did not know she was watching him from the corner of her eye as she worked, Simon stood, unfastened his shirt, pulled it loose from his breeches and removed it. He hung it on the iron pothook for the fireplace, positioning the hook so that the shirt was far enough away not to burn, but close enough to dry quickly in the heat from the fire.

He seated himself on the stool, removed first one boot, then the other, placing them neatly beside a dusty pile of blankets. He stood up, reaching for the fastening of his breeches.

At last, she gasped. "What are you doing?"

He turned slowly to savor the sight of her, jaw agape, frozen in surprise with a bowl of fruit cradled in her arms, as if for protection. Wickedly, he spun the moment out just slightly longer than necessary before he answered, "I'm ensuring that I don't take ill. Shouldn't you do the same?"

At that, she looked down at her own gown, the skirts dragging the ground from the weight of the water, then back up at him. There was a puzzled frown on her face that deepened as he started to peel away his riding breeches. But she did not turn away from him as he had expected. Instead, she stared at him, up and down the length of him, with a hint of wonder.

Suddenly, with her gaze transfixed upon him, he felt as shy as an untried boy. He snapped, "I am not a ham, Miss Fenster. Kindly stop gawking as if you were at market."

He was warned by the flash of fire in her eyes. "If I were at market, and you were a ham, I should certainly not ogle you. You are no gentleman to insult me so." She whirled away, but not so quickly that he couldn't see her mouth twist in pain as her injured ankle gave way and she lost her balance.

Simon started forward to offer a steady hand as she struggled to maintain her balance against the hampering cling of her wet skirts. Before he could reach her, she lost the struggle with a last toss of her arms. The bowl of fruit she had held struck him in the chest, taking his breath away. She landed in a sprawl on the floor.

He held out his hand to her, unable to resist a gentle barb. "You can see now how dangerous wet clothing can be."

She refused his hand as she rose. Without looking at him, she swept her rain disarranged hair from her cheek where it clung. She had the grace to blush and suddenly he was not so much angry as sad. A woman with such courage and loyalty, not to mention that unique flair for skirting disaster, would have made an unforgettable duchess—under his tutelage to smooth out the unfortunate tendency to impulsiveness, of course.

But that was not to be. Anything he had to teach her must be taught tonight. He felt the old emotional wound open as he stared at her hair, half fallen out and curling with the damp. And she certainly deserved a lesson for this foolishness. If he were any other man, he had no doubt that she would have her skirts around her ears, by now. The thought made him groan aloud as he captured a handful of damp curls, the same color as cinnamon, and let them rest in his open palm. "You should see to your own health, Miss Fenster. You are as wet as I."

Her eyes were huge, but still trusting. He wanted, more than anything at that moment besides to make love to her, to make sure that she would never put herself in this position again. He stepped closer. "It would be a misfortune should you take ill . . ." When she tried to back away, he closed his hand over the hair that he held and pulled gently until she was so close that one exhalation from him stirred the drying curls on her brow. ". . . before I have received my compensation for the trouble you have put me through."

She breathed shallowly, as she tried to avoid the bare flesh of his chest and arms. "I agree that you deserve some recompense, Your Grace. Perhaps I might shine your boots?"

He was tempted to laugh, which amazed him. He had not laughed in a long time and Miss Fenster had coaxed the urge more than once in under an hour. "I would prefer payment of another kind. Do I dare hope that the infamous Miss Fenster will agree? I well remember the black eye Grimthorpe sported the morning of the duel."

Her trembling lips tightened and her voice was a soft whisper. "Mother never told me that I'd blackened his eye. I'm surprised she didn't add that to my long list of sins." Her chin came up a fraction more, and suddenly the blade of the paring knife rested against the flat of his stomach. "As you were not harmed by my actions, Your Grace, I cannot believe you would allow me to be harmed by yours."

Though he was relieved that she had the sense to realize she was in danger, Simon reacted as swiftly as if she had been a London cutthroat, disarming her of the knife before she blinked.

Her eyes wide, she stared at the knife he now held, as she cradled her wrist gently in her other hand. He had not the slightest doubt that she would not have harmed him. Still, it was better that she know she was outmatched. She might take the lesson to heart, at last.

A smile twitched on her lips as she breathed out softly. "You are magnificent! How could you disarm me so swiftly?"

Magnificent? He was magnificent? He was seducing her! Simon stroked the back of his hand gently from her chin to her ear. She stood still for his caress, making no protest, not even the softest of sighs. Her eyes captured his. He did not know how to read them, did not know how to look away. Her skin was firm and silky under his fingertips. Simon closed his eyes briefly. When would she protest? When would she finally believe he had gone too far?

Goading her further, Simon drew his forefinger across her lips. They parted slightly, her breath came warm on his finger. And all the while, her gaze was upon his, trusting, worshiping and, dear God, desiring. Simon fought his urge to touch her lips with his own, or to allow his hands to explore the curves displayed by the clinging of her damp clothing.

He reminded himself sternly that he wanted a reaction from her, not from himself. But Miss Fenster swayed toward him slightly, apparently unable to oblige him with the affronted response he was seeking. And all he could think of was that she could have been his wife. He could have had her in his bed every night. Pain supplanted desire at the thought; he could not bear to seduce her and discover fully what it was that he had lost.

With a sigh, he grasped her shoulders and turned her away from him so that he could unfasten her dress. Her shoulders stiffened in his grip. "What are you doing?" Her voice was husky—with fear, he hoped.

"Helping you out of your wet things. You can drape yourself in a blanket." He wondered if his impertinence would finally spur her into response. But she stood silently as he peeled the clothing away from her back.

Simon exhaled sharply. "What is this?" Through her damp, practically transparent chemise he could see the faint, but unmistakable white scars that came from a severe lashing. One of his fingers came up to trace a scar that snaked wickedly down to the small of her back and beyond.

She shivered and pulled away from him. "My father did not approve of my outspoken nature, as I am only a female." Her shoulders stiffened, and he heard the ring of defiance in her words. "I will never let another man have such complete power over me that he could beat me for my belief in my own abilities!"

Anger swept through him and made his words intemperate. "You say you will not give a man power over yourself and yet you stand here, uncorseted, in a dress so damp it hides not one curve—except for at the bosom, where it threatens very enticingly to fall away and display your breasts." She stared down at her loosened bodice and clutched it tight.

"You have allowed me to all but undress you, Miss Fenster. I daresay I could take you here and now if I wished." She opened her mouth as if to protest, and then closed it. For a moment, uncertainty crossed her features.

She blinked rapidly, saying nothing for a moment, until Simon turned away from her. He crossed the room and tossed a blanket to her across the few feet between them. And then she blushed crimson and said, "I was not thinking . . ."

"That, my dear Miss Fenster, seems to be a trait you and your brother both share."

He had hit a nerve with that he saw, when she replied, "Valentine's integrity is as great as yours, Your Grace." She crossed the few feet of distance between them to stand close enough to burn him with the heat of anger in her eyes.

He realized that she still had no idea what she risked being here alone with him. Her head was full of dreams and ideals of love and honor. It struck him that she was still as naive about men and women as she had been five years ago. So far, she had been fortunate to have been pursued by men for whom she had felt no physical passion.

He shuddered, thinking of how willing she had been for his caresses. All because he was a hero of some trumped-up tales of bravery she had heard secondhand. He closed his eyes. In London there would be dozens more "heroes" who could ignite that same fire, no matter how much his ego cried out that she felt such things only for him. And, despite her father's cruel discipline, she had no defenses in place to prevent her own ruination.

His urge was to call upon Valentine and insist that a husband be found for Miranda at once. But he had no right to do such a thing. And he could not, without Valentine learning the whole story. Still, he felt a strong desire to . . . to show her just what danger she courted.

Even as he took her in his arms and bent his head to kiss her, he told himself he intended to give her no more than a taste of what could happen when a woman was at the mercy of a rake. But when she opened her mouth under his in a small gasp of surprise and then curled her hands around his neck, he forgot all but the taste of her.

Chapter Three

A noise from the loft above cut into Simon's consciousness.

Reluctantly, he pulled away from Miranda, holding a finger to his lips that turned her bemusement into a narrow-eyed silence. He was fleetingly glad to see that her cheeks were flushed. He hoped it was a sign that he had taught her to be wary.

With the stealth and silence that had kept him alive more than once, he grasped the frayed rope that hung from a ceiling beam and handed himself slowly and silently up into the tiny loft area. Except for a little moldering hay put by in one corner, the rest of the loft was swept bare of anything but a layer of mouse and owl droppings.

Simon grabbed up the pitchfork, brandishing it as if it were a bayonet. "Come out of there now," he said in the voice that had made his bravest men jump.

There was a twitch in the hay, but nothing more. Simon directed his attention to the area of the twitch and swore softly at the sight of a bare foot protruding from the hay. It was covered with grime—and small. "Come out, boy."

There was no movement from the hay. Behind him, Miranda gasped. "It is but a child you're frightening?"

He turned his head, surprised to see that she had climbed up after him. There were not many women of his acquaintance he'd credit with the ability or inclination to climb a rope. "I can see you've forgotten London life, Miss Fenster. Can't turn your back on the little beggars."

To his surprise, though nothing he had previously done had eradicated one glimmer of the hero-worship in her eyes, his comment seemed to have brought him down a notch.

"Little beggars!" With a scornful look at him, she marched up to the pile of hay, which was trembling now, and knelt beside it. "I'm sorry if we frightened you." When there was no further movement from within the pile of hay, she coaxed, "You must be hungry. Would you like food? I have apples and cheese and fresh bread. Why don't you come out?"

Her voice was soft and persuasive, but the child remained hidden in the hay.

Simon's gaze, trained as it was on Miranda's slender back, still bared by her gaping dress, was caught by the series of shivers that shook her. With an impatient oath, he dropped the pitchfork and reached out for the child's exposed foot. One swift pull, accompanied by a soft squeal, revealed a young girl, no more than three or four, with long blond braids and big brown eyes.

Even Simon could not be wary of the girl once he saw how tiny and frightened she was. As he held the child in his arms and jumped from the loft to the floor below, he felt a flash of gratitude that she had made her presence known when she did. He could think of no more effective means to prevent him from seducing Miss Fenster tonight. Certainly his own willpower had failed.

He left Miranda to tend to the frightened child while he gathered wood. When he returned, chilled, but with what he hoped was enough wood to last through the night, he was not surprised to find Miranda draped in a makeshift toga, with the child beside her, cleaned up and bundled into a blanket of her own. The child held a half-eaten slice of bread in one hand and was well into the story of how she had come to be at the cottage.

"He said I was pretty as my Mam, and he gave me a sweet before he went in to her." Her eyes rested on Miranda with complete trust, as a child might look at her mother. Simon's gut clenched with shock at the unwelcome realization that he and Miranda might have had a child this age by now. He dropped the wood into the basket with a thunk.

"Why'd that handsome gennulman tell me he dropped a gold piece at the crossroads?"

"I don't know Betsy, but I can't believe he knew you'd go looking for it and get lost." Miranda met Simon's gaze.

He wondered, seeing her doubtful expression, how much of what was an obvious attempt to distract a child while the "gennulmun" tumbled the mother, was apparent to Miranda. The girl's clothes, though carefully patched, were little more than rags. She probably came from one of the poorer of the village folk, grateful for money any way they could earn it.

"Do you come from Watson or Nevilshire, girl?" he asked.

She smiled proudly, "Nevilshire, Your Grace." With

a gleeful glance she checked with Miranda, as if to ensure that her salutation had been correct. She was rewarded with a smiling nod from Miranda.

Simon sighed inwardly. Doubtless Miranda had not thought of a child's wagging tongue before she'd informed the girl of his title. "I'll take you back to your Mam tomorrow. Tonight you'll bed down with us."

Her eyes sparkled as if he'd promised her a pony. "Yes, sir. Thankee sir." And then her eyes darkened. "My mam will be sore mad at me. She told me not to never go too far away."

Miranda said gravely, although Simon suspected that a smile lurked under her sober demeanor, "I'm sure if you convince her that you've learned your lesson, she'll forgive you, Betsy."

"Indeed?" Betsy looked doubtful.

Miranda smiled at her. "Why, I remember when I was your age and did something similarly naughty. My nanny told me about another young lady who also wasn't the best at heeding her mother's warnings."

Betsy's eyes were sparkling once more. "What was her name?"

Miranda's brows knitted. "I don't think Nanny Hilda ever told me the girl's name, now that you ask. But she did tell me about the wonderful warm cape that her mother made her, of a most beautiful red, the color of a cardinal. So why don't we call her Little Redcape, as my nanny did?"

Betsy nodded her approval, and despite a mouthful of bread, asked, "Did she get lost too, like me?"

Miranda shook her head. "No, not exactly. You see, her grandmother was ill, and Little Redcape's mother asked her to take a basket of herbs and some soup and fresh bread to her."

"And she didn't?"

Miranda laughed. "She did indeed—and met a wolf on the way."

"A wolf!" Betsy's round face was a study in delight.

"Truly." Miranda began her tale as she took the remains of the bread from the child's fingers and smoothed back the blond hair. Simon was tormented by a vision of how it would feel if those fingers were smoothing back his own hair. As she spoke, she quietly tucked Betsy in, smoothly unbraiding and rebraiding her hair. Without a peep of protest from the unwary child, Miranda had readied her for sleep. He watched her expression change by turns from happy to ferocious to frightened to cunning as she told her fairy tale. He wondered if Miranda understood the allusions to straying from the path—and the danger of the wolf.

He found no answer; her attention was all for her story, and for the child listening raptly, right up until Redcape used the ax she had hidden in her cape to free herself and her grandmother from the wolf's stomach. And then, to Simon's utter amazement, the child let out a contented sigh, turned over, and began to snore very quietly.

Miranda eased herself away from the sleeping child, rose, and came over to him by the fire. "I expect she will sleep now. She was so frightened. I thought a story would calm her."

"Indeed. But I imagine the lesson would have gone more deeply if Little Redcape had realized she was not capable of saving herself from the wolf after she'd been eaten."

"Nonsense." She shook her head, strands of cinnamon-colored hair falling from the loosening knot at her nape. "Redcape has a happy ending. She learned her lesson. You'll never find her talking to strange wolves again."

"Happy endings are rare in life, Miss Fenster. Look at what happened to you when you ran into a London wolf."

"I?" Her gaze reflected her puzzlement. "What wolf have I . . . ? Oh." There was a fierce light in her eye. "So such men are called wolves? It suits their predatory nature even more than the term rake, I think."

He noticed that she stood close to him without fear. Obviously, she did not consider him a rake. "Indeed. But my point remains, Miss Fenster. And the wolf did no more than taste you." He couldn't help adding, "And I'm none too convinced that you've learned your lesson."

Impulsively, he reached out and pulled the few anchoring pins from her hair, allowing it to fall about her shoulders. "What if he had managed to eat you, my dear?"

Her color heightened, she snatched the pins from his hand and said sharply, "I refuse to believe there are no happy endings, Your Grace—for Little Redcape or for Valentine and Emily." She looked at him, a challenge in her eyes as she said softly, "I even believe you, a man of two-and-thirty might still have a happy ending for yourself."

No. That was not possible. Simon closed his eyes to block the sight of her, hair tumbling down over one bare shoulder, as enticing as a nymph. Was she trying to drive him mad? Or was she playing a game? He knew that a woman could seem innocent and honest and be rotted inside with guilt and lies. His own mother had taught him that truth. Somehow, he didn't believe it of Miranda.

Without opening his eyes, he said, "The rules are different for men and women. You are a woman. I am a man." He wondered if there was any possibility that she was as aware as he was of that simple fact.

There was a bare hesitation before she answered. "The rules make no sense. They put restrictions on women, who are not ruled by physical attraction, and allow men free rein to indulge themselves with the naive and unwary, as Grimthorpe did with me."

Her naïveté amazed him. He gave in to his urge to touch her and grasped her lightly by the shoulders, caressing the soft, exposed skin. "What might have happened if you *had* been aroused by Grimthorpe's attentions?"

"He was a toad!"

"Agreed." Simon asked a question for which he was not sure he wanted the answer. "What of your country suitors? Did none of them make you wish for a stolen kiss?"

"I am well able to control my actions, wishes or no."

"Then the answer is yes?"

She hesitated, but his trust in her innate honesty was rewarded by a sharp, "No."

"And my kiss left you unmoved?" She tried unsuccessfully to pull away from him, but he continued relentlessly. "If we had not discovered Betsy, would you have allowed me to make love to you, Miss Fenster?"

He opened his eyes. Instead of the expected dawning of wariness in her eyes, her gaze seemed fixed on his face, as if she sought to puzzle out a mystery. It was clear that she had no idea of her current danger. Or perhaps she did not recognize this feeling between them as dangerous. He felt pushed to the wall. With an angry growl low in his throat he loosed her shoulders, swept her off her feet, and carried her the few steps to where the blankets had been laid for the three of them to sleep.

"As you pointed out not that long ago, Miss Fenster," he said as he brought the both of them to the floor and pinned her beneath him, "I am a man of two-and-thirty. Has it ever once crossed your mind that I might not connect seducing an innocent but foolish young woman with any sullying of my honor?"

She lay stiffly beneath him, and he was satisfied to feel the rapid beat of her heart against his chest as she stared up at him, finally wary. After a moment's silence, she said quietly, "You would regret it in the morning, Your Grace. We both know that."

He brought his head down, as if to kiss her, pleased to note the sudden catch in her breath. His face was so close to hers that he could not see her expression as he whispered softly, "I would not regret it half so much as you, Miss Fenster." Abruptly he pulled away and flicked the last of the blankets over them, satisfied to see relief in Miranda's expression, worried lest she see the same feeling reflected in his own. He had doubted his own sanity for a moment.

He turned his back on her. "I pray that you have learned your lesson, but if you have not, I am content to let some other man give you the proper ending to your fairy tale."

Ignoring the little quiver in his gut that indicated he was lying, Simon lay his head on his arm and forced himself to remain still atop the cold hard floor.

An hour later, still unable to sleep, he heard the slow rhythmic creaking of cart wheels. He rose, crept to the door, and cautiously cracked it open. The rain had ceased. Lantern lights dotted the field and glimmered at the edges of the wood. After a moment, the night's breeze carried the sound of a woman crying, and then a deeper voice, calling, "Betsy? Betsy, my pet? It's time to come home."

He could almost hear laughter in the creaking of the wheels of fate as they drew closer. Someone had come looking for Little Redcape.

Miranda woke to the warmth of Simon's breath in her ear. "Wake up, Miss Fenster." She tried to speak, but his hand crushed her lips closed. His lips brushed her ear and a shiver ran down her spine. "Little Redcape's Mam is searching for her, and she apparently has half the village with her."

Miranda stilled, and he rose abruptly. By the light of the single candle he had lit, she could see that he was dressed as neatly as his wrinkled clothing allowed. Despite the state of his breeches and shirt, the villagers would know they dealt with no ordinary man.

"You must leave, Your Grace, or we will be compromised."

He turned toward her, his expression calm, and there was a hint of a smile on his lips that made her uneasy. "They are nearly upon us. Hide in the loft while I get rid of them."

The urgency in his voice, and the sound of approaching villagers quieted her urge to argue. Snatching up her clothing, Miranda quickly climbed into the loft. She lay still in the shadows, positioned by the large gap between the boards that gave clear view to the room below.

Hidden now, she spared a glance for the sleeping Betsy. Earlier, she had wondered what kind of woman would entertain strange men in her cottage, leaving a child like Betsy to wander away in her little patched dress that offered no shelter from the night chill. But any mother who would come searching in the dark and rain must care for her daughter greatly. The patches—and even the visitor—must be for want of funds, not want of love.

It was much too easy for Miranda to imagine her youngest sister Kate like this. She was not much older than Betsy, after all. Though they still had silver to sell, and there were investments that held hope for the future, putting bread on the table was difficult at the moment. Simon's intervention in Valentine's elopement was more unfortunate than she was prepared to let him know.

Simon's swift movements caught her attention. He plucked an apple from the floor where it had gone unnoticed earlier and tidied the pile of blankets to make two neat heaps: one for Betsy, she realized, and one for himself. Swiftly, he was hiding all evidence of her own presence.

"You should hide my boots," she said the third time he walked past them.

He looked up, and Miranda would have sworn he could see her, though she knew darkness made that an impossibility. "Miss Fenster, if you do not wish to suffer any embarrassment, may I suggest that you remain perfectly still"—his voice deepened—"and completely silent."

Still, he swept her boots under one of the piles before he slipped out the door.

Miranda heard the sound of a horse being brought up short, and a faint, desperate voice. Moments later Simon reentered the cottage with a young woman. She held her lantern high enough that the light bathed her face. Her resemblance to Betsy was slight, just the heart shape of her face, and a certain arch of her brows. Behind the two of them followed an older man, bent with years.

He, too, carried a lantern, as did the three or four

others who crowded into the doorway. Suddenly the cottage was fully lamplit.

The woman's gaze flew to the mound of blankets where Betsy slept. With a cry of relief, she hurried across the room and flung herself on the sleeping bundle. "Bets! Bets, my love. What were you thinking of, running off?"

Betsy woke, and her thin arms went readily around her mother's neck. "Got lost," she said sleepily.

Miranda recognized blazing anger and fear in the woman's gaze as she lifted it to Simon. "Didn't I tell you to stay near to home? What were you doing going off with a stranger?"

"Didn't go with 'im Mam, I'us looking for the gold piece that fancy gent who come to see ye dropped on the road. Then I couldn't find home again."

Betsy continued her story, oblivious to her mother's sudden pallor. "I hid in the loft, but 'ee found me, and the lady was so nice. She gave me something to eat and something to drink and told me the story of little redcoat. . . ."

Miranda's stomach knotted as she realized that Betsy was about to unravel whatever careful fiction Simon had established. "She was purely kind, Mam . . ." Betsy's tale broke off at this point as she searched the cottage with a puzzled frown.

Her bright eyes rested on Simon. "Where's your wife gone, Your Grace?" There was an audible intake of breath from the assembled villagers, accompanied by an embarrassed rustling of hasty curtsys and hats being removed.

"The little girl must still be dreaming," Simon said. It was an absurd statement, but to Miranda's surprise, no one in the tiny room reacted to it as if it were anything but the honest truth.

"Of course, Your Grace." The older man spoke,

his eyes narrowing and his lips thinning. "I've seen you riding this week past. You be up at the Camberleys', do you not?"

"Aye," Simon assented. "But I sheltered here from the rain and came upon your granddaughter doing the same. I would have returned her to Nevilshire in the morning."

"Thankee, sir." The old man answered before Betsy's mother could speak, but his eyes grew no less wary than they had been—nor did his daughter's.

Just then, a man shouldered through the crowd in the doorway and entered, his face momentarily obscured by the shadow of one of the larger men in the search party. "See here young woman, if you have Damaged Atlas, I shall see that you pay dearly. . ." The voice trailed off in shock, but in an instant the newcomer had regained his equilibrium. He inclined his head to Simon. "Kerstone."

He stepped from the shadows, and Miranda blinked quickly, at first feeling that the strain of peering through the floorboards had ruined her vision. *Grimthorpe.* The cause of her scandalous retirement from society stood in this very room, lamplight glinting from the carefully tended auburn curls.

She had thought she did not care. But anger shook her at the sight of him. His sneer was the same one that had burned through the shock Miranda had felt at being dragged from the dance floor into a secluded corner and kissed despite her protest. That sneer had been the reason she had gone beyond a gentle protest to give him, so Simon had told her, a black eye. In his eyes was a look of gleeful malice that took her breath away. Quite obviously, he had never forgiven Simon for seconding Valentine—or had he some other reason for disliking the duke?

"Kidnapping young girls now, Kerstone?" He

spoke in the same half-amused, half-derisive voice that Miranda remembered.

Simon stood as still as stone. "Grimthorpe. What brings you out?"

With a sniff that made his ridiculous handlebar mustache twitch, the man grimaced and pointed to Betsy's mother. "The fool woman lost her wits when she found her urchin gone. Took Atlas. I've been following her afoot half the night just trying to get close enough to regain him."

The older man spoke deferentially, but his hostility was readily apparent in the tense set of his shoulders and the clenched fists of his hands. "Your horse has come to no harm, my lord. My daughter was foolish to take him, but Betsy is her only child, and she was out of her head. Please forgive her."

"I shall hardly take your word for the matter, fellow. You should pray tonight that Atlas is not even sweated, or she shall pay a pretty price. Theft of a piece of horseflesh like that could get her hung."

The old man lowered his gaze to the floor. "I beg you to consider her distress, sir." Miranda could guess at the sick fear that ate at him, but his face was so lined from a hard life that it did not show.

"*I* beg *you* to consider having her chained to her bed. Atlas has a sensitive mouth, and she could well have ruined it with her clumsy panic."

"Perhaps you should see to Atlas's mouth before he wanders off." Simon had not moved, nor taken his eyes from Grimthorpe.

She resisted the urge to sneeze, holding her breath against the hope that Grimthorpe would take Simon's suggestion. For the villagers to find her would be misfortune enough. That devil could attach a scandal to her name that no one could deny.

Apparently, Atlas's welfare was no longer foremost

in his mind, however. "Indeed I shall, Kerstone, as soon as I find out why you are spending the night here, instead of your own most comfortable guest bed. Or were your accommodations less satisfactory than mine?"

"I am not here by design," Simon answered sharply.

"No?" There was a malicious pause. "You did not have an assignation, then?"

Chapter Four

Miranda held her breath. She dared not move lest the straw rustle or drop down through the loose flooring.

Simon said curtly, "The child was lost and came here to escape the rain. I was unseated from my horse and did the same. There is no source for gossip here."

Miranda marveled at his sangfroid. If she did not know that he had someone hidden in the loft, she would never have believed it. His entire bearing, even to inflection, spoke of aristocratic contempt. Not even Grimthorpe could guess that this man could have held her in his arms, kissed her, nearly made love to her but an hour before. She scarcely believed it herself.

Grimthorpe laughed sharply. "You? Unseated? I should have liked to see that. Perhaps this has not been a tedious waste of time after all. This will be a worthy story to tell—"

"Shame on you!" The outburst came from Betsy's

mother, who now stood, clutching her daughter in her arms, her eyes burning with fury. Her words were practically incoherent as she forced them from her tear-choked throat. "Taking advantage. First of me, now of him."

Grimthorpe gaped at her, as if he'd been suddenly addressed by a wayward carp. And then his thin lips thinned even further. "How dare you speak to me like that. I've a good mind to see that you *are* prosecuted for horse theft."

Miranda felt a shiver of fear, as her eyes darted back to the mother and child, clinging together protectively.

Betsy's mother was evidently beyond any such fear. Her eyes flashed with fire and her chin was held high as she spoke with intensity. "It's you who should be hanged. My Bets told me you said there was a crown in the crossroads."

At the murmur of the crowd, Grimthorpe stepped back. "My good woman, I assure you the child is mistaken."

The woman hugged her daughter tighter. "Of course. You're a gentleman." She sobbed softly. "I should never have let you in my door. I knew you were trouble the moment I saw you. You are nothing but a pig."

"You . . ." Grimthorpe, his face reddened to indicate that he was angered beyond words, stepped toward the woman, his arm raised.

Somehow, Simon inserted himself deftly between them and stood there, making no further threat. Miranda was not even sure how he had moved; he was simply there, between one blink and the next.

Grimthorpe stopped as if held in a grip of steel. He threw Simon one furious glance, and then turned his attention to the woman who had dared to criticize her "better". "I paid you good money for your services, woman. I merely wanted the brat out of the way for a time. You should have taught her the way home. Children are known to wander."

Especially when promised a gold coin, Miranda added silently, her dismay at the sight of Grimthorpe rapidly growing into panic. The man seemed to be intent on shaking Simon's secrets out of him, no matter what kind of fool he made of himself.

With a whimper of rage, the woman tore at a small leather bag around her neck. Coins clinked in her hand for a moment before they littered the packed dirt at Grimthorpe's feet. "Keep your coins, then. I'll have nothing more to do with you."

Grimthorpe bent with self-conscious grace to sweep the coins into his hand. "I'll consider this repayment for the use of Atlas."

His smile burned fury into Miranda when he said, as if amused, "After all, your brat led me into the scandal of the century—the upright Duke of Kerstone prefers little girls."

Simon's fury was apparent to all in the room, judging by the way everyone seemed to shrink from him, including the fool Grimthorpe, who had baited him. "You go too far. These people were distraught about a lost child. They have found her and do not need your insinuating lies."

The troublemaker's smile flashed as Simon scowled. His silvery tone reminded Miranda of the time when a younger Giles Grimthorpe had chided her for being missish. "You should thank me, Kerstone. Once the mothers know of your predilection, they might stop throwing their daughters at your head." He laughed. "Even Camberley will think twice about allying his daughter with you, dukedom or no."

Miranda's breath caught in her throat. Had Simon

been planning a marriage with Celine Camberley? She did not want to believe it, even though she knew that she herself did not want to marry any man—not even Simon. To kiss him further perhaps, to feel his hands on her bare arms as she had this evening, those things she wanted. But they only came with marriage—and marriage was too high a price to pay for the dizzying taste and feel of the Duke of Kerstone.

Betsy's grandfather had had enough. His spare form straightened and he said softly, "Come, daughter. We must get the child home." He put an arm around the woman's shaking shoulders and cupped Betsy's chin in his hand to give her a reassuring smile. The child did not seem to notice the sad cast to her grandfather's expression, for she beamed at him with all the brightness she had shown earlier in the evening.

Miranda vowed to herself to stop in and make certain that Betsy and her mother were not harmed by this night's events. Perhaps some of the fruits of Anderlin's gardens would be welcome to mother, daughter, and grandfather.

A moment more and she would be free, she hoped. And then Betsy said, "I want to say good-bye to your wife, Your Grace."

The room fell silent, every eye on Simon. Inside him the quiet certainty that, for once, Fate would be thwarted, died. He wished he had thought to stuff an apple slice in the child's mouth, while he was hiding all other evidence of Miranda's presence. But, truly, what could he expect? He had heard Fate laughing.

Grimthorpe's eyebrow raised. "Have you married since I saw you this afternoon, Kerstone?"

Simon tensed. Under no circumstance would he

allow Miranda and Grimthorpe to meet. Not here. Not like this. "No."

Not content with his answer, Grimthorpe turned to Betsy and asked with a charming mockery of a smile that indicated he did not care about the dislike shining from the child's eyes, "Just what does the Duchess of Kerstone look like, child?"

"She's beautiful and kind," Betsy said with a hint of belligerence.

"Of course. But I must know if she's fair or dark."

Betsy remained obstinately mute, for which Simon blessed her. He would need to marry Miranda, now, of course. But he would prefer that no one know for a certainty that she was with him tonight. Inexplicably, even as he focused on protecting Miranda from humiliation, his thoughts raced ahead to marrying her. There was not a trace of regret, despite the shambles it made of his careful plans.

Grimthorpe coaxed with false sweetness, his gaze trained on Simon. "Perhaps I know her—the lovely new Duchess of Kerstone that we knew nothing about. . . ." His glance slid to Betsy, who was saying nothing further.

"How long were you planning to keep this marvelous news a secret?" Giving up on the child, he turned his attention back to Simon. "How interesting the ton will find this, Kerstone."

All Simon's concentration was on removing this man from the cottage so that he could be alone with Miranda. Her naïveté was such that he could not be sure she understood the implication of their predicament. "The child needs to go home. She is tired."

As if set in motion by his words, the villagers quickly nodded respectfully to Simon and filed out of the cottage. Grimthorpe did not.

The cottage was eerily silent with just the three of

them. Poking idly at the basket of food, at the blankets, Grimthorpe suddenly bent over and plucked up Miranda's boots. "Care to tell me whose feet these boots might grace?"

Simon said nothing, his jaw tensed with anger. For a moment he considered simply confessing all—he was going to marry her, after all—though his preference was to tear Grimthorpe's head from his shoulders.

Miranda lay frozen in the loft, realizing that she could be discovered at any moment. The thought of the consequences of discovery for her did not distress her as much as she knew they should—it was Simon whose reputation she feared tarnishing.

"Well, since they're certainly not yours, and there 's no one about . . ." Grimthorpe pointedly glanced at the loft. With a triumphant glance at Simon's booted feet, he tucked Miranda's boots under his arm. "I expect these were left by some previous occupant?"

Simon shrugged in response to the other man's inquiring glance, reaching out for the boots.

Grimthorpe smiled, bringing them more tightly into his grasp. "Never mind, old man. I found them. I shall make it my business to return them forthwith— as soon as I locate the owner."

Before Simon could react, Grimthorpe was gone.

Even though he left without checking the loft, even though the sound of Atlas's hooves was clear as he rode away, Miranda hesitated to move.

Simon said, with—unbelievably—the faintest of laughter, "Come down Miss Fenster. He is gone— with your boots, I'm afraid. I suppose this might well teach me not to dare Fate." He sighed. "Oddly enough, I am pleased you will be my Duchess." As she scrambled down from the loft, ready to protest, she thought that he added, faintly, "for as long as I live." Miranda was too disturbed by the beginning of his sentence to worry about the oddity of its latter half.

Walking home barefoot—with one turned ankle, took quite a while. Dawn had been well broken before she arrived at Anderlin, soaked to the skin and furious with the sanctimonious Duke of Kerstone. At least she had retained her dignity by refusing to allow him to sweep her up into his arms again. She wished she could have persuaded him that she required no escort on her walk. Instead, she satisfied herself by refusing to speak to him.

At the edge of the wood, she stopped and made her position clear one final time. "I must insist you accept that I will not be your wife." She looked up into his rain-slick face and said quietly, "I am honored that you think my reputation worth the protection of your name. I assure you that I am no Rapunzel trapped in a tower of shame in need of rescue."

"You do not understand these matters, Miss Fenster." He moved as if toward Anderlin, and Miranda let out a cry of sheer panic that stopped him. Impatiently, he explained, "I must discuss this with your brother."

"My brother? The very man whose elopement you prevented just two days ago? Do you think he will greet you with open arms when you tell him you have spent the night with his sister?" She tried to put scorn and disbelief in her voice, but truthfully, she did not know if Valentine would even acknowledge the duke's words—perhaps not even the duke himself.

Her brother, the last time she'd seen him, had been

dead of heart, dead of soul, and beyond communicating even rage or anger.

"You are so certain your brother is honorable, yet you doubt that he would do the right thing if he were to know the circumstances of our evening together?" He reached out and brought her to him, surrounding her with his unyielding arms.

"Do you love me, then?" She barely dared believe she had uttered the words, but she could not breathe in the space between the question and his answer.

He appeared as startled as she, and then pressed his lips together as he shook his head.

"Do you trust me enough to let me see what you have in that leather pouch?" Again, she knew she dared much. He did not love her, though. Could he trust her?

"Don't be silly," he said brusquely. "It is business, not meant for a woman's eyes." And then, to her surprise, he whispered, "We will suit, Miranda. I am sure of it. Marry me."

She bristled. "What does that mean? Suit? Does it mean that you can order me to do what you wish me to do? Think what you wish me to think? Share nothing of yourself?"

He smiled and nuzzled her ear briefly, then pulled away to look into her eyes. "Think of it, Miss Fenster—wed, we could do as we please without cost to your reputation. . . ."

She searched his gaze as her pulse beat in her temples. Marriage . . . no. The price was too high. "The thought is tempting," she answered him honestly. If only she knew she could be a duchess he might trust, he might one day come to love. But that was unlikely. Her talents lay in creating mayhem out of order rather than the reverse.

His arms tightened around her.

She pushed at his chest. "I'm sorry. I know I would regret it within the year."

His arms dropped away, leaving her exposed to the chill of the morning air. His whole expression shuttered closed. "Within six months is probably more accurate," he said, followed by a small harsh laugh. He closed his eyes and muttered softly to himself. "You are right, if we can avoid this, it would be best for both of us."

Miranda smiled, though she was not truly inclined to do so. "There, you see, we can just pretend that this never happened. Grimthorpe may have my boots, but he does not have my name, nor my description."

Simon's gaze lingered on Miranda's face until she felt herself flush with heat. She wondered if he was beginning to realize just how unsuitable she was as a candidate for his duchess. With a shake of his head, he said, "Should Grimthorpe discover the truth, we *will* marry."

Miranda shook her head. "You will see. He will never discover that I own those boots."

Afraid that he would take her in his arms again, Miranda quickly hobbled away toward Anderlin. She forced herself to stop thinking of him, of last night when he had kissed her, when his fingers had gently traced the scars on her back.

Perhaps on the physical level they suited very well, but he was too eager to take control of her life for her own peace of mind. As her father and mother— as Grimthorpe himself had learned once upon a time—she was not willing to be forced into being or doing something against her will.

She let herself silently into the kitchen at Anderlin and made her way down the darkened hallways to the study. The study door was locked; faint flickers of fading firelight showed infrequently. Miranda knocked softly but received no response. She pressed her ear against the door, suddenly afraid that Valentine had taken his own life. But then she heard the sound of shattering glass and a muttered round of unintelligible curses.

She decided to take it for a good sign. After all, he had not spoken two words together since he came home in disgrace, his elopement forestalled. Perhaps tomorrow he would be able to deal with the problem of their dwindling finances.

Not really believing that possible, Miranda decided she would settle for his taking breakfast and shaving as a sign that he might soon return to a semblance of his normal personality. If not, she would have to do something about their finances herself—again. She closed her eyes, leaning fully against the door as she remembered warm lips covering her own. But, despite that memory and the problems of her family's finances, marrying the Duke of Kerstone was not in her plans.

Chapter Five

Miranda took the bundle from deep within her cedar chest. It was wrinkled and gray, and as she removed the items that had been rolled within it and fruitlessly tried to shake the wrinkles from the cloth, a smell of stale grease surrounded her.

"Are you sure you should go?" her younger sister Hero asked, hazel eyes reflecting her worry even as her nose wrinkled in distaste at the odor.

"Yes." She had hoped never to have to wear it again. "Valentine is being stubborn. He insists that he will find a way to keep Anderlin afloat."

"Perhaps he will." There was little confidence in Hero's voice.

Miranda was tempted to shelter her younger sister, but she could not. Hero was the next oldest after Miranda and Valentine, and she must be prepared to shoulder the responsibility of the younger girls while Miranda was gone. "He is coming around from his disappointment. But not fast enough for us. He has not stirred from the study in two days, except to bathe and shave.''

Hero protested. ''If you give him just a little more time, Miranda—''

''We've barely any flour left, and the vegetable garden will not produce enough for eight people this month,'' Miranda interrupted, trying not to breathe too deeply, as she donned the wrinkled gray gown over her own plain blue, giving her figure a bulkier look. ''Help me with this, please, Hero.'' Miranda turned away from her sister's stricken look and quickly tied the hideous yellowed linen cap onto her head so that it hid every lock of hair.

As she had in previous trips, Miranda took two balls of spun wool and stuffed them into the sagging bodice of the gown until it was rounded and taut. One glance in the mirror convinced her that no one would recognize her. But the final coup de grâce was the pair of padded bags that she tied under her skirts. Before she tightened each bag's drawstring, she inserted two carefully wrapped sets of silver candlesticks and the glittering ruby neckpiece that had been her mother's prized possession.

''Oh, Miranda.'' Hero took the necklace from Miranda's hands and unwrapped it from the velvet cloth that protected it. ''Must you pawn Mother's necklace? She left it to you to wear when you are married and give balls of your own.''

It was truly a work of art, with its intricate workings of diamond-eyed gold swans, each with its neck curled gracefully around a ruby the size of Miranda's thumbpad.

The jewels themselves held no dazzle for Miranda. It was the memories that the piece conjured for her— her mother, dressed for a ball in a beautiful gown, sweeping down the staircase at Anderlin under the awed gazes of her children.

Miranda sighed. "Well, I have no better use for these jewels, Hero, than putting food on the table. I'm afraid Mother would be disappointed, but I don't believe I'll ever marry. Like the girl in the tale who would do anything to release her brothers from the evil spell that has turned them into swans"—she ran her finger over the swans, feeling the hard smooth swell of the jewels under her fingertips—"I would give up anything for my family." She smiled at her sister and gave her an impulsive hug.

Hero's eyes shone with hope. "Perhaps the duke will come for you like Cinder Ella's prince. You'd make a better Cinder Ella than swan princess."

Miranda frowned. "It's Grimthorpe who has my 'slippers', Hero, not the duke." She shuddered. "And I pray that he never finds out that they belong to me."

Hero laughed. "That would certainly change the way you told Cinder Ella's tale. You'd have one of the stepsisters fit into the boots, then, wouldn't you? Still, you'd be a marvelous duchess, even without boots. Wouldn't Mama just be delighted if she could look down and see her daughter a duchess?"

Miranda's smile died on her lips as she thought of her mother looking down from heaven. What would Mama have had to say about Miranda's folly? She had allowed the Duke of Kerstone unforgivable liberties.

Worse, in her own mind, as she was sure it would be in her mother's were she alive, Miranda had desired his kisses, his caresses. Silently she answered the question he had not made her answer that night. *Yes.* She would have allowed him to make love to her if they had not discovered Betsy in the loft. Indeed, she ached at the thought of what she had missed.

She knew with certainty that were he to climb into her bedroom window, like Rapunzel's love, she would give herself to him without hesitation. It was only marriage she didn't want.

What kind of a wanton was she to feel that way? If Grimthorpe had discovered her, her escapade would have afforded a week's worth of scandalous gossip in London. Miranda herself might have been completely ruined, but she gave little credit to that.

It was Simon's reputation that concerned her. The Dukes of Kerstone had been above reproach since the title was conferred—before that even, when they were mere earls. Should Simon be made a mockery of for a situation not of his own making?

True, it would be a minor blot, nothing like the shame attached to her. But Miranda had been in London briefly. She knew the avid joy with which this piece of news would be passed from vicious tongue to jaded ear. No one was more mocked than a fallen saint. And no one deserved that mockery less than Simon.

Putting those thoughts aside, Miranda briskly hugged Hero and pushed her out the door. "Please make sure there is no one in the kitchen to see me slip away." She added, hoping to vanquish the odd stare her sister had given her as she turned away and headed down the stairs, "I have no wish to marry, Hero. Truly I do not. Not even the Duke of Kerstone, as much as I admire him."

Becoming his mistress would have been a more likely outcome—though, of course, she would not have considered such a thing. One night, that was all she would have wanted—one night to know what it was that his kisses promised her.

Thankfully, he had been too much of a gentleman to take advantage of her. She had to be honest—he had been meddling when he had kissed her the first time. Trying to teach her a lesson had taught him one. She smiled. Even though the kiss he had given her was more in the way of a lesson than a liberty, she knew that he had enjoyed it much more than he had expected.

Her smile died. He would have insisted that they marry if he had made love to her. Perhaps Valentine was right. She was foolish to think life was like a fairy tale. Maybe there were not always happy endings. This ending was the happiest she would get—no marriage, no more of Simon's kisses.

Still, there was a touch of regret she could not explain. Perhaps it had to do with the longings that had plagued her daydreams since he had kissed her. She closed her eyes. Daydreams were all she had of him. Though, perhaps if she had not been a silly young girl five years ago. . . .

Her mind refused to consider the painful possibility. She would simply have to be grateful that Valentine would never learn of this. He had become such a prude since his return from the military, he'd probably lock her in her room and feed her bread and water for the rest of her life. Or, he would try, anyway.

There was a tapping on her door, and before Miranda had more time than to snatch the cap from her head and conceal her disguise in a swirl of dark gray cloak, her youngest sister dashed into the room, blond curls straggling from the ribbon meant to hold them tight.

"Kate, you naughty girl, why aren't you taking lessons with Juliet?"

The six-year-old's lower lip extended in a pout. "She called me a terror and boxed my ears."

Miranda suspected there was more to the story. "Whyever did she do that?"

Kate looked briefly discomfited. "Well . . ." But then, remembering something more important than her sad tale, the imp smiled. "I forgot, Miranda. Valentine needs you in the drawing room right away."

"He does?" Miranda considered letting him stew until she got back from London, but decided that she couldn't risk it. The trip would take the better part of today and most of tomorrow.

Absentmindedly, she stroked her sister's hair back into place. "Go and make peace with Juliet. You know she has the most beautiful voice of us all, and I shall see that she gives you a singing lesson if you behave for her."

"Will you also tell me a story?" the child wheedled.

Miranda had no time to bargain. "If you behave, sweet, I will tell you a story tomorrow when I tuck you into bed."

Kate nodded, then dashed madly out of the room, unheedful of Miranda's warning. "Don't run, it is not ladylike."

Miranda felt the weight of the silver thud against her legs, giving her strength to face Valentine. If only she could confide in him . . . but no, he was no longer the loving, trusting brother he had been.

Responsibility was a weight on his shoulders he would not share. She pulled her cloak tightly about her so that the gray gown was not in evidence and quickly hurried to the drawing room.

She was shocked to find that Valentine had company. The visitor's voice was unmistakable, and the muscles of her stomach tightened in dismay. Valentine's guest was none other than Simon Watterly, Duke of Kerstone.

She paused, wondering if she dare enter. Surely he would not have spoken of their encounter to Valentine. That would be tantamount to ruining her. Her heart soared with hope for a moment. Perhaps he had come to help Valentine win Emily back? After all, he had had time to think over everything that Miranda had told him.

Miranda took a deep breath and swept into the room, prepared to be surprised to see the duke after five long years.

Valentine's frown stopped her cold.

His face was white and his lips were drawn into the scowl that he had inherited from their mother. "Have you completely lost your sense of propriety, Miranda? How could you have done this?"

"Done what?" Miranda asked innocently, refusing to believe that Simon would have told her brother the truth. After all, he had as much to lose as she. She would never forget that bitter laugh of his when she reminded him that they would not suit.

"Is something wrong, Valentine?" she asked, hoping that his anger had some other source than her ill-spent night with Simon. Perhaps Valentine had missed the silver candlesticks she planned to pawn in London?

"I expected you to have told your brother everything by now, Miss Fenster." Simon was having none of the pretense. He made it clear with one crisp sentence that the truth was out.

Miranda spent one frozen moment in silent distraction as she stared at his beautiful, strong mouth. She could not help the rebuke that fell from her lips. "Some people keep their secrets, Your Grace—in leather pouches, perhaps, but they keep them."

His lips pressed tightly together until they were a white line. But he said nothing in apology.

And then, turning to her brother, she tried to recover the situation before it got out of hand. "It

was a dreadful mistake Valentine, but don't blame
His Grace for it, please. . . ."

"You had to try to save the family your way, didn't
you, Miranda?" She'd never seen him look so drawn.
There were lines of worry creasing his face that had
not been there a few short weeks ago. His blue eyes
showed clearly that he had lost all shreds of faith in
her. "Why didn't you tell me your plans?"

Miranda was incensed at his accusation. He was
speaking to her as if she were a child, not his twin
sister. "If you recall, you were not speaking to anyone—including me when I climbed through the
library window!"

"Then you should have waited until I was better
able to deal with your foolishness."

His words, so very like their father's, stung
Miranda deeply. "I don't see any point in telling you
anything anymore, Valentine. You're not the brother
I knew."

"I am the head of this household. You should have
told me your plans."

Miranda felt the tears start in her eyes and was
surprised to find that they were tears of happiness.
Her brother was fighting with her again. "You'd have
locked me in my room." She smiled.

Though Valentine did not return her smile, irony
was all that was left when he replied, "I'd have locked
you in the attic; you would just escape your room.
Miranda, do you realize what you've done?"

Miranda glanced nervously at Simon. How much
had he told Valentine? Surely not about the kiss . . .
or anything else. "No one knows, Valentine. I'm sure
that Simon will be discreet."

"Simon?" Valentine's eyes widened and his mouth
tightened again into a scowl.

Miranda blushed. The familiar address had become natural in her daydreams.

"I mean His Grace, of course, Valentine. I'm just rattled that he brought this matter to your attention. I thought we had settled it satisfactorily between ourselves."

She turned a stern glance on Simon. "It was to be a secret between the two of us. No one else was to know."

"What of Grimthorpe?" Simon asked in amazement.

Valentine exploded. "Grimthorpe! I don't know how you manage these things, Miranda. To accost the duke was misguided, but to be caught by Grimthorpe is beyond the pale."

"You sound as if you believe that was part of my plan, Valentine. And His Grace is overstating the incident. Grimthorpe saw naught of me. He simply has my boots."

Seeing her brother's stubbornly set face, Miranda abandoned the attempt to reason with Valentine and turned on Simon. "We agreed to keep this between ourselves, sir."

"Unfortunately, I could not persuade Grimthorpe to see it our way. He is on his way over here even as we speak."

"What?" Valentine and Miranda spoke together, their voices blending into one.

"He cannot know for sure it is me," she said firmly, though she didn't believe her own words. *Grimthorpe coming here?*

Her eyes studied the walls, where rectangular patches of lighter-colored wallpaper indicated the paintings that had been sold to cover her father's debts. The mantel was nearly bare, when it had once held porcelain boxes and figures, as well as the two sets of candlesticks she had weighing heavily against her legs.

These were details in which Grimthorpe would delight. But that was of no importance at the moment. She turned to Valentine. "You must tell him that I am away visiting a sick relative."

"Miranda . . ."

"Tell him I've been gone for weeks and will not be home again for a month. That will convince him that he is mistaken in his assumptions. And no one need know."

She threw a reproachful glance at Simon. "I wish that you had come to me first, Your Grace. You have shared our secret with Valentine, and it will be a hard one for a dutiful brother to accept."

"It will be impossible," Valentine sputtered.

"There is no need for upheaval, Valentine," Simon said smoothly. "Your sister and I are now officially engaged. I sent an announcement to the *Times* last evening with my manservant. It should appear tomorrow."

Miranda and Valentine were both stunned into silence.

After a moment, Miranda demanded, "How could you have done such a thing?"

Simon addressed Valentine, brushing off Miranda's question as if she had not spoken. "The marriage will take place in six weeks' time, if that is satisfactory."

His eyes touched on Miranda in a way that made her heart beat faster. "Since Miss Fenster and I were introduced five years ago, perhaps we could put it about that we nursed secret longings in our hearts that came to a quick fruition this past week, during my stay at the Camberleys' estate." His smile had a twist of irony in it. "No one should find that difficult to believe of her that she wished to live out one of her own fairy tales."

Valentine bristled. "How could you put an announcement in the paper without speaking to me first? That is simply not done, Kerstone."

Miranda added, "I have no intention of marrying you." Neither man paid her the slightest bit of attention.

Simon spoke, his attention focused on Valentine. "You must see that I had no choice, given the situation."

"I should call you out for this."

"Valentine." Miranda was truly alarmed now. Shattered as he was at losing Emily, she was afraid that he meant what he said. "You may not call out the duke. He was not at fault in any of this." Simon was a crack shot—and to have either man wounded would be unbearable. To have been the cause of their dispute would be ten times worse.

Valentine brushed off the restraining hand she laid on his arm. "Keep out of this, Miranda."

Exasperation made her shout. "How I wish I had!"

Both men, again, ignored her.

Simon stood straight, looking magnificently autocratic. "I should be the one calling you out. You are responsible for her. And she has made one hell of a mess of my life. I shall be months untangling this foolishness."

For one moment Miranda thought her brother would strike Simon. She again rushed to grasp his arm. "Valentine, be reasonable. You of all people know how my plans sometimes go awry."

Her brother looked at her as if she were a stranger. Miranda continued, her heart squeezed with pain. "I simply wanted to help you and Emily be together."

He stared blankly at her, and she continued, not looking at Simon. "Simon has been very understanding, except for this nonsense about marriage. Can't you find it within yourself to be the same?''

The old Valentine suddenly returned as his blue eyes gazed at her. There was warmth and amusement and affection radiating from him as he said, ''You are right, Kerstone, she is my responsibility. Until you are wed. And then I'll leave her to you.''

''Valentine! You cannot agree to this preposterous farce!'' Her brother merely laughed and moved to embrace her.

Aware of her bulky disguise—and somewhat miffed— Miranda stepped away. ''Would you sell me to the duke, then?''

''Mother always told you to think of the consequences before you acted, not after.'' He reached for the brandy—the last of their father's stock, Miranda knew—and poured two liberal drafts.

''As I am. Should this marriage take place, the consequences are too horrible to detail.'' When Valentine did not respond, Miranda continued. ''You promised me that I would not need to marry if I could not find a man content to let me run my life.''

Still he said nothing. ''Valentine, this man kissed me and unfastened my dress simply to teach me a lesson!'' Miranda blushed, realizing that she had gone too far in her desperation.

As if he had not heard her, Valentine handed Simon a glass. ''She is a fine woman. You will not be sorry to have her to wife. Certainly, Kerstone, you are the one man who just might manage to slip the bit in her mouth and charm her into liking it.''

Simon spared her one grim glance before he swallowed down his brandy. ''I will consider it my very first duty as her husband.''

Miranda watched the two men talking each other around to the reality of the marriage with growing frustration. They treated her statements as if they were less than the flap of gnat's wings.

Worse, she realized, she had no time for this nonsense if she were to catch the coach to London. "I've no intention of marrying you, Your Grace. Grimthorpe knows nothing for a certainty."

She faced her brother. "Valentine, you must tell Grimthorpe that I am away, and have been for the last two weeks. I am certain he will lose interest in this matter in less than a week's time."

With that directive, she spun around and left the room to the two men. Perhaps their drink would bring them back to their senses.

If not for the imminent arrival of Grimthorpe, Miranda would have exited from the front entrance to save precious time. The past few days had taught her to opt for discretion, though. She turned toward the back hallway and found two stunned men standing at the library door, their eyes trained on her.

She realized that she had forgotten to give her brother an excuse for her upcoming absence. Just what she needed, Valentine trailing her to London now. "I'm sorry I can't stay to discuss this further with you, Valentine, but I am late already. I have promised to help an invalid."

She pulled her cloak tight around her, hoping that he wouldn't notice that she wasn't yet wearing a bonnet. "She's seriously ill, so I don't know when I'll be back."

The silver thudded against her legs as she said encouragingly to her brother's blank face, "Perhaps you might tell Grimthorpe that I won't return for an entire month. I'm sure that will put him off the scent."

Chapter Six

Simon stared in bemusement down the hallway after Miranda. It took several moments before he registered that she had refused his offer—again. Would he have had this much trouble if he had proposed marriage five years ago? Several more moments of astonishment were spent before he realized that she meant to leave the house as if that were the end of the matter.

His surprise was quickly overtaken by a trifling sense of something out of place, not quite right in Miranda's hasty departure. He carefully reviewed the previous conversation.

She had been nervous, but that was to be expected; she had thought to escape unscathed from her escapade. He frowned, she had even dared to chide him, reminding him of the leather pouch of papers she seemed to be so damnably curious about.

Still, Simon held an unshakable conviction that something was off. A small yet significant inconsistency came to his attention. Miranda had not been wearing a bonnet when she left.

To his knowledge, young ladies, even unconventional young ladies like Miranda Fenster, did not go visiting engulfed in shabby, oversize cloaks and forget their bonnets.

Sprung into action by that small inconsistency, Simon clapped Valentine briefly on the shoulder. "Don't look so glum. I'll have her smiling at me when we take our vows."

Valentine looked at him dubiously. A smile crept to his lips, chasing away the shadows in his gaze for a moment. "You will, if anyone will. Good luck, Your Grace."

Even though the smile faded quickly, the deep weariness that had etched his face when Simon first approached him as he sat in the study foxed and distraught, was somewhat faded. There was a spark of life in the blue eyes that had not been there ten minutes ago.

With a confidence he had not felt but a moment ago, Simon held out his hand to Valentine. "I'll leave you to handle Grimthorpe alone. Perhaps it might be wise to tell him our engagement is of long-standing."

Valentine shook his hand heartily. "Certainly. Anything but Miranda's tale—can't count how many people may have seen her about, even these last few days. She's always been one to fly off to someone else's aid."

Simon wasted no time getting to the stables. There was no sign of Miranda. Both of her horses were unsaddled. Where the devil was she? Before he could come out of the stable, he heard voices.

Quietly, so that neither of the speakers would notice, he slipped to the door. His view of the yard was good, but he was disappointed to see that it was not Miranda, as he had first thought, but a heavyset older woman, obviously a servant, dressed all in gray with a yellowed linen cap covering her head, obscuring her face.

"Where is your mistress," Grimthorpe demanded for the third time. Simon could hear the exasperation in his voice.

The servant, her head bowed low, spoke in a heavy German accent. "Vich mistress do you mean? His Lordship ist not married und he hast six sisters."

"Do you expect me to be interested in any schoolroom misses? It should be obvious that I mean his eldest sister—Miss Miranda Fenster."

"Oh. Dat one." The servant's voice grew bored. "She hast been gone two veeks, a mont'."

"Gone? Gone where?" The doubt echoing in Grimthorpe's question mirrored Simon's own. When had she had time to coach her servant about her story?

"Avay. Far avay. She'll not be home for veeks."

"Nonsense. I'm certain I saw her but a day ago."

The servant shook her head impatiently and began to sweep the courtyard vigorously, raising a large cloud of dust. "Be off vith you foolish boy."

Grimthorpe raised his handkerchief to his face. "Tell me the truth, woman. I know I saw her just yesterday."

With a swoop of her broom, the servant aimed an extra large cloud of dust at Grimthorpe's insolent frame. "I told you Miss Fenster is avay. Go and ask His Lordship if you cannot believe the likes of me. I haf no more time for you. I haf vork to do."

With an oath that made the servant's jaw drop, Grimthorpe shouldered past her, into the kitchen entrance of the house.

Wishing Valentine well, Simon prepared to step

out and question the servant woman himself. Before
he could move, however, she dropped her broom in
the dust and took up the dark cloak that had been
slung over a nearby crate. She started down the garden path, moving with a speed and grace that greatly
belied her age and bulk.

As she passed by the stable doors, Simon heard her
utter an oath, and though he did not recognize her,
he definitely recognized her voice.

The little minx! She had fooled Grimthorpe, and
almost fooled Simon himself. What the devil was she
up to? He doubted that it had anything to do with
someone's illness.

He watched as she took the path that led toward
the village. He'd have to follow her. And he'd have
to be very careful to make sure that she didn't see
him. There was no telling what she'd do next if she
knew he had penetrated her disguise.

Shortly thereafter, Simon waited in an inconspicu-
ous seat at the side of the livery barn, hidden from
casual sight by the team of horses that had just been
unhitched from the London coach.

He had tethered his own horse out of sight. He
didn't know if Miranda would know his stallion by
sight after her brief encounter with his rear quarters,
but knowing Miranda as he was beginning to know
her, it was better not to take chances.

Calmly, he waited, hoping she had not switched
costumes yet again before emerging into the village,
or he would have no hope of spying her. Fortune was
with him. Shortly afterward, he saw her gray, matronly
figure, dingy gray cap hiding the lustrous curls. She
crossed the street and calmly shouldered her way onto
the top of the coach just as the new team was tethered.

Simon resisted the urge to mount his stallion and
head for London. He remained where he was, ever

conscious of Miranda's impulsive nature, until the
coach lurched off and he could be absolutely certain
she was indeed on her way to London.

When the dust had settled, Simon followed and
soon overtook the coach. With only a moment's inde-
cision, he passed the lumbering vehicle in a wide arc
that kept him out of sight of the passengers. He
wanted to arrive well before she did. As he rode, he
considered how to organize his campaign to find
out what she was about, leaving her home in such a
disguise without her brother's knowledge or consent.
He urged on his mount. He would need several hours
to gather the things he needed for the plan he had
in mind. . . .

Hours later, he watched as Miranda, clad in her
bulky disguise, climbed from the coach. He was
relieved to see that she had actually arrived, and not
alighted at some earlier stop. It was obvious she knew
where she was going. She asked no directions, spoke
to no one, and was careful to avoid the less respectable
of those abroad the teeming streets.

He followed her for a short distance, careful to stay
far enough away that she would sense no danger.
Fortunately for his temper, her destination was not
far. He recognized the street they were upon, a block
of lesser-known jewelers he had never frequented
himself, but he knew of others who had bought their
mistresses' trinkets in these streets.

A burst of intuition told him that she was going to
sell some of her few remaining valuables in order to
keep her family in funds. He wondered for a moment
at his assurance, and then remembered the faded
patches of wallpaper and nearly bare mantelpiece he
had noticed at Anderlin. There was no reason for the
relief that flooded through him at the realization.
After all, Miranda had turned down marriage with

him under the very mistaken impression that she could take care of herself. What else might she be capable of?

He had not truly thought that Miranda's errand might be a visit to a lover, or something more sinister. Now that he knew her destination, it was time for him to teach Miranda Fenster a lesson of which she was sorely in need. When next she met the Duke of Kerstone, she would fling herself into his arms and beg for marriage.

He adjusted the padding of his own hastily acquired costume so that his right shoulder seemed to reach to his ear. With a squint on his mud-daubed—and now whiskery, thanks to a theatrical friend—face, he hunched low to disguise his true height. He enjoyed the irony of playing the beast to her beauty. He wondered if she would appreciate it once he was through.

His powerful, fluid gait transformed into a more awkward, rolling one, as if his legs were of two different lengths. The distance between them closed rapidly. He was confident that Miranda would not recognize him when he drew up to her side and bore her into the nearby alleyway before she had any notion of what was happening to her.

"How dare you, sir," she said, struggling against him. "Unhand me."

There was no immediate sign that she understood the dangerous situation she was in. He did not find that a surprise.

"Where be ye going, girlie?" he asked in a harsh rasp as he pinned her up against the rough brick and deliberately let his breath assault her. It was worth the three cloves of garlic he had chewed to see the expression on her face.

"That is none of your concern, sir," she answered sharply.

But he noticed her lower lip begin to tremble as she realized the depth of trouble she had gotten herself into. He hoped that she realized she had been a fool to come unescorted to London.

She drew breath to scream, and he pressed his hand against her mouth. He did not want his prized pupil rescued before the lesson had even begun. "Be quiet, girlie. I've got a knife. Do you understand?"

Fighting tears, she nodded.

"Where be ye going?" he asked again.

"I have business in the street," she answered. Though her voice was shaky, her eyes were fierce as they trained on him.

He was thankful for the dimness of the alleyway, not certain his disguise would hold against her inspection if given the full light of day. "Would your business be with any of the jewelers?"

"No." Her eyes narrowed, betraying the truth even as she denied it.

"Ah. Would it be Dofflinger ye be seeing?"

She shook her head. "I told you I'm not—"

"Wendell then. Wendell would be a good man for buying from a pretty piece."

"A pretty piece!" Miranda's eyes widened in astonishment. "I'm as large as . . ." She clapped her jaw shut, cutting off the words. With a lift of her chin, she started over. "Never mind, that is of no consequence. My business is my own, sir. I choose not to share it with you."

"I've no wish to share yer business—only yer profits."

"Then you must free my arm so that I can reach my purse."

Simon stepped slightly away, but warned by the

light of hope in her eye, he drew his forearm across her throat, keeping her pinned to the wall.

The reticule she had clutched so carefully to protect it from the pickpockets was quickly fished from a deep pocket. She held it out to him. "Here. This is all that I have."

Simon accepted the bag with a small bow, although he kept his forearm tight across her throat. He dared not lower his guard where Miranda was concerned. She was likely to contrive to bring her lesson to a premature end by getting rescued by some courageous swain.

He rummaged in the bag, but there was nothing of value save a few coins, not even a single strand of pearls. He realized she would expect him to find those few coins interesting, but he knew there had to be more. "Is this it, just a few shillings? Is that the best ye can do when ye have business in this street?"

Miranda shook her head. "I am not a wealthy woman. I am a simple fishmonger's wife."

"A fishmonger's wife, eh?" He eyed her speculatively. "I've known a fishmonger or two in my time to make good money. Perhaps you have some silver hidden away?"

Her face went white, and he knew. He knew. But where on earth did she have it concealed? She carried no more bags with her.

Unless . . . of course, it had to be hidden in the bulk of her costume. But where?

A memory came to him unbidden, of Miranda with her gown clinging damply to her. Even in the candle glow of the cottage he had seen enough of her to know her true shape. Perhaps she had hidden her treasure in the bosom of her gown—much fuller than the Miranda he remembered. Or under the bulky skirts?

He hesitated, reluctant to physically search her. It was more than the lesson that he had intended. But for someone such as Miranda, it might not be going too far. She had taken an awful chance to be here. He could be a real cutthroat. And a real cutthroat would have no mercy on an unprotected woman.

"Have ye nothing under your skirts, girlie? I know some women what hide things under there. Ye've enough room under there for a set of silver."

Again Miranda blanched. "You are mistaken. Take what I have given you and go. The money is all I have, including my fare home. You are stranding me in London. Isn't that enough for you?"

"Nay, girlie," he answered. "Give up what's under your skirt—or perhaps tucked in your bosom—" He tried for a leer, and found it easy as he visualized her real shape beneath the padding.

Miranda clutched her hands to her bosom. "No!" He sighed loudly, making sure to aim his garlic-laden breath directly in her face, but she only said, "I am as poor as Cinder Ella before she married her prince. I assure you."

She was not going to make this easy. And Simon did not want to prolong this lesson for too much longer. Any moment someone might rescue her. "I've no time for this." Quickly, he lifted her skirt, just enough to let her know that he was serious.

She snatched it away. "Just a moment." Her voice trembled as she turned away from him with a dignity and modesty that surprised him. Truthfully, he could not understand why she was not down on her knees, in tears, begging for her life. He was a sight with the bushy, unkempt beard he had borrowed, and the clothes that stank from unwashed years on the beggar he had bought them from.

Impatiently, as she fumbled with the ties, he moved

to help her. The back of his neck was beginning to prickle with the second sense that had kept him alive through many a battle.

She started at his touch, and a bag fell at his feet with a clink. Silver, definitely. She picked it up with a nervous laugh, then handed it to him. He opened it to see the silver candlesticks that were to afford her family some ready.

"Thankee, girlee." As he turned to leave, he saw the look of overwhelming relief on her face and stopped. Was she holding something back? he wondered. "Is there any more, ma'am? Perhaps yc've something to balance you out?"

Again, her face betrayed her.

He did not want to wait while she fumbled yet again with nervous fingers to release the second bag. Drawing her against him, he untied the bag hanging against her slender hip. Her heart was beating rapidly. This was a lesson he hoped she would never forget— although he would see that she should not be in such want ever again. He found himself fiercely glad of that fact. He took the bag without checking the contents.

Remembering that he held all her money, he withdrew a few coins from the reticule. "This is good booty. I think I will be generous and leave you fare back home. Such as you should not be visitin' London."

The tears welled in her eyes and he flung a few more coins at her. "Here's enough for a room for the night and a cup of tea while yer waiting for yer coach."

He turned to leave, and then stopped once more. He couldn't have her enlisting the aid of any sympathetic young gentlemen as soon as he'd left her here. "Don't be calling for help, girlie. Don't think there won't be questions about where a fishmonger's wife got her hands on a set of silver candlesticks.''

As he left the alley, he was accosted by a sharp-eyed older man who wore clothes almost as disreputable as Simon's. ''Hold, guv'. Those bags look heavy. Show me what ye got.''

Simon held the bag up, as if to show his booty, and then, using one of the candlesticks as a club, he struck the man a blow to the side of the head. The man's hand released him, and Simon turned to see Miranda staring straight at him, as if she might challenge him. He frowned ferociously at her, satisfied to see her turn and walk away at a fast clip, staying far from the entranceways and alleys.

The man at his side made a feeble grasp for his coat, but Simon struck his hand aside easily. Free, he ran.

''Simon? It *is* you? I was convinced Cedric was mistaken. But it is you.''

''Yes, Mother. It is I.'' He ignored the plea in her eyes. She might have fooled London with her fragile blond beauty and her gentle voice, but he knew the true woman beneath her soft manners.

Seeing that he intended no gesture of peace, she settled into a chair by the fire. He ignored her gesture for him to sit. ''Have you come then, to tell me . . .'' Her voice faded for a moment, then regained its strength. ''. . . to say good-bye?''

''I am to be married.''

She gave a shocked exclamation. ''Married? Have you gone mad?''

Stiffly, Simon answered, ''The matter is settled. I see no point in discussing it.''

''Then why did you come?'' she asked bitterly.

"I did not want to cause you any undue embarrassment, should you appear ignorant of the engagement of your only son. I would do nothing to break the promise I made the old duke, as you know." He would have turned and left, but she laid a hand on his arm.

Sudden hope kindled in her eyes. "Simon, does this mean that you have decided not to go through with your foolish plan?"

"No, Mother." He should have guessed that would be her first question. Ever her thoughts revolved around her position and her image in society.

"Then why, Simon?"

"It is a long and uninteresting story, Mother. One I do not wish to share with you. Suffice it to say that my bride is a resourceful, impetuous woman, whose parents did a lamentable job with the extraordinary daughter they were given. I have decided to amuse myself in my last months with turning her into a woman suitable to live in the world in which she was born." He added, as a muttered afterthought, "Without turning it upside down and inside out."

His mother flushed. "You cannot marry when you have no intention of remaining a duke. Do you plan to walk away from your wife in six months' time? You'd do better to leave her jilted at the altar."

"Perhaps that is true, Mother, but I am not about to do so."

"I see." The cold woman he was more comfortable dealing with came again to the fore. "You are just like your father. What you want, you take, no matter the consequences."

"Are you referring to him?" Simon nodded toward the portrait of the former duke that hung above the mantel. "Or were you speaking of my true father?"

Her cheeks grew red. "How dare you be so insolent. The duke acknowledged you, Simon. He was your father in the eyes of the law."

"And in the eyes of God?"

With cold precision, she said, "Truly Simon, you are as unfeeling as both of your fathers. You care nothing for this girl or her welfare. You wish only to satisfy your own whims."

His mother was more furious than Simon had ever seen her, except perhaps at his father's deathbed. The words she had spoken were still burned into his memory. *I find I cannot pray that the devil takes you, Sinclair. Though I wish I had never clapped eyes on you, though I wish my father had not sold me to you before I even had a chance at the marriage mart. I would not have Simon if it were not for you.*

Simon had not understood, as he stood listening unseen from the doorway, until his mother had answered his father's inaudible whisper. *Yes. he is a fine boy. My bastard son will make a successful seventh duke.*

Bringing himself back to the present, Simon said curtly to his mother. "You give me no credit, Mother. It is not merely my whim which compels the marriage." He wondered very much the truth of that—he had evaded marriage traps before with great skill. This one, it seemed, he was springing on the bride. Was it only a whim?

Her eyes narrowed. "You have gotten her with child?"

"No, Mother. Though you are hardly one to comment, are you?"

"Simon, I am your mother."

"Of course. Please excuse my intemperate speech, Madam." He felt a twist of pleasure and pain at the color that washed her cheeks yet again. He sighed.

"Miss Fenster and I have been discovered in a compromising position by a person who would delight in trying to embarrass me, for which I care little. But I promised the old duke I would not harm the family name, and I will not allow even a trace of mockery to be attached to it as long as I am duke. After all, I know what my proud lineage is, do I not?"

Her mouth twisted as she let out a cry. He had never seen her lose control like this—except on the day of his father's death. She gazed at him steadily and said in a cold, hard voice, "Simon, you might not be his son, but you are more like Sinclair than you know."

She closed her eyes and whispered, "How I wish it weren't so." And then, her anger returned, she added, "And so will this girl you intend to marry—unless you give up your plan to run away from your title and the duty you were bred to perform."

"I believe we have covered that completely in the past, mother."

"The duke knew, Simon. He . . ." Her voice trailed off, the emotion that had burst from her words going flat in a way he knew well from the days when he had thought himself his father's son, the legitimate heir, and had listened to her rare arguments with his father. No one ever won an argument with his father. After a while, most learned not to try. "He wanted you to inherit. If he had not, he would have disowned you without a moment's hesitation."

"Good day, Mother."

"Think of that innocent young girl, Simon. Does she deserve what you want to put her through? Just so that you can amuse yourself for a few months' time? You will ruin her!" When he would have answered, she allowed her voice to rise. "I don't mean her reputation, Simon. I mean her heart and soul."

He thrust that thought away from him. He wanted Miranda as he had wanted no other woman in his life and Fate had dropped her into his arms. No matter that it was foolhardy to marry for the few months he had left, he would do so. He would be a good husband to Miranda, no matter how brief their time together. And for the rest of his life, he would know that he had had at least a tiny part of the life he had dreamed of once long ago.

He was not without self-control and he knew several methods that would assure he left no child behind. He was not, in truth, being unreasonable. He could not risk marrying in his new life. Years of deception would wear him down to nothing. But six months was a heartbeat in a lifetime. If he could have her for six months, then so be it. Still, he could not help his urge to justify himself. "She will be ruined if I do not marry her, Mother. And she will only be a widow—heart, soul, and jointure in her possession— if I do."

His mother winced. "Simon, reconsider this fool-hardy action of yours. If you are determined to keep the integrity of the Watterlys unscathed by scandal and pass the line to a true descendent, you do not want to bring a wife into this mess."

Simon refused to listen. She was not one from whom he would take counsel. "I must go, Mother." He bent to press a light kiss against her cheek, avoiding her clutching hand.

Chapter Seven

Miranda slipped soundlessly into the darkened main hallway of Anderlin. She stopped for a moment to shoot the bolt, leaning against the sturdy oak door. *Safe.*

Gradually, the trembling within her abated as she drew strength from the peaceful familiarity of Anderlin at night. No servants or younger sisters stirred to ask embarrassing questions, or silently note her discomposure.

The incident yesterday had affected her more than she supposed. As she walked the familiar pathway from the village to Anderlin she had seen highwaymen in every sway of a tree branch in the breeze.

She straightened and headed for the library to check on Valentine. What was she going to do now? Simon seemed intent upon marrying her, Valentine upon marrying her off. And now, at the whim of a scoundrel, she had lost her chance to put the family finances back in order for a while longer.

Her hands clenched. If she had carried a knife or a pistol with her, maybe she would have had a chance to fight the cutthroat off. It was amazing the way he had known she had something hidden beneath her skirts, almost as if he could read her mind.

She felt a shiver go through her. He had been one of the meanest, ugliest creatures she had ever had the misfortune to meet. She would never forget the stink of his breath, nor the bushy dark beard that hid his face from her. She hoped never to come across him again.

She entered the darkened study quietly, so as not to disturb Valentine if he was sleeping. The fire had burned low and she could make out only a shadowy outline in the chair by the fire. The sound of his breathing was even and light. She hoped he slept soundly, for then she could avoid any awkward questions.

With an ease born of a lifetime's familiarity, Miranda moved carefully through the darkness. One thing she needed, whether he approved or not, was a medicinal glass of brandy to steady her nerves.

She nearly dropped the crystal decanter when she heard Simon's familiar voice. "How was your sick friend, Miranda?"

She whirled to face the figure in the chair. If he was still here, it meant that he intended to try once more to convince her that the marriage was necessary. She would need all her wits about her. Looking at him, she had to suppress a shiver of anticipation when it crossed her mind that he might kiss her yet again in his attempt to change her mind. "Where is Valentine?"

However, Simon dispelled the image of a passionate embrace when he said calmly, "I imagine he has quite sensibly retired, considering the hour. I expect he thought you would stay the night with your sick friend.''

She flushed in the dark, wondering what had possessed her to think of kissing when she needed to think of how to convince Simon that she was not interested in marrying him. ''Yes. Well, as you can see, I did not.'' She replaced the lid on the decanter, and put the bottle back. She wasn't comfortable taking a drink with Simon present.

''What kind of an illness was it, Miranda, to be over so quickly?'' he asked.

Miranda frowned. She felt that if she told another lie to him she would become the poor bitter girl in the tale who spit frogs and snakes when she spoke. ''That is of no consequence, Your Grace. No doubt you wish to discuss another, more pertinent matter, but I'm afraid this very conversation with you is improper. Perhaps we should continue it tomorrow, in Valentine's presence.''

''I will be taking my leave at sunrise.'' He rose from the chair and crouched by the fire. ''Besides, I find I enjoy speaking with you at night, by firelight. And my question is a simple one—do you wish to be married here?''

Unbidden, the image of Simon in the old chapel, smiling as he awaited her vows, came to her. Miranda brushed it aside. ''What has made you change your mind about marriage? I recall when you thought I was trying to entrap you, you were quite certain that you did not want to marry me.''

He did not look at her as he answered. ''I'm surprised you need to ask, after the night we spent together.'' Suddenly, he looked deep into her eyes. ''Remember—you are the one who is so certain that physical attraction can cause a man to behave foolishly. Surely you can understand that I have accepted that the only way for me to have you in my bed is to marry you."

Miranda felt the heat of his words all the way to her toes. She refused to give in to it, however. "But I am a woman, Your Grace. And my mind has not been changed. I do not want to be married to a man who does not love or trust me—" Afraid her words were too harsh for his, after all, gallant behavior, Miranda tried to soften them with a touch of honesty. "Even though there is a physical attraction between us."

His whisper was as loud as a shout in the silent room. "A strong attraction. The kind worth risking a little pain for."

"Surely you would not force me to marry you when I am so set against it? This is not the eighteenth century, sir!" She appealed to his honor, knowing how much a part of him it was. "You are too fine a man to do so."

There was a short silence and then the shadowy figure stood. "Perhaps it is the taint of bad blood in me, Miranda, but I want you and I will do everything in my power to have you."

"Bad blood! The Earls and Dukes of Kerstone have an impeccable line."

He stirred restlessly. "Perhaps from my mother's side, Miranda. One never knows these things, does one? Now, about the wedding—will it take place here? Or shall I make arrangements at my seat? Or would you prefer London, perhaps?"

Discomforted, Miranda noticed that there was an edge about him that there had not been that morning. Somehow, he was quite certain she would marry him—and it was not simply masculine arrogance. That she had dealt with before.

This was more, and she was afraid of his intensity

as he stared down at her in the darkness of the quiet study.

"Why, when we neither of us have a true desire to be wed?"

In the darkness he moved to light the candles, lighting them one by one from the dying glow of the fireplace until the room was filled with leaping shadows and she could see Simon's implacable eyes. "That makes us a perfectly matched pair."

Knowing that a scream would merely complicate matters, and bring the rest of the household down around their ears, Miranda settled for grinding her teeth. "Your Grace, please, I would prefer that you allow me the liberty of crying off."

He came toward her, until she could see his face clearly. "But Miranda, the ink on our engagement announcement is still wet. Surely you will not embarrass me so?"

Miranda bit her lip. That was a dilemma, was it not? If she cried off . . . "Well, then, you cry off. My reputation and feelings are of no consequence."

He shook his head and smiled. "I cannot humiliate myself that way. I made a promise to my father on his deathbed never to disgrace the family name. I have made an honest bid for you, and Valentine has accepted it."

"Valentine is not thinking clearly."

"Valentine knows his duty, Miranda. I don't know why you persist in fighting it. Why is it that you object to a match with me? Have you a *tendre* for some other fellow?"

"Of course not."

"Then why, Miranda?"

"Because Grimthorpe is the only reason you feel this need to marry me. I know it is not physical attraction that impels you to make the offer—it is your damnable sense of honor!''

He interrupted her with a deep, short laugh that held an irritating amount of smug satisfaction. ''I think you have mistaken the reason for my offer, Miranda. Though, of course, it might not have happened if not for Grimthorpe. I look forward to the task I have set myself.''

Miranda was confused. ''Task?''

''I have decided it is my job to make you into a wife any man might take pride in—especially your next husband, should you decide to marry again.''

Miranda felt the sting of his insult first, then took in the import of his final words. ''My next husband?''

He sighed. ''I want you Miranda, but I cannot keep you.''

''You are making no sense. Are you drunk?''

''No, I have not been drinking. I am trying to explain that you will have me as husband for only six months' time.''

''Are you going away?'' Some former soldiers did that, she knew, to explore India and Africa. But, as duke, Simon had responsibilities. Surely he would not shirk them?

''You might say so.''

''Do not be cryptic with me now. Where will you be in six months' time?''

His gaze focused on the leaping flames in the fireplace. ''In six months' time, Simon Watterly, Duke of Kerstone, will be dead.''

Miranda gasped. ''But how? Have you the pox?''

It was Simon's turn to gasp. ''Where the devil did you hear about something like that?''

''I overheard Valentine's friends. They said many soldiers . . .''

''No, Miranda, I do not have the pox. And I assure

you that you will not be overhearing such conversations in the future. As my wife, you will begin to keep suitable company and discuss suitable subjects."

Miranda ignored his comments, more intent on the unbelievable thought that this vibrant man was dying. "You are certain of this? Perhaps if you see another doctor?"

"There is no hope, Miranda. I have seen all the doctors I need to see to be sure."

Miranda stared at him as she reeled under the impact of the news, unable to accept it. Her objections to the marriage were swept away in a single breath. "Perhaps we should apply for a special license."

For a moment, there was the faintest of smiles on Simon's lips. "I would not be averse, but do you think Valentine can stand the strain of gossip?"

"Valentine admires you very much. I should think he would be happy to know that I will be applying my abilities toward getting you through this crisis and making you well again."

The smile on Simon's lips was not at all faint this time. "Ah yes. I would delight in as quick a recovery as your patient had today."

He looked at the mantel. "It is quite dark in here, Miranda. I can't see your face. Perhaps that is because of the lack of candles. You really ought not to allow the servants to polish the silver without replacing the candlesticks promptly."

Miranda blushed. The candlesticks would never be back and it was certainly not the servants' fault. She realized, very suddenly, that if Simon married her, all would be well for her brother and her sisters.

It was only her own foolish, miserable heart that would suffer. And certainly she deserved that. "I hope you never regret marrying me. I am impetuous and . . ."

In a moment he had crossed the distance between them and swept her into his arms. ". . . And loyal and brave and sweet." His lips brushed her neck as he whispered.

"I don't know what good I can do your health, Simon, but I will do all that I can and more to see you well."

"I won't need anything but your companionship." His arms tightened around her, leaving her in no doubt about what he meant. "Although perhaps your nursing skills might be brought to bear upon my heir apparent. He always seems to be sniffling—when he isn't falling off his horse."

"I have enough patience for two patients." Miranda gave herself entirely up into his embrace. "I shall do my best to make you a good wife."

She had expected a look of subdued triumph to overtake his features, not the bitter twist that came to his mouth. "I think, Miranda, that I will be the one to make you an excellent wife. And your next husband will no doubt thank me."

Miranda would have protested, but his mouth came down on hers and all thoughts were swept away in the pleasure of the kiss.

Betsy swept a pretty curtsy as Miranda came up the pathway to the neatly kept cottage. Unfortunately, in her excitement, she forgot that a young lady never ran and dashed away behind the cottage calling loudly for her mother.

Miranda had to quickly stifle her laughter behind her palm as Katherine came running, clutching two handfuls of uprooted herbs. Her eyes lost some of their panic when she saw Miranda. Her face became quite pretty when she smiled.

"How did the wormwood tonic do?"

"Oh, quite successfully, thank you. Valentine's spirits and his appetite have both picked up," Miranda answered, her smile disappearing as she remembered her task here. "But I'm afraid I need more than a simple remedy this time."

Katherine's expression grew grave. "For yourself?"

Miranda shook her head. "No." She looked into eyes she had learned to trust, after only one short meeting a few days ago. Katherine had been nothing like Miranda expected. She was indeed a good mother—and no lightskirt. Grimthorpe had come to her for a remedy of a very personal—and herbal— nature.

Though it was obvious the family had no money, the garden and pathways were well kept, the cottage itself in repair and neat. Miranda took a deep breath, knowing that she was trusting Katherine with a very important secret. "His Grace has confided in me that he is very ill."

Katherine murmured in shock. "No!"

"His doctors have told him that he is to die within six months' time." Miranda grasped the other woman's slender arm. "Can you help him? He sounds as if he's given up hope."

The healer frowned. "He certainly seemed healthy the little I saw of him. What are his symptoms?"

The logic of the question caught Miranda by surprise. She had been so shocked by Simon's news that she had not thought to find out. She shook her head in annoyance at her own stupidity. "I never thought to ask."

Katherine smiled sympathetically. "Will you see him sometime soon? Could you ask him then?"

"We are to be married tomorrow—"

Katherine laughed, and Miranda was surprised to

hear it. Such a serious demeanor had led her to believe that the healer was incapable of laughter. Then she realized the cause and blushed. "It is not what you think—"

"I think nothing but that when you speak of him your eyes glow. And I shall do my best to see that you have him for as long as you live." Her eyes darkened. "Although, knowing nothing, I cannot promise. . . . Still, he seemed so hale I can't believe . . ."

Her voice drifted off as she looked full at Miranda. "My goodness, if you are to be married so quickly, how shall I find out the cause of his illness. Will you write?"

Miranda shook her head and began to guide her into the cottage. "No. I have a plan—"

Chapter Eight

It was done. She was married. Standing in the only home she had ever known, her beloved Anderlin, Miranda realized she could no longer it call "home" now that she had wed. Miranda stood quietly for a moment in the corner of Anderlin's dining hall, amazed at the transformation that Simon's army of newly hired servants had wrought for their wedding feast. The silver and gold gleamed. For a moment she felt doubt assail her. She hoped she was not making a mistake, marrying a man who did not love or trust her. And, truly, what did she know of him? For all she could be certain, beneath the saintly demeanor might lie the heart of a robber bridegroom waiting to chop her up and eat her in a bride stew.

She frowned and walked nearer the mantelpiece, Somehow, candlesticks had been found that matched the ones from the study, the very ones that had been stolen from her in London. She sighed. She had almost put that incident from her mind—Simon was no robber bridegroom, and he would not let her family starve. And Valentine had given up his depression to throw himself into new plans to revitalize Anderlin.

"How does it feel to be married?" Hero's smile was shy as she joined her sister in the corner and took her turn surveying the changed room. "To command such an army of servants?"

"At the moment, I confess I feel somewhat numb." Miranda's heart ached at the thought of leaving her sisters, but Hero, at eighteen, and Juliet, at sixteen, were at least old enough to understand what marriage meant. Indeed, they were no doubt dreaming of being married themselves shortly.

What Rosaline, Helena, and little Kate thought, she had no notion. They had been kept away from her by Hero and Juliet so that she could finish up the endless fittings and little details that brought her wardrobe and her wedding together in under a week. She had missed them terribly, even though they were just in another part of the house. How much harder would it be when she was gone from Anderlin?

Hero did not smile. She was such a serious child that her anxiety was etched upon her thin face. "How should I address you now that you are a duchess? It seems so strange to think of you that way." She blushed as she realized that her words could be taken as an insult. "I mean . . ."

"I know exactly what you mean." Miranda glanced across the room toward the bent head of her husband of less than an hour. "It is odd. A few vows, a simple ceremony, and we are bonded for life. What has always been the ending for our fairy tales is, in truth, the beginning of a very different life."

Hero nodded, her eyes flitting around the room, as she whispered, "He is like a fairy godfather, is he not?" When Miranda did not immediately agree, Hero faltered and added softly, "Instead of a godmother, I mean. . . ."

"In some ways I think he's more in need of a fairy godmother." She thought of Simon's disclosure but said nothing of it to her sister. A wedding day should be joyous.

Hero shook her head soberly. "Oh, he's in no need of that anymore, Miranda. Not now that he has you." A sudden sadness obscured her features.

Miranda reached over to squeeze her sister's hand. "But I shall always be the sister you knew. My becoming a duchess changes nothing between us."

Juliet had come up behind them and slipped an arm around Hero's waist for a brief moment, saying, "Except for removing you from our household, of course."

Miranda nodded, once again looking toward Simon. Her heart hammered inside her chest. "I have every confidence in your abilities to manage the household, Hero." She tried to coax a smile out of her by adding, "And I know Juliet will help you as she has always helped me."

Hero, her quiet, bookish sister, had a disconcerting gleam in her eye as she laughed. "And since the duke has agreed to give me a Season this year, I daresay you will soon be trying your wings at managing things, too, Juliet."

She found it somehow frightening to think of her younger sisters trying to manage Anderlin, never mind trying to find husbands. For a moment she fought a strong desire to go jump up onto the table and announce that she had made a terrible mistake.

Hero, ever sensitive, leaned over to whisper in her ear, "You look less than happy, Miranda. You should smile more or some will say you are a reluctant bride."

Miranda grimaced and then quickly fixed a smile upon her expression, as she searched the crowded room for Grimthorpe—who, as a cousin, no matter how distant, had somehow managed to attach himself to a group of wedding guests and insinuate himself into the celebration. He was the only one who might suspect the circumstances of her sudden marriage. "The broken stay has slipped a little and is scratching my side."

Her sister winced in sympathy. "Stubborn contraption. I thought we had it well fixed. Perhaps we can manage to slip away and exchange stays? I don't need the new ones that Simon had made for you. I'll return them to you."

"No!" Miranda shook her head firmly. "I don't know what help Valentine will take from Simon, and I'll not have you running the household with a broken stay jabbing your ribs when you move."

Hero hugged her. "You are a thoughtful sister. Thankfully you'll never have to worry about such things again. I'm certain Simon will see that you have as many new stays as you need."

Miranda frowned. "I hadn't thought of that." She sighed. "I suppose a duchess must always wear her stays?"

"Do you really mind?" Juliet looked incredulously around at the remains of the magnificent feast that Simon had supplied. "Think of all your new clothes. I would have chosen my wardrobe already."

Miranda smiled, "I was too busy dreaming of presenting Hero to the new queen. I hadn't even given a thought to how it would feel to be married, never mind how I would dress."

"I daresay you'll be used to it by next year." Hero's hazel eyes danced with mischief. "And then you'll be getting used to motherhood, no doubt."

Miranda blushed scarlet. "Hero! What if the twins or little Kate heard you say such a shocking thing?"

As if on cue, Miranda's youngest sisters crowded around her, exclaiming how beautiful she was, while at the same time preening in the finery that had been hastily stitched for them with no spared expense. It had been years since they had been able to afford silk and satin. The girls had had new stuff gowns once a year, but Miranda had not had a new gown since her London season.

"Miranda," Kate confided sotto voce, "I don't think there's anyone here more beautiful than you." She gazed wistfully at her own pink satin gown, and then added, "Except for me."

Miranda smiled at her sisters, thinking how glad it made her to know that her marriage would assure that each of them would come out properly and find a husband worthy of them.

She looked at Kate, twirling around in her finery. Except for Kate, perhaps. Kate herself would require an extraordinary man to be a patient husband for her. She looked up with a wistful smile on her face at the thought of Kate grown and married, and found Simon next to her, gazing at her with an unsettling intensity.

"Excuse me, ladies," he said gently as he extracted Miranda from the center of her sisters, "but my wife and I must be on our way home."

Miranda felt a clutch of fear. "Home," she repeated without a smile. Home had always been Anderlin, and now, because of a simple ceremony, a few words, and a ring on her finger, home was no longer Anderlin. It was far away—with Simon.

As one, her sisters' smiles fell. She had prepared them for what would come after the wedding, but she understood their dismay, as she was feeling the same herself. Hero was the first to recover her composure. There was only a hint of moisture in her eyes when she gently kissed Miranda's cheek and pressed a quick embrace upon her. "We're going to miss you."

"Must you go?" Kate asked. She stared at Simon angrily. "Why can't you stay here? Anderlin is the best home that ever was. Who will tell me stories if you take my Miranda away?"

Hero, stepping almost naturally into the role of eldest sister, chided Kate gently before Miranda could open her mouth. "I will tell you stories, Kate. Don't be a baby."

Kate, disliking the change of command, stared stubbornly at Miranda, the sister who had mothered her for as long as she could remember. "She can't tell stories like you can. Please don't go."

Simon knelt down until he was at eye level with Kate. "When a man marries, his wife goes to live with him. One day, Kate, you will do the same."

"Never," she declared. "My husband will live here at Anderlin."

Juliet chided her. "Hush silly. Don't you know that Valentine will take a wife and they will live here. You will go with your husband."

Kate, ready to cry, was enfolded gently into Simon's arms and lifted up to face him. "Just because Miranda's home is now my home, little one, doesn't mean that you won't be welcome to visit."

Kate looked at him wide-eyed through her tears. "Will you take me with you?" Miranda was ashamed at her leap of hope that Simon would agree.

Valentine, who had come up beside Miranda in time to hear the last part of the exchange, gave her shoulder a quick squeeze. She relaxed and reached for his hand to give his fingers a return squeeze. He would not let Kate—or any of the others—feel too much loss. He had promised letters and visits.

As if to show her the truth of his words, Valentine held out his arms to his little sister and said, "Kate, you cannot leave me now. First I must learn to run the household without Miranda, and I need your assistance."

Kate looked doubtfully at him for a moment and then came into his arms with a little sigh. "Very well. But then, I must visit Miranda. After all, you have Hero to help you."

Valentine nodded. "Of course, and Miranda will always be welcome here." He looked at his sister, to emphasize the full implication of his words.

Miranda smiled at him, glad that they were of one mind again. She did not fear that she should need to take up his invitation. But she knew how rare it was for even a loving brother to boldly declare that he would interfere in another man's marriage if his sister was hurt.

Simon added dryly, as he firmly took Miranda's elbow, "And your family is welcome to visit at any time. Consider our home your own."

Our home. How odd. She smiled at her sisters until they returned smiles of their own, though mere pale imitations of their usual ones.

Simon squeezed her elbow gently, an intimacy that startled her. "Come, my dear. The coach is waiting."

Miranda nodded and followed slowly. It felt strange to have Simon's hand on her arm. And tonight it would be like it had been in the hunter's cottage . . . except he would have no reason to pull back from her. He was her husband, now. She looked down at the strong fingers that held her, and felt a soft fluttering inside her. What on earth had she done?

Before entering the carriage, Miranda crushed

each of her sisters to her for a final hug. Juliet, who would come out next after Hero and was already well grown; Hero, who wanted to live up to the reputation of the Shakespearean character for whom she was named; the twins, Rosaline and Helena, who had been the despair of their mother when they cut their hair and declared that they did not want to be "silly girls."

And Kate of course, the baby who remembered no mother but Miranda. How would they fare without her? Or she without them?

But then, she comforted herself, Simon needed her more than her sisters.

"Wait a moment, Kerstone." Valentine was suddenly by her side, looking into her eyes, and she saw the panic she felt mirrored in his eyes. "You will be happy." He enfolded her in his arms as he spoke. "If not, your husband will answer to me."

Valentine's embrace twisted the stay into her side, but Miranda did not protest. "I have not married a robber bridegroom. He will be good to me—and I shall help him get well." She threw her arms about her brother and whispered hastily, "I shall speak to Simon about Emily as soon as I am able, Valentine. And I shall not abandon our family simply because I am now married. I shall find a way to increase our fortunes."

He said sharply, not bothering to whisper, "Emily is beyond me, Sister. Please accept that. And about our 'fortune', it appears to have turned." Miranda was startled when Valentine grinned broadly. "It seems that one of our investments has paid off at last. I heard from our solicitor late yesterday."

"What? How could you forget to tell me until now?" Those investments that she had made while he was away had been a nagging source of guilt for her for so long. Miranda breathed deeply as the weight of guilt finally eased.

"I thought you had more important things on your mind." He smiled, and her heart twisted at how easily he was shutting her out of her former life. "It is not great wealth, but it will keep us afloat." He hugged her once, tightly, and released her into Simon's care. "Don't worry about us, Miranda. We'll be fine."

"Of course they will," Simon added. His deep voice sent a shiver up her spine, beginning just at the spot at the small of her back where his hand gently rested. "And none of you need worry about Miranda. I will take good care of her."

Valentine met her eyes and smiled. "And she will take care of you, Kerstone. Won't you, Miranda?"

Would she? Could she? She struggled not to reveal the crushing load of doubt that suddenly oppressed her. Simon's life, not just his future happiness, lay in her hands.

He handed her into the carriage. The vehicle swayed as he followed her inside. To Miranda's surprise, he intended to ride inside with her. Could he be in pain? He seemed healthy enough. Indeed, his presence filled the carriage.

As the cheerful well-wishing of the wedding guests faded into the distance, and the sharp pain of watching her family's faces grow into indistinguishable dots of color dulled, she found herself nervous to have him so near. The intimacy again reminded her of their sojourn in the hunter's cottage—the very reason they were now here as husband and wife.

Wife. She felt a liquid settling in her middle as the word struck her, with all its attendant responsibilities. Not the least of which was the getting of an heir. She owed him that, after all, if he was not to live long.

She hoped she would not fail him in such an important task.

"Why are you staring so?" Simon asked her. But there was a smile upon his lips that suggested he knew very well in which direction her thoughts had wandered.

Miranda flushed. "I was wondering if you were feeling well."

His lips tightened in annoyance and then relaxed into a smile as he edged closer toward her. "I am fine."

Miranda, knowing that she was a coward, whispered, "I feel so tired, I think I shall nap." She closed her eyes upon his amused expression and, to her surprise, found herself waking up hours later.

Her waking position was in Simon's arms and she hastily righted herself, but he did not allow her to edge to the other side of the seat as she would have liked. "Are you still feeling well?" she asked as the carriage jounced over a particularly bumpy portion of the roadway.

"I did not marry you to acquire a nurse." He took her into his arms and his lips began plying small, disturbing kisses against the skin of her neck.

Miranda sat captive, able only to offer token protest. "A wife must worry after her husband's health. . . ."

"Does that mean satisfying his every need?" His breath was warm on her ear as he spoke.

Miranda tried to keep her mind on the conversation, to stop the strength from sapping from her limbs. "Now that I am your wife, Simon, I must see to your comfort, your hunger—" She grasped the straw of hope that came to her. "Are you hungry? Should we stop for the basket of delicacies that Cook prepared?"

He laughed low in his throat, and she could feel

the vibration to her toes. "We agreed not to stop, except for fresh horses, but to press on so that we could reach home tonight. But I am hungry, wife." His arms seemed to tighten around her infinitesimally.

"Should I unpack the basket here, then?" Miranda pulled away to reach for the wicker container stored under the seat.

Simon pulled her back into his arms. His hands were gentle and warm on her hips as he settled her in his lap. She looked up into his eyes and recognized the passion glowing there. Her own senses ignited.

Feeling as if she was so warm she must burn him wherever she touched, she smiled and held herself still. Was it seemly to remember so vividly what had happened once, by mistake? To want it to happen again? She fought the urge to lean forward and press her lips to his. "If you are hungry, Simon, I must feed you."

Her heart beat harder when he leaned toward her to whisper, "Then kiss me, Miranda, for I am hungry for your touch." His mouth took hers with gentle persuasion, and Miranda found herself more than willing to return the kiss. He did not seem to find her too hot to the touch, no matter how she burned inside, because his hand quickly moved upward from her hip, past her waist, toward her breast, and then slipped into her low bodice.

His other hand left her shoulder and she felt his fingers brushing through her hair, making a tingling, melting sensation flow from her scalp downward. He said softly, "Rapunzel, Rapunzel, will you let down your hair for me?"

Dimly understanding that he was asking far more of her than his words suggested, still she could not speak. Her answer was to lift her own oddly heavy arms and begin removing the pins. In a moment, her hair was heavy upon her shoulders and Simon's fingers combed through it freely, every stroke of his fingers vibrating, magnifying inside her.

"What are you doing to me?" She gasped, at last frightened by the intensity of her pleasure. "I cannot breathe. I cannot move."

Simon pulled back for a moment. "Am I crushing you?"

Miranda shook her head, feeling completely unable to express what she was feeling. "No. I just . . . the pleasure . . ."

His eyes widened as he understood her dilemma, and the smile of male pride mingled with desire might have irritated her if she did not desire his lips upon hers so desperately. "I had thought to suggest cards as a way to spend our traveling time, but if this pastime pleases you more, so be it."

Without quite knowing how, Miranda found herself shifted in such a way that she reclined halfway against the seat, Simon half on his knees, half lightly but firmly atop her. His breathing was harder, but his hands were still gentle. She quickly realized the advantage of their new position as she felt the shocking heat of one of his hands against her bare thigh, even as the other cupped her neck and his lips brought more heat to hers.

As she daringly tried to imitate his kiss, and darted her tongue between his lips, he groaned softly into her mouth. The hand that cupped her nape slid lower, to her waist and his arm tightened, pressing her closer to him. There was no way she would not burst into flame, but he did not seem to know the danger he was in, and Miranda wondered, as she looked into his glowing eyes, if he felt the same.

A stabbing pain in her side cleared the heated fog

of pleasure from her mind in an instant, and Miranda gasped and tried to pull away. Simon's arm tightened, and he murmured a protest.

She stilled instantly, afraid that his arms would increase the pain in her side.

Unaware of the reason for her stillness, he buried his mouth in her neck. "Miranda, you are more than I dared to dream," he whispered, claiming her mouth with his so that she could not explain her plight. She gasped in pain and began to writhe as her broken stay jabbed more deeply into her. Her knees drew up and locked around Simon as she attempted to keep him from tightening his embrace any further.

He broke the kiss for a moment to whisper urgently, "Miranda, my love, we should not hurry this moment. . . ." Before she could gather the breath to speak, his mouth was again on hers, gentler now. But still his restraining hands caused the stay to dig deeper and the pain was so unbearable she could not suppress a moan.

Simon answered her moan with a low groan of his own and pulled away to whisper, "You are so beautiful."

"My gown must come off." She gasped, but got no further before his mouth came down more passionately upon hers.

Deciding that she would be better served to struggle with her gown rather than with Simon, Miranda began tearing at the buttons. Miraculously, he began to help, tearing at her clothing until she was afraid the gown would be shredded. In no time, with the both of them working frantically, the laces of the stays were undone.

Suddenly with a sharp cry, she found herself free of the painful broken stay. Simon pulled back from her abruptly. "What is the matter Miranda. Have I hurt you?"

Miranda shook her head. "My stay was broken and we have just now disengaged it." She glanced down to see the expanse of herself exposed to his sight and blushed. "I'm sorry to have behaved in such an unseemly manner."

His expression swept from a puzzled frown to a short laugh. "My God. I thought I had transported you to frenzied passion, and you were merely trying to escape a broken stay. Come, show me the injury."

He examined the abrasion with a worried frown. "It will heal, but I suspect you'll have a bruise in the morning."

The feel of his hands brought back some of the pleasure Miranda had felt before the pain of her broken stay. She was disappointed when he lifted them away and stared at her accusingly. "I shall have the staymaker shot. These cannot be more than a week old at most."

"Oh, no, that pair was my mother's before it was mine. I should have replaced it years ago." He stared at her uncomprehendingly, his breathing still rough and ragged. "I'm sorry Simon, I thought it would hold until we reached your home. I had it taped. . . ."

"I thought I told you to have whatever clothing you needed supplied by the milliners I sent from London."

"My sisters needed new stays more than I," she confessed. "I thought to do without for a while longer."

He frowned. "No more taped stays for you." His eyes swept her nude form and then, shockingly, he bent to press his lips where the stay had scraped her skin. His lips were warm. Her heart began a double beat, and every sound and feeling seemed magnified. "Simon—"

"I want you." His lips covered the distance from her bruised side to her breast and he gently took the sensitive tip into his mouth. Impossibly, once again she found herself dizzy from the heat that rushed through her.

She gasped. "I want you, too." Her surprise at her own boldness was quickly lost in the feel of his strong muscled shoulders, as she allowed her hands to roam his body as his roamed hers.

And then the coach rolled to a stop. They had barely enough time to shield Miranda from the coachman's eyes before the door was flung open. "Welcome home, Your Grace."

Chapter Nine

The chill evening air that had swirled in with the opening of the carriage door brought a gasp from Miranda and a return to reality to Simon. Briskly, he sat up and began rearranging his clothing. Fortunately, his servants were well trained, and the door had shut almost as quickly as it opened.

He could hear Miranda frantically attempting to arrange her own clothing, and he had no heart to tell her how fruitless her attempts were. In the darkness, the clothing that had been so easily discarded would be impossible to right. He distinctly remembered feeling tiny buttons pelt his cheek when her bodice had finally given way.

A frantic elbow jabbed him in the ribs and a knee connected painfully with his hip before he relented. "Miranda, I'm afraid the task is hopeless."

She stilled, and the rustling of clothing ceased so that he could hear the sob that caught in her breath.

"It cannot be. I will not be seen like this by your . . . our staff."

As if on cue, there was a timid knock on the carriage door. "Your Grace? Would you care to dismount—"

There was an awkward pause, which Simon used to offer a thankful prayer that Miranda had no understanding of William's careless double entendre.

William's strained voice began again. "I mean, Your Grace, would you and your wife care for any assistance?"

Before he knew what she would do, Miranda said imperiously, "Please hand in your lantern, my good man—and give me a few minutes. The pins have fallen out of my hair from the jouncing of the journey." She opened the door only enough to receive the lantern. The light, however, served to reveal the disaster he had expected.

"Oh, my God, Simon. What have we wrought?"

In the bright glow of the lantern, Simon could clearly see that the fever that had engulfed both of them had left Miranda. She stared at him with embarrassment and confusion, her hair down around her bared shoulders, her arms clutching the remains of her bodice to cover her breasts.

Surprisingly, he felt his desire flood through him again. If she did not look so much like a lost child, he would have ordered William to give them a half hour of privacy. It took great strength for him to remember that she was his bride and deserved a proper wedding night in a proper bed.

"What shall we do, Simon?" Miranda gave up trying to repair the disaster of her new traveling gown and stared at him in complete dismay. "I cannot be seen like this!"

"On the contrary, my dear. I believe I very much enjoy seeing you this way."

Miranda's gaze flicked with obvious annoyance over his own clothing. "Your attire looks no more rumpled than one might expect from such a journey. But I look as though . . ." She blushed.

Reminding himself that Miranda was now his duchess and suffering from the indignity of having been discovered in dishabille by a servant in her new home, Simon put aside his own feelings for the moment. The night was young. And he was certain he could return them both to their abandoned state as soon as he closed the bedroom door behind them.

Swiftly, he covered her with his cape and lifted her into his arms. She protested, embarrassed, but he swept aside her objections. "It is the bridegroom's prerogative, Miranda, to carry his sleeping bride into his home so that she might rest in comfort on her wedding night."

"Sleeping . . ." Her eyes searched his for a moment, as if for the first time she was realizing that what had passed between them in the carriage was not an isolated event. To his delight, a small smile curved her lips as she obediently snuggled her head on his shoulder and feigned sleep. For the first time since he had thrown caution to the winds and decided to spend his last few months in England with Miranda, he was unreservedly happy with his decision.

Mrs. Hoskins, the housekeeper, had lined the servants in two neat rows to welcome Miranda. Simon looked at her apologetically. "Tomorrow will suffice for introductions, Mrs. Hoskins," he said softly, feeling the rapid beat of Miranda's heart. "Your new duchess is worn out from the ride."

For a moment, until she quickly bobbed her head and curtsied to him, Simon thought he saw a tremor of shock cross her features. But that could not be true, Mrs. Hoskins had never displayed anything but respectful acknowledgment of his orders. In fact, he thought, as he surveyed the line of servants, none of them had. As his eyes swept the row of servants, they bobbed, hiding their faces from his scrutiny.

"Your Grace, might I inquire—" Dome, the butler, tried to accost him.

"Tomorrow, Dome." Simon had no time for household matters at this moment, his intent went no further than to carry Miranda upstairs, shut the door to his bedroom, and make love to his willing wife. She was his wife for only the shortest of times and he wanted her all to himself now.

Halfway up the flight of stairs leading to the second floor, a familiar, and unwelcome voice stopped him cold.

"Simon. Where are you going in such haste?"

He turned slowly and faced his mother.

She nodded in greeting, her eyes on the cloaked figure in his arms. "The evening is early yet. Have you no time to spare for a greeting to your mother?"

He did not answer, but stood there, unable to move. Just as if they had never fallen out, she beckoned. "Come, I would like to meet my new daughter-in-law."

He could feel the tension in Miranda's body, and a quick glance told him that her cheeks were flushed and her eyes were focused self-consciously on her new mother-in-law.

"Let me down," she whispered.

He held her more tightly.

His mother's eyes narrowed as she took in the sight. She turned her gaze upon Miranda. "Some men are so impatient, my dear. What we women must put up with!" And then she said shortly to Simon, "Can't you put the girl down, Simon? How long have you been wed? Hours at most."

"Miranda is exhausted, Mother. I am helping her upstairs."

"After you help her up the stairs, Simon, will you tell her? Have you told her yet?"

He shook his head. "That is none of your business, Mother."

"I beg to differ, Simon." She focused once again on Miranda, and Simon panicked, afraid she would tell his new bride everything.

"Wait in the study for me, Mother," he commanded curtly. He quickly turned and proceeded up the stairs.

Miranda looked at him questioningly. "I should go down. . . . Why didn't you warn me that your mother would be here? I can't imagine what she thinks of me!"

"What can she think of you, but that you are a charmingly exhausted bride," he soothed her, though inside he was raging. How dare his mother be here? How dare she! His letter had been very clear. She was not to set foot in this home for the next six months.

He should have known that she would not heed him.

He should have given clearer orders to Dome. Damn his promise to the old duke. He could not bar her from the house. The servants would talk.

"Simon, I don't want to begin badly with your mother."

"There's no need to worry, my dear. No one could be on a worse footing with my mother than I am, nor she with me."

Miranda said nothing as he set her on her feet in her own bedroom. He noticed that in accordance with his orders, the room had been well polished, dusted and swept. There was no sign that this room had been unoccupied since his own birth, when his mother moved into a different wing and lived separately from his father.

"Simon, you should not speak disrespectfully of your mother. It is not seemly."

"Am I to take it that you are the arbiter of what is seemly, Miranda?" He smiled at the thought as she stood before him with her traveling dress in tatters around her.

He was glad to see that she smiled at his teasing, and did not take it amiss. They were comfortable together, and it pleased him. Though soon he intended to show her there could be more than comfortable companionship between a man and a woman. "Why don't you prepare for bed as soon as the maid comes up with your things. I will be back shortly."

"Don't be ridiculous. I intend to come down as soon as I am presentable."

That was the last thing he needed. "There is no need, Miranda. My mother was told that she is not welcome here. She requires no greeting, and I hope she will be gone by morning."

"I am sorry there is a rift between you and your mother, but I cannot allow it to continue. After all, if you—" She could not quite bring herself to say it, which was a relief to him. Lies upon lies.

But he didn't care. He wanted her and now he had her. She was his wife, and his mother was leaving. There was nothing more to be said about the matter—except to make the situation clear to his mother. He left Miranda to make herself ready for the night and went to beard the lioness in what was no longer her den.

She nodded her head in his direction as he entered the room. "Your bride—what little I saw of her, seems charming, Simon."

"Mother, I gave you specific instructions not to come here."

"Yes, Simon, I know. But it is fortunate that I am here."

"And how is that?" he asked coldly, willing his anger to subside. He did not want to go up to Miranda with this rage inside him. He needed to treat his new bride gently.

"If you plan to go ahead with this foolish idea of disappearing from the face of the earth, you cannot afford to create a child. You cannot make love to your wife."

Simon was shocked by her blatant statement almost as much as he was dismayed by it. He refused to discuss with her his knowledge of the measures to ensure there would be no child from his brief marriage. "That is not your concern, Mother."

"It is not my concern?" Her voice rose. Simon realized that it had been years since he had seen a break in the icy composure she cultivated. His marriage must be more disturbing to her than he had realized it would be. Good. It would serve her right to see what she had denied him a lifetime of: family.

There was a discernible tremor in her voice as she continued. "Simon, nothing would delight me more than for you to get a child upon your wife. For then your foolish plans would die stillborn."

He opened his mouth to deny her words but she gave him no chance. "Could you deny a child of your own his birthright? Could that girl upstairs? And what would you tell her?"

"There are ways to prevent a child, Mother." He had not meant to say it aloud. Not to her. For a moment, though, he had felt like a child caught in an act of folly.

"Yes," she said with a depth of bitterness that he had not expected, "And I can tell you, you would not be here if they were infallible."

He looked at her in shock. Though he had hated her for a long time, he found he hated her even more now. And he hated himself. For her words revealed him to himself—as a fool. Who knew the number of lovers she had had over the years? And she had never borne a child from her liaisons. Except for Simon himself.

If he used every trick he had learned to prevent conception he could not be absolutely certain there would be no child. And that was only if he used the tricks. He shuddered as he remembered the carriage ride home. He had not thought once of the french letter in his pocket. He doubted, if they had been granted the time to complete their lovemaking, that he would have withdrawn in time.

He saw his mother's triumphant smile. She knew him too well, all those years when he had not known of her treachery and he had exposed his soul to her and thought that she nurtured it. She knew him too well.

He fought her with the only weapon he had, keeping his expression as unreadable as possible. "You have cast your final stone, Mother. It is time for you to go home. Or do you forget this is no longer your home?"

She did not even blink, although her lip curled up in disdain. "I have no intention of going home, Simon. What have you told the girl? Have you prepared her at all?"

He did not want to answer, but something in her

expression dragged the words from him. "I have told her that I am dying."

"Dying!" In the lamplight, her skin seemed to lose all color. "It is not true?"

"No. It is a lie." He shrugged. "It was simpler in the end."

"And she married you anyway?" His mother's head tilted to the side, her eyes took on a thoughtful look. "Probably hoping to get an heir from you before you die. She could then run through the estate during his minority."

Stung, Simon retorted before he could stop himself, "Miranda married me because she was convinced she could find a cure for my 'illness,' Mother. She is not like you."

"Indeed." As if he hadn't just grossly insulted her, the dowager duchess said quietly, "I would like to meet her, Simon. Very much I would like to meet the woman who was willing to marry you, knowing that you were dying, hoping to bring you a cure. Poor thing."

Simon looked at her in confusion. "What?"

She shook her head. "And for a woman with that kind of loyalty, Simon, you would abandon her with child?"

"I have taken your point, Mother. You can be assured that there will be no future dukes coming from my bastard line."

"Simon, I beg you for the last time to give up this foolish notion. Arthur is not a suitable replacement."

"He is the true heir."

"Pish tosh. The true heir is the son your father cherished and nurtured for the role. He made you as consciously as he would have if he could have done so with his own body. You are his son, much as I wish it were not so."

"Arthur . . ."

"And if Arthur dies? Certainly he has no more fortitude than a rosebud in winter."

For a moment he wondered just how evil his mother really was. He had never rid himself of the suspicion that some malignant fate had played him for a fool, removing three of the scarce Watterly direct descendants from the living before they could be named as his heirs. The carefully researched document that enumerated remaining heirs had seriously thinned of names.

Just as quickly as he had considered the thought, he dismissed it. If his mother had had murder in her, she'd have murdered the old duke years before he had died of old age and overindulgence. And Arthur was here, and alive, if not the most suitable candidate for a duke's responsibilities. But Simon could change that, given a few months. He had to.

"Did I hear my name spoken?" The man upon whom, in six months' time, the dukedom would devolve entered the room hesitantly. "Did you require my assistance, Simon?"

Simon noted the pale cheeks. "Have you been ill?" he asked, intending to divert his mother.

"No," Arthur sniffled. "Nothing more than my usual rails."

The dowager duchess smiled maliciously at her son and he wished he could bring himself to toss her out bodily. But he had promised the old duke. And Arthur's rails were quite well-known. They kept him up at night, they kept blue circles under his eyes. His valet often spent the night providing steaming pails of water just so Arthur could breathe.

Simon refused to allow himself to consider Arthur's worthiness—or unworthiness. His extensive search for an heir, a true heir, had dug up Arthur and that was all there was to it. If Simon himself had been dead, there would have been nothing for it but for Arthur to take up the title.

He could not bear to think of the dukedom lapsing after so many years of vigorous and healthy service. Just as he could not bear the thought that a man without a drop of the Watterly blood might insinuate himself into the proudly unbroken lineage.

Unaware of the serious bent to his cousin's thoughts, Arthur beamed and clapped Simon on the back. "I hear you've brought a bride home, Simon. I hope that means that I'll soon be an unnecessary appendage and you'll have a full nursery."

Simon bit back a sharp retort. His cousin was nothing if not sincere. There was no hint of disappointment—in fact there seemed to be a touch more relief than boded well for the future heir to a dukedom. "Your wishes show what quality of man you are." He stared at his mother in challenge as he spoke. Arthur was a good man, sterling in character. It was his force of will and his health that were easily destroyed. And he was damnably accident-prone. . . .

His mother nodded. "Yes, you are a good man, indeed, Cousin. And wouldn't it be grand to have a houseful of children who looked just like Simon— or perhaps like his bride."

She looked at Arthur as she spoke, but Simon knew the words were meant to cut her son deeply. He wished that they didn't.

He thought of Miranda, waiting upstairs for him. He thought of his heedless rush to make love with her in the carriage, and realized with a thread of disgust that he would now be worrying that they had conceived a child with his bastard blood had not the stay broken—or the carriage door flown open.

He could not think how he had made such a mistake. He was married now. He could not set Miranda aside. He would not. But he must find a solution. He bowed slightly, wanting only to leave his mother's despicable company. "I must bid you both good night."

"Ah, yes." His mother smiled at Arthur. "His bride awaits upstairs."

"I have other matters to attend to, Mother. Please excuse me if I do not see you off tomorrow. I regret that you must leave so early in the morning, but it is for the best, is it not?"

She nodded. "Who can say what is for the best, Simon? One must do what one must do."

Fury gripped him as he realized that he was trapped. He could not go up to Miranda; he could not trust himself not to make love to her yet. And he must keep the fury from his face, from his action. He must, in order to keep the truth from Arthur.

"I bid you a pleasant evening, Cousin. I must make sure the horses have been taken care of after our long journey." He turned on his heel and left Arthur speechless and his mother smiling with smug triumph as he sought the solace of the stables.

His poor excuse rang in his own ears and he could imagine what Arthur was thinking—he had never questioned the day to day running of the stables before. Why start on his wedding night?

Chapter Ten

Miranda stood by the window in the vast bedchamber that was now her own. Fairy tales rarely went beyond this point. The weight of her responsibilities as a duchess were emphasized in the very gleam of the polished hardwood of the solid, centuries old furniture and in the tapestries that hung on the wall—tapestries created by Simon's ancestors.

She ran her hand absently over the smoothly carved bedrail, able to feel the grain of the wood with her fingertips. How old was this bed? Had the first, newly made earl had it commissioned to celebrate his success? Or was it the first earl to be made duke? Her wedding night was taking on more import.

If she could not find a cure for Simon's illness, they had little time to make sure there would be at least a chance for a male heir to inherit. Instead of a bridge between two people, they held the responsibility to create a bridge from the present to the future. She knew how Simon valued his lineage. What if she failed him?

She smiled as she traced a golden thread through its path in one of the tapestries. The historic significance of what would pass between Simon and herself was not nearly enough to sober her. An impatient joy bubbled in her. Simon would come to her tonight. She wondered why she did not feel more sorrow, for if Simon was right, then he would be dead too soon and her joy but fleeting.

Yet she had her plans—Katherine would arrive soon. If her healing skills were as good as the villagers attested, Miranda had hope that the village healer might succeed where Simon's doctors had failed. She must.

She held her impatience at bay until she had finished tracing the golden thread. What could Simon be saying to his mother that would take him away for so long? Surely he was not nervous; such vagaries of the nerves were for the female on her wedding night, not the male.

She drifted toward the gilt-edged looking glass. She had long since changed into her wedding nightgown, a frill of lace and silk that made her blush, even after she had covered it with a robe of silk.

Where was Simon? If he did not come to her soon, she would be too nervous to ensure that things went smoothly between them. As her mother had often lamented, Miranda was not by nature a person able to wait quietly. She must do something. After a moment more staring at the bed and its imposing grandeur, she looked down at her attire.

Impulsively, she chose a gown from her trunk and dressed quickly. She found her way to the front hall with only a little difficulty. There was light from under the drawing room door, but no sound of conversation—or argument. Hesitantly, she opened the door.

"I'm glad to see that you have recovered from your earlier indisposition," Simon's mother said calmly. Her steel gray eyes missed nothing as she examined Miranda from head to toe. "I wanted to meet the woman who could convince my son to marry her considering his . . . condition."

Miranda was too distracted to do more than blush lightly. "I am honored to meet you, Your Grace. I apologize for my earlier indisposition. Our trip was long and exhausting, and neither Simon nor I expected a guest."

A true smile, with a bitter twist, softened the dowager's features briefly. "I hardly think I qualify as a guest in the home I came to as a bride—or that I raised Simon in." She looked directly at Miranda, as if issuing some challenge.

Feeling as if she was being ensnared by a careful spider, Miranda decided that directness would be the best course. "Where is Simon?" *Goodness,* she thought to herself, *I sound as condescending as the dowager.*

"I should try the stables, my dear. I don't believe he trusts himself in the house at the moment." Her voice sounded almost amused.

Miranda searched the impassive face for a clue as to how to take such a comment coming from Simon's own mother. Was this woman evil inside, as Snow White's stepmother had been? Would Miranda be safer refusing apples from the dowager, lest they be poisoned? Or was her poison one of the soul rather than the body?

After a moment's silent clash of gazes, she bit her lip and turned to look out into the hallway. What was wrong with Simon's mother? Miranda, her sense of alarm aroused, had no time to find out. "I shall try the stables, then."

"Steady, boy," Simon soothed as he brushed his skittish stallion. He knew that the stallion's ebony coat needed no more brushing; it shone in the dim lamplight from the hour that Simon had already spent on it. Still, he could not face the end of the task. What could come next to fill the hours between now and dawn?

He moved the brush slowly over the horse's coat. He had trapped himself in an impossible situation. He was a fool. Even the servants could see it.

Barcus, the head groom, had looked at him as if he'd gone daft, coming into the stables when he had a new bride in his bed. The man's mouth had dropped open when Simon ordered his stallion saddled.

Though Barcus had been reticent about refusing, Simon recognized the behavior. All his servants exhibited it at inconvenient times—just when he was most out of sorts. Barcus had acted as if he were unsure how His Grace would react when told he could not ride his stallion into the dark as he wished.

Would it make any difference to the man to understand it was the tempting thought of his bride that had driven Simon to make such an unreasonable request in the first place? But Miranda was exactly what had kept Simon in the stables when informed that his stallion had turned up with a stone in his shoe and needed rest more than a fierce ride across a darkened landscape.

Thus, his stallion was receiving a brushing and currying the likes of which he'd never known, and all of the stablemen thought Simon had completely lost his wits. Simon himself wasn't absolutely sure that he hadn't. He had planned everything very carefully— or so he'd thought.

The idea of never making love to his wife was unbearable. He had married her in order to take her to bed, to enjoy his last days as duke with a semblance of what he might have had in other circumstances. But could he risk a child? His mother's revelation had driven the risk home to him too well. With Miranda so near and so willing, how could he limit himself, as he had intended at first?

And what if, despite everything, she got pregnant?

That was unthinkable. He would not have his plans turn to dust this close to realization. In six short months he meant to be done with all his false ties to the dukedom. A child would not be a complication— a child would be a disaster.

The only answer was to remain celibate. He could do it; the consequences of not doing it were too disastrous to dare. But what would Miranda say?

As the stable doors swung slowly open and the glow of a lantern appeared, Simon groaned softly to himself. He had forgotten for a moment that the woman he had married not only had a passionate nature, but a curious and persistent one as well.

When she came to the door of the stable, he was surprised to see that she had taken the time to don one of the new walking dresses he had chosen for her, of a deep gold hue that, just as he had expected, brought out the golden highlights in her tawny hair.

With a muttered oath, he sternly repressed the image that he had enjoyed before, of himself slowly removing that gown from her, her hair hanging loose.

"Simon?" Her voice was a whisper as she came down the length of the stalls until she saw him. She smiled, but he was not fooled by the gesture. She was very aware that things had gone seriously awry between them and this intelligence shone in her brandy-dark eyes.

"I thought you would be asleep by now," he lied, applying the brush as vigorously and unnecessarily as he could to his stallion's withers. "Our traveling was most exhausting."

She looked at him in surprise, taking a moment to respond. "On my wedding night?" Her voice was soft and chiding, though he knew it must cost her to keep her fear and uncertainty from him.

"What difference would it make what night? The trip was long and . . . wearying." He cursed himself the moment he saw her eyes light with misunderstanding.

"Oh, Simon, why are you currying your horse if you are tired? Come to bed and I shall rub your back."

"I referred to your exhaustion, Miranda, not my own."

"But I am . . ." Her voice trailed off.

She had meant to say that she was not the one who was dying. His hatred focused on his mother and his black mood darkened.

He did not meet her eyes as he searched for a reason that would make her turn and leave him in peace. "I'll not come into that house until my mother has seen fit to depart."

"Do not damage your health because you are vexed with your mother, Simon." She moved toward him as she spoke, and he carefully stepped away, keeping the horse between them.

Vexed? She thought him vexed? *Leave it,* a cautious voice in his ear warned him. If he let even a scrap of his true feelings for his mother surface, Miranda would not rest until she knew every bit of the truth. And that he would not allow.

"I cannot sleep." That was certainly the truth. He

would be hard-pressed to stay in his own bed knowing that Miranda was one door away and legally and willingly his.

She said nothing for a moment, but he could feel her gaze burning on his back. He hoped she would turn and leave. Her voice was gentle as she finally asked, "Are you afraid of making love with me Simon?"

"Afraid?" He strove to hide his incredulity from her and his voice was a bark. How had she hit upon that so quickly?

"Afraid for your health, I mean," she amended hastily and he could see that she believed he was angry for the affront to his manliness. "It seems to require some exertion . . . and . . . I did notice your heart beating violently when . . . when . . . in the carriage." She smiled. "I'm sorry for my missishness, Simon, but it is difficult to find the appropriate words for our situation."

"Had you any fear for yourself, then, Miranda?" She looked puzzled. "Your own heartbeat was rapid, as I recall." With vivid clarity, Simon thought ruefully, as he remembered the eagerness of her response to him.

She blushed. "I presume, then, such a reaction is natural?"

He nodded, and continued unwisely, "It is terribly natural although many proper ladies are said not to be able to react so with their own husbands."

"So I do have improper feelings?" She looked chastened. "And I am too much for you, my poor Simon? You require a proper, calm lady for your wife and I am too wild?"

He suppressed the urge to laugh at her suggestion. It offered him a surcease, for this evening at least. Hesitantly, he nodded at the absurd idea that a night with her would be too much for him. A thousand nights would be too little to satisfy him. He wanted forever. But it did not matter what he wanted. He could not have it.

"Come to bed, Simon. I will not trouble you. I will stay in my room. There is a door between us. I will not disturb your rest."

He was considering her offer when she continued. "And when your health has recovered, I shall endeavor to be calm during our encounters. After all, I will not have broken stays next time."

He wondered how to convince her that there would be no "encounters." "I do not need more than your company, Miranda."

"Of course you do. You must have an heir. Why else would you have married when you believed yourself dying?"

He looked at her, shocked. She had said nothing to him about children and heirs before the marriage. Foolishly, he had assumed that meant she did not consider it a possibility. Indeed, he had thought she would not have wished it, as a child would put a halt to much of the coveted freedom that her widowed state was to offer her. He didn't know whether to laugh or to curse.

Misinterpreting his silence, Miranda stepped closer to him and laid her hand on his chest. "I know I behave in an unladylike way at times. But I promise I will do my best to remain calm and not strain your health."

The scent of her came to him, despite the stronger odor of the stables that surrounded them. It triggered his anger. "Miranda, I do not require your coddling. And my cousin Arthur is all the heir I need." Even as he said it, he vowed to see Arthur wed before he left. To a strong young woman with broad hips.

"Please come to bed, Simon. Don't hurt your health because of this discord with your mother—or because you fear I will endanger your health."

He turned his back on her. "I will retire when I wish to."

"Promise me you will come to bed soon."

He ignored her.

"I will not leave until—"

He sighed. "I will retire when I wish. Now, go to your room and leave me in peace. I won't last another hour, never mind six months, with you nagging at me this way."

His harsh words worked as reason had not. He did not turn around to watch her defeat, but he heard the swish of her skirts and the rapid beat of her feet that indicated that she nearly ran. For a moment, when she spoke of being "gentle" with him, Simon had seen true anguish in her eyes. She didn't want to hurt him. Which meant that he would have to hurt her. Often.

He felt remorse for the course he had set by marrying her. But he ruthlessly crushed it. He had made a mistake and they would both pay for it. He could not make love with her and he could not trust himself not to take her to his bed. She would need to exert the control that would keep them apart and prevent a child of his bastard blood from inheriting.

Chapter Eleven

"Had you no luck?" The dowager duchess stood in the hallway, as if she were still the house's mistress and going about the unappetizing chore of questioning the help. Her spine was straight; there was not a wrinkle in her glossy black silk skirts. Her dark gray eyes bored deep, as if to delve the depths of Miranda's soul.

Despite the older woman's air of composure and command, Miranda had the odd impression the dowager had been standing there, unmoving, ever since Miranda had left the house.

"What did you say to him? He was not in the least unhappy until he spoke to you." The harsh words came unbidden.

Though she was horror-struck at her own audacity, she was still reeling from Simon's painful rejection, unable to temper her words with the respect due the dowager's position.

Most frustrating of all, from her perspective, was

the ambiguity of her mother-in-law's expression. The older woman's face was serene, as if she had asked after her son's choice of apparel for the day—as if Miranda's reply had been coolly civil and not flagrantly rude and angry.

Nothing in the woman's expression seemed concerned, yet there was an air of expectancy emanating from her as she said, "The question seems more to be—what did he say to you?"

Even though the dowager waited silently for her answer, Miranda could feel the other woman's eager impatience as if it were a force of its own. And yet her features were so composed that she gave the impression of a pond that had frozen over.

Had this woman no heart? To distress her dying son in this manner and then act as if she were blameless?

Reining in her temper, she answered as politely as she could manage, "He will be in shortly."

"What a pity." Again, the dowager's face held no clue to her thoughts.

Miranda, her temper at the boiling point, had no notion of how to respond to such blatant incivility. She finally decided to do her best to match the dowager's sangfroid. "I feel certain you will excuse my wish to retire now."

The dowager smiled, a simple lift of her mouth. "I had held some hope that the young woman who persuaded Simon to marry her at this juncture of his life could persuade him to be civil to his mother."

Miranda stood rooted to the spot. For a moment she thought she had not heard correctly. Stiffly, she responded to the dowager's attack. "My concern at this point, as I'm sure you understand, is his health."

Though she had sworn to herself not to lose her temper again, she could not resist adding, "I don't pretend to understand what is behind his unfilial behavior toward you, Your Grace, but I cannot worry about that when he is dying."

"It is all that I can worry about." The deprecating smile was so fleeting that Miranda almost believed she had imagined the slight quirk of the dowager's mouth.

Her temper flared, and she was too exhausted to fight it anymore. "Do you not care about him?"

The anger that she was poised to vent disappeared in an instant, though, at the sadness that shadowed the dowager's features as she spoke. "I regret that our relationship must be unmended should I never see him again."

It seemed a cold way to discuss her son's death, as if he might simply be leaving for an extended trip. "That is between the two of you. For my part, I can only do what Simon will not."

"Indeed?" The dowager's brow rose. "And what is that?"

"He will not consider doctors; apparently they have failed him in the past. So I have found someone to minister to him."

The instant the words were out of her mouth, Miranda regretted them. She had not confided her actions to Simon, yet she had just told his mother, knowing the two of them could not bear to be in the same room with each other.

Though the dowager seemed not to move, her skirts rippled slightly, as if she had suppressed a start of surprise. "Simon has agreed to this?"

"He has been disappointed by doctors, he says. But a healer is a different cup of tea," Miranda sidestepped, not wanting to divulge any more to the woman Simon so obviously didn't trust.

As if sensing that Miranda did not want to lie, the dowager would not be put off. She leaned toward

Miranda and fixed her with a stare. "Does he know?" Her voice had the stern tone of Miranda's old nanny.

Responding to both the tone, and the need to explain what she intended for Simon, Miranda looked steadily at the silver locket that hung starkly against the dowager's black silk. "I hadn't intended to tell him the exact purpose this person will serve."

The dowager leaned back and sighed, almost as if she were a tutor who had been disappointed by an errant pupil. "Dishonesty so soon, my dear? Whatever will Simon say?"

Miranda felt as if she were five again, and being scolded for not confessing her part in a midnight raid on the biscuits in the kitchen. "My concern is Simon. I believe that he will resist the healing if he knows about it."

"Indeed?"

Miranda blushed lightly. It was embarrassing to speak to his mother, who had known him all his life, as if she knew Simon well.

But her feeling about this was strong, and soon, when Katherine arrived, there would be someone to agree with or dispute her deeply held belief that Simon was preventing his own recovery. "I think he is not pursuing all the avenues available to him for a cure, for some reason. I cannot help but hope, like Briar Rose, a curse of death has been laid upon him and can be lifted."

Again, Miranda looked up to meet the dowager's intense gray eyes. The woman's words were softly spoken, yet there was a tension within her that Miranda could not fathom. "You are a very perceptive young woman. I wonder if Simon knows just how perceptive a young woman he so rashly married?"

Uncertain of the meaning of the dowager's words,

Miranda answered lamely, "I have never considered Simon rash."

"And yet he chose one day, without warning, to cast his own mother out of his life."

Miranda had been taught to respect her elders, but caught between Simon and his mother, she knew she must defend her husband. "I cannot think the problem all rests with Simon," she addressed the dowager duchess warily. "In the short time I have known him, I have given him several reasons to hold me in contempt and he has always listened to my explanation and understood—as best he could—my reasoning, faulty though he might think it."

"Indeed?" The dowager's right eyebrow lifted elegantly. "Certainly he has refused to listen to me. But then, I talk plainly, and not all people care to hear the truth."

Miranda bit back a harsh defense of Simon and said mildly, "Perhaps, but I have always found Simon to be above all interested in the truth."

As she stood in the doorway, with the cold night air encroaching from the hallway, she found herself no longer in such pain over Simon's rejection. This was a house of coldness that sprang from more than the night air. There was much more here than was fathomable in one night.

Whatever drove Simon to refuse a doctor's help with his illness had its root here in this house, and with his relationship with his mother. Miranda hoped she would be equal to the challenge of divining what ailed Simon's body—as well as his soul.

There was a flash of some emotion in the dowager's eyes that was quickly masked by her usual enigmatic expression. "Be cautious child, thinking you know any man. They are all capable of bending truth to the breaking point if it suits their needs."

"Not Simon," Miranda countered flatly.

The dowager smiled. "You are very young, my dear."

"Good night, Your Grace." With a weak smile and a nod of her head, she turned and fled up the stairs to her new room and her new bed. Somehow, the thought was not quite so appealing now that she knew Simon had been diverted from his initial intentions.

Hours later, as she sat listening, unable to relax, she heard muffled sounds from the room adjoining hers. Murmured voices—Simon and his valet. A thump as something hit the floor—a boot? Two? And then, presently, silence. She waited, but there was no indication that he even glanced at the door between them, never mind thought to come through it.

She woke from her fitful sleep, forgetting for a moment where she was. She lay half awake, half asleep, unable to pinpoint what had disturbed her. The bed was strange, not her own familiar little one with its cheery yellow curtains.

Behind the massive oak-paneled door that joined her chamber with Simon's, she heard the faint sounds of groaning. Instantly she came fully awake. She heard nothing more. Could it have been her imagination? What if Simon needed her? She stared at the door. Unable to deny her worries, she slipped quietly to the door, careful not to use a candle lest the light disturb Simon. As the door silently opened into the other room, she heard no more groans.

Still, a nagging worry made her creep into the room, until she was at the foot of the bed. He lay there, his even breathing a testament to his current well-being. Miranda felt a knot of fear ease and she turned to go.

Just then, Simon groaned again softly. Miranda halted. He had said nothing to her of pain, but surely there must be some?

Through the dim moonlight, she could see that he was restless as he slept, his bedcovers were twisted and pulled askew. Her heart went out to him. Even in his sleep he could not be at peace, his illness still touched him.

The need to soothe him was too strong to resist. Cautiously, she approached the bed. Simon's face was in the shadows. The moonlight illuminated only a cheek and a wing of his golden hair, giving him a magical, illusive air. She reached out to touch his face and reassure herself that he was real, and without warning, found herself staring into his alert gaze.

His voice was soft. "Have you come to tell me a bedtime tale? What one have you chosen? Goldilocks and the three bears? The child who's so bold as to go wherever she will?"

"There is no need for you to be sarcastic. I have every right to worry for your health. I am your wife."

"I have not forgotten our marriage." He was silent for a moment, staring into her eyes as if he could not look away. And then he sighed and turned his back to her. "I am well enough, just bedeviled."

"Is the pain so awful?" Miranda bit her lip, afraid to hear the answer. Simon coughed. If the subject had not been so serious, she might have thought that he was hiding amusement. No, it was a trick of the night.

His voice was gruff and rasped out at her. "Almost unbearable right at this moment. But I am sure it will ease if only I could know that you slept soundly."

"Perhaps if I remain here tonight?" The idea came to her unbidden and she was suddenly warm, even in the night chill. She smiled. "Didn't Goldilocks try out all the beds?'' It was a pleasant thought, lying next to him, being held in his arms. Perhaps even—

"No. And, if you remember, Goldilocks ran screaming from the bed in terror."

The cold rejection hurt more than Miranda expected, although after the events in the stable, she had been forewarned. Still, she was reluctant to release her pleasant dream. "But I could—"

He turned back to face her and sat up slightly, so that his whole face was lit by moonlight. "Believe me, Miranda, you would cause me greater pain that way."

She found her gaze caught by the smooth bare shoulder the moon exposed with its silver light. "I should have realized that." She admired him for keeping the depths of his pain a secret from her. That having her next to him would hurt had never crossed her mind.

She laughed, as if to make light of her suggestion. "I suppose it is just that I feel so alone here. There are no sisters to slip into my room and ask for a drink of water or a story. I am not used to being so . . . unnecessary."

He was silent for a long moment and she met his steady eyes. It made her shiver to see the same intensity that had been in the dowager's eyes only hours before. He said, "I have told you before, Miranda. I do not need a mother—not even the one I already have."

"I know, Simon. I don't want to be your mother. I want to be your wife."

He sighed. "Please, go to sleep now. I promise I shall introduce you to your new home properly tomorrow. Such an introduction will require you to be well rested. I can't have my servants thinking their new mistress is dull and foolish, can I?"

Miranda sighed in unconscious imitation of him,

seeing the sense in his words and trying hard not to be too disappointed. "Very well. I shall see that your mother is gone in the morning."

"If you can dislodge that woman before she is ready to go, I really will begin to believe in happy endings."

She smiled. "Then you will believe in them very soon. I'll leave you to rest." Impulsively, she bent to kiss him. Her hands came down on his shoulders to brace herself for the light peck on the cheek she intended. But the feel of warm bare skin under her fingers send a shock of wanting coursing through her and she sought his lips instead.

He did not respond. Indeed, he remained still as stone as she pressed her lips to his. The sting of rejection left her feeling the cold night air and the flimsiness of her thin nightgown and robe. When she pulled back, she could not look at his face. "Good night."

His own "Good night" in answer to hers was terse. She could not doubt that he wished her out of his room. For the first time, she began to wonder if he regretted their impulsive marriage and wished her out of his life, as well.

Chapter Twelve

Simon opened the door to Miranda's adjoining room quietly and glanced inside. If she was not yet fully clothed, he wanted to be able to perform a rapid tactical retreat. He told himself he was relieved when he saw that she was almost ready to go down to breakfast.

Something made him pause in the doorway, though, just watching as a maidservant fluttered around, offering scents and powders. He smiled at Miranda's courteous rejection of all offerings. He liked the vanilla scent of her and the near perfection of her powderless skin.

He stepped into the room. "Are you ready to meet Arthur this morning?" He kept his tone light and bantering, hoping that a maid's presence would encourage Miranda to do so also.

She whirled from her toilette, surprised that he would just walk in on her as she dressed. The maid, too, seemed more startled than she ought. For a moment he considered turning around and leaving them in peace to get on with the business of dressing. The impulse passed quickly as he savored the view of Miranda with her hair still down, as she had come to him last night.

Though she was already dressed for the morning in a peach gown with cream trim, the fall of her hair made her seem barely decent. It was a luxury he had decided to allow himself.

There was little danger of anything untoward happening between them once she was safely dressed and the day had begun. It was evening—and the middle of the night that were dangerous.

Miranda smiled uncertainly at him and once again settled herself so that the maid could pin up her hair. Her eyes met his in the looking glass. "You seem to be well rested and cheerful again."

The little maidservant seemed unnerved by his presence, and Miranda winced as a lock of her hair was clumsily tangled in the brush. As she let out a soft cry of pain, the girl stopped her ministrations and looked as if she might burst into tears.

He stepped forward and took the brush from the maid's trembling fingers. "You may go."

The girl stared uncomprehendingly at him for a moment. "But Your Grace, I must see to Her Grace's hair."

"I shall take over for this morning." Simon gave the girl a slight push toward the door, afraid if he didn't she might remain rooted to the floor forever. With a muted cry, she ran from the room, her cheeks blooming scarlet, her eyes filled with tears.

Simon brushed Miranda's hair gently. "I'm sorry, my dear. I know she is inexperienced, but I thought you might prefer to hire your own personal maid, so

I had Mrs. Hoskins promote her into the position of temporary maid.''

"She has done her best, Simon. She is simply very young.'' There was a reproachful look in Miranda's eyes that suggested she was displeased with him, almost as if he had beaten the girl instead of dismissing her from the room.

"Of course. I would never have promoted her—not even temporarily—to this position if she had not shown promise.''

"She just needs someone to show her how to behave as a lady's maid.'' Her eyes met his in the mirror and she smiled warily. "Someone to show her how to brush hair as well as you do it. I must wonder where you learned such skills. Did you ever serve as a lady's maid?''

He laughed and kissed the top of her head. It was sweet torment to go no farther, and he began to regret having sent the maid from the room. "It is not proper for a wife to be jealous of her husband's acquired skills, merely to appreciate them. Some things a wife is not meant to know.''

In the mirror, he could see the confusion in her expression. He did not want to explain himself, or last night, however. Explanations would close the distance between them, and for his sanity he needed to keep Miranda a few steps away from him, emotionally as well as physically.

So instead of answering, he concentrated on brushing out the tangles he found, reveling in the smooth silky feel of her hair in his hands. He had decided during his sleepless night that he would enjoy every aspect of being a husband, except one. And he meant to record each day in his memory to warm him in the long, lonely years ahead. He absorbed the feel of her hair into his fingertips as he brushed.

Very soon it lay shining and tangle free as it fell down her back. His very own Rapunzel. Simon enjoyed the sight for a moment before he lifted his gaze to hers in the mirror. "I'm afraid my expertise ends here." He sighed, laying the brush on the table beneath the looking glass. "I could no more put your hair up than I could stitch you a gown of moonbeams and sunlight."

His words surprised him, coming from nowhere. But he could see her thusly dressed and suddenly wished he could order it done. Impossible dreams, like the ones he sometimes had of a wife, a family, a life that was truly his own.

"Perhaps you can. Hero once called you our fairy godfather." She smiled, her eyes alight with imagination at his fanciful analogy and he felt a breath of relief that she had put aside her questions about the previous evening. "I can put it up, Simon. I haven't had a maid since—"

She paused. Her eyes darkened briefly before she smiled again. "Hero and Juliet used to help me, but I've often done it myself. I suppose I shall have to get used to doing without their help in the future."

He heard the lonely note in her voice and stilled the hands she had raised to pin her hair. "Leave it like this for today, and come and meet Arthur."

She lifted one hand to her hair. "He shall be forever shocked. I cannot meet him like this." She looked at him uncertainly, and he cursed himself for bringing her to this. She was bright and beautiful, not meant to be buried in a mausoleum, as this house was. And it would be dangerous for him to offer her too much companionship to ease her natural loneliness.

"Of course you will not shock him. He will be charmed by you, my dear. And jealous of my having rescued my own Rapunzel." At her continued doubt, he added, "I'll take all the blame upon my head—for not finding you an experienced lady's maid."

An idea came to him, one that might cheer her up slightly, and possibly keep her too busy to feel neglected. "We'll find you an experienced maid immediately—in London."

Her eyes widened. "London? Oh no, Simon, that will be too tiring for you. I'd rather we stayed here where it is peacefully quiet and—"

Damn these lies. "Nonsense. A young woman needs laughter and dancing." He saw that she intended to argue, so he continued. "And I need to show off my beautiful bride. How can I do that if I don't find an experienced lady's maid to make sure that all the young bucks are green with jealousy?"

She smiled at him, suddenly nervous. Her eyes did not meet his as she confessed, "Actually, Simon, you needn't bother about the lady's maid. I hired one before the wedding. She should be arriving soon."

He was surprised. Though, of course, since he was dealing with Miranda, he should not have been. "When?"

"I should have told you. I'm sorry. But it's done now. She's very experienced." Miranda smiled and stood, coming up on tiptoes to press her lips to his cheek. "Now let's go meet that heir of yours—and see if your mother has taken herself off as promised."

The reminder of his mother stopped him from giving in to his impulse to pull her into his arms. He followed her, drinking in the scent of vanilla that seemed always to surround her.

Briefly, he wondered what kind of a woman she might have found in the vicinity of Anderlin who would have experience at being a lady's maid. No doubt one who was supremely incompetent but in dire need of a job.

He sighed. Perhaps it would not be wise to bring her to London just yet. A few weeks spent to acquaint her with the reticence of a proper duchess might prevent another scandal. He knew he should be applying himself diligently to molding her into a proper wife, but he did not want to spoil the magical spell she had woven over his life and his home with the discord that was sure to result.

She stopped at the top of the stairs and turned to him. "Have you done with the idea of taking me to London, Simon?"

He nodded. "If you do not wish to go, I will not press the issue." Yet, he added silently.

She smiled at him, her eyes glowing, despite his behavior toward her last night. Was that his fate then? To take her trust in him and twist it until her eyes no longer reflected a belief in the goodness of life? "Thank you for considering my wishes, Simon. You cannot imagine what that means to me."

It chilled him to think of her at the mercy of the wolves and rakes in London. No doubt the lot of them would scent her innocence and devour her whole, as Grimthorpe had tried five years ago. But how to bring her some worldly ways and keep that beautiful core of sweetness?

It would take weeks, perhaps months, to give her a polished shield to safeguard her. Would there be time to introduce her to London and make certain that she would be safe after he was gone? He took her arm to lead her down the stairs and the feel of her hand in the crook of his elbow was pleasure and pain in every pulse of blood through his veins.

Downstairs in the breakfast room, there was blessedly no sign of his mother. Arthur, however, was enjoying a plate of eggs and smoked sausage. He rose when Simon and Miranda entered the room. "Simon,

I beg to be introduced to your lovely new bride." He came around the table and clapped Simon on the shoulder as he beamed at Miranda.

Simon could not help reflecting that Arthur would have been just as effusive if Miranda had been four feet tall and possessed of hairy warts on her nose and chin. Arthur had always been a bit unsure of his ability to carry out the duties of an heir. Simon's mother had sarcastically called him the "heir-reluctant." Simon might have laughed, if it were not so patently true.

He patted Miranda's hand briefly and then released her. "Yes. Miranda, I am pleased to present you to my cousin Arthur. Arthur, this is my bride, Miranda."

Arthur beamed. "Welcome to the family, my dear. I have been telling Simon that what he needs is a bride and children—not a distant cousin culled from nowhere to learn to perform duties he's not very good at to begin with."

Miranda looked at him in puzzlement. "Culled from nowhere? Surely not."

Arthur colored. "Of course I am a bona fide Watterly. I am just from a very distant branch of the family. We'd quite forgotten our ties to the Dukes of Kerstone until Simon reminded us, I daresay."

And happy to have done so, Simon thought to himself as he remembered the arguments that had preceded Arthur's agreement to be trained as Simon's heir. It was only the fact that, as the closest male relative, he would indeed inherit the title and lands whether or not he trained for the task that convinced him to take the offer and come to learn about his future duties.

Arthur seemed also to be thinking along those lines. "He is trying to mold me into a proper duke." He smiled gently as he spoke, as if the outcome—failure—were assured.

"Come, come, Arthur. You have improved greatly in your abilities since you've arrived. You will make an excellent duke."

Arthur raised a skeptical brow.

Simon continued, embellishing upon Arthur's small strides forward in ducal behavior. "Haven't your accidents been much more infrequent of late?"

"Accidents?" Miranda's eyes widened with curiosity and Simon was suddenly sorry he had brought up the subject. The best thing he could do for Arthur was steer them away from this discussion before his cousin became a fresh target for her ministrations.

Arthur, aiding Simon unaware, blushed at her interest and quickly downplayed his string of mishaps. "Trivial incidents, really. I just seem to be a clumsy thing."

"I think you are much less clumsy," Simon added, to help ease Arthur's obvious discomfort at the discussion.

"And a duke must not be clumsy?" Arthur smiled again, refusing to take offense, or, Simon thought with chagrin, to take seriously that he would be the next Duke of Kerstone. At least, Miranda was diverted. For that he was grateful.

As they spoke there was a discreet cough from the direction of the door. Dome stood patiently.

"Yes?" Simon asked.

"A young lady and her daughter have arrived, Your Grace. The young lady claims to be a new employee?" His eyes were frosty and his back rigidly straight as he glanced at Miranda. "She claims to have been hired by Her Grace."

Simon was outraged. "My mother has hired a servant? For my home? Send her packing at once."

Miranda touched his arm, checking his outrage. "No. I hired her, Simon. She's my new lady's maid."

His sudden rage receding, Simon noted Miranda's unease and wondered what sight would meet his eyes. "Very well, take her up to the servant's quarters and get her settled in."

The butler nodded, and asked, "And her daughter, Your Grace?"

"Put them in a room down the hall from me." Miranda said.

Everyone stared at her. Dome, his reserve breached, colored slightly. "Servants, Your Grace?" His eyes fastened onto Simon in a silent plea for a return to sanity.

Miranda seemed unperturbed. "Yes, but her daughter is quite frail and needs to be in a room with a nice big hearth."

Simon's neck began to tickle with suspicion. "Send the servant and her daughter into my study for an interview, Dome."

Miranda protested. "I'm certain they must be much too tired for an interview at this point, Simon. Why don't we let them get settled in and then you can meet them."

It did not escape his notice that she had attempted to change a formal interview into a casual meeting. But his new wife would soon find out that he would not allow her to turn his household upside down.

If he could not bed her, he could at least see to teaching her how to conduct herself now that she was a duchess. "Send them to me immediately," he told Dome. He had an uncomfortable feeling that he was going to recognize the "servant" in question and he was not at all happy about it.

As he waited in his study, Miranda anxiously watching him, he soon found his suspicions confirmed. The woman from the village . . . and Betsy. They stared at him with their big blue eyes, both seeming to recognize that he was not pleased, and that their fates hung in his hands.

Nervously, Miranda performed the introductions. "I have hired Katherine Lawton as my new lady's maid. Perhaps you remember her from the night we—"

"I remember her well." Simon interrupted Miranda's attempt to force him to accept the hiring of this woman as a *fait accompli*. "But I do not recall it being said that she was a lady's maid." He wondered if Miranda had hired her knowing what the woman did to earn her living. Surely she could not have.

Just then, like a tiny whirlwind, Betsy broke from her mother's side and ran up to Simon. She stood there, her blue eyes trained on him as she gave him a wide smile and asked, "Do you remember me? I'm the little girl you rescued."

Simon surprised himself when he found that he had no difficulty in smiling back at her. "I remember you very well Betsy." He lifted the little girl into his arms and she laid her arms around her neck. "Just as I remember your mother." He gave both women a measured glance, to ensure they knew he had not gone soft-hearted because of the child.

He said steadily to Katherine. "So you want to be a lady's maid? For what reason?" The flicker of surprise over the woman's features as she quickly sought Miranda's gaze for guidance confirmed his suspicions. She was no more than another of his bride's misguided attempts at rescue.

Miranda stepped toward Katherine, one hand outstretched. But her eyes were on him, pleading in the oddly imperious way she had. "Simon, I know that Katherine will be an excellent servant. Let us call a halt to this interview now, and let them get settled."

He opened his mouth to tell her clearly and com-

pellingly that he was master in his own home, when
a new voice interrupted. "Simon, what is going on?
Why is this woman—dragging a child along, no less—
here? Surely she is not claiming the child is your by-
blow."

Katherine paled and Miranda tightened her grip
on the other woman's arm as she addressed her
mother-in-law, "Of course not. How could you think
such a thing?"

The dowager turned her attention to Simon, who
was still holding Betsy in his arms. "He seems comfortable enough with the child. It was a natural mistake
to assume he was her father."

Simon loosened his grip on Betsy when she
squirmed, and he realized that his hold on her had
become ironbound. It was a long practice for him to
tamp down his anger and pretend to a cold civility.
"Good morning, Mother. When I did not see you at
breakfast, I thought you had taken your leave."

"That would have been quite rude of me, Simon.
Your bride should certainly appreciate the benefit of
my experience as chatelaine of this home for more
than half my lifetime."

She turned to Miranda and inclined her head
toward the doorway. "Would you like to start with a
tour of the main house, my dear? Perhaps the family
wing? I promise not to tell you all the stories today,
just the ones that seem the most important."

Simon cut off his objection before it began, realizing that for once his mother was working in his aid.
He would be able to deal with Katherine and her
daughter without interference. "An excellent idea.
Miranda, I will handle this matter. You go with my
mother."

She looked from Katherine to Simon and he could
feel her dilemma as if it were his own. Fortunately,

it wasn't his to decide whether to try to cushion the interview with Katherine or bear the cold company of his mother.

It wasn't hers either. He had decided for her. With a firm hand on her back, he propelled her toward the door. "Don't be shy. I'm sure my mother will be her usual informative self."

"But . . ." Her eyes were locked with Katherine's. And then something so subtle seemed to pass between them that Simon nearly missed it. Only the fact that Miranda nodded and turned toward the dowager made him realize that some form of communication had occurred. He wondered briefly, as his wife left the room, if he had made a bad bargain in being left alone with Katherine and Betsy.

Chapter Thirteen

The dowager's method of touring seemed to consist of walking briskly through room after room while reciting capsule histories of the room's flaws. The Elizabethan Parlor, a quite charmingly sunny room, was too warm in the summer. The formal drawing room, in which hung a beautiful tapestry in scarlets and bright greens and golds, possibly done by one of Simon's ancestors, had a persistent leak on days with heavy rain.

As the dowager led her quickly through the various and sundry parlors and drawing rooms, Miranda abandoned all attempts to commit the lay of Simon's home to her memory. There were rooms that could not be got to by any method but an excellent memory.

Off the White Duchess's parlor—so named for a three-generations-removed silver-haired virago—was a tiny, exquisitely designed reading room with a comfortable chaise longue, a large sunlit window for light, and several shelves of books meant expressly for feminine tastes.

Miranda would have lingered, but the dowager had no such intention. The room's flaw seemed to be that it encouraged an unhealthy degree of solitude.

She found herself only able to concentrate on the whirlwind of information with half her mind. The other half she was unable to pry from the study where Simon was undoubtedly cross-examining Katherine. She believed she could trust the healer not to spill the true reason she had been hired. Simon would be furious if he found out. Worse yet, he might refuse the remedies.

Hopefully, Katherine had said nothing to Betsy. The child had not yet learned to be discreet, as they all had well to remember. She smiled, remembering how easily Simon had swung her into his arms. It was heartening to see that he held true affection for the child, despite the way he had spoken of "urchins" in the loft. He would make a good father, if he were given the chance.

Miranda hastened her steps, in danger of losing her companion. Curious, she followed the dowager into a gallery with a high ceiling that arched overhead. Imposing portraits of men in heavy and ornate gold frames lined the left wall, while somewhat less imposing portraits of women hung opposite.

Although they had been painted hundreds of years apart, by different artists, the eyes in the portraits were all of such a compelling nature that Miranda felt as if she were being observed by every one of Simon's relatives. Their expressions were all so uniformly solemn she had no doubt that she had been found distinctly lacking.

For a moment, the two of them stood without speaking, as if the dowager recognized that the overwhelming watchfulness of the room was unnerving and was allowing her a moment to recover. And then her acerbic words made Miranda doubt that she could possibly have had such a kind motivation. "Impressive lot, aren't they? I wonder if they cowed the portrait painters as effectively as they do anyone who enters this room."

She stopped at a portrait that held a strong resemblance to Simon, but seemed somehow wrong. "Is this one of Simon?"

"No, that is Peter, his older brother." Oddly, Miranda noticed, the dowager deliberately did not look at the portrait before she answered.

"I never knew that he had an older brother." The man in the portrait was young, but not a child. "They are very alike."

As if drawn against her will, the duchess slowly turned her head to look full at the portrait. She moved closer. Her hand hovered near, but without touching the bottom of the gilded frame. Miranda noticed that the slender fingers shook ever so slightly. "Yes. They were indeed alike."

The older woman shook her head slightly, as if it took great effort for her to remove her attention from the portrait and turn her gaze to Miranda. "At least in looks. They never had the opportunity to meet each other, since Peter died not long after Simon was born."

Miranda's breath caught in her throat. Somehow the long ago death of the brother seemed to make Simon's own impending death a reality. Her sympathy was entirely genuine when she said, "How awful for you."

But the dowager seemed to have recovered from any passing weakness that came from strong emotions. She waved her hand in dismissal. "He was not my son. Sinclair's first wife was his mother. He was older than I by several years."

Miranda had no answer for such a cold statement. "Then I'm sure it was difficult for the late duke."

The dowager gave a tiny, graceful shrug. "I'm sure he grieved—in his own fashion. But he had Simon as an heir to replace him."

Miranda thought of Valentine and the girls. They were irreplaceable. Were she to lose one, it would be a permanent and irredeemable loss. As would Simon's death be, if she could not prevent it.

If she and Katherine could not cure Simon, she would soon be without him. The sense of loss took her breath away. How had she come to care for him so much in such a short time?

Certainly he was a brave and honorable man, his loss would be a grave one to society. But it was not a general sense of loss that she felt. Her feeling of loss came from the thought that she would not be able to receive one of his quick smiles, and from the realization that she might soon hear only in her memory the rich voice that set her nerves atingle.

She pressed a hand below her heart to ease the ache. Not being kissed by him ever again. Not touching him, smiling at him across the table. No, her feeling of loss was personal indeed, for a husband she had not really wanted and who was, for the most part, maddening in the extreme.

She looked at the portrait again. The man in it had the slim build of a young man still approaching his majority. And he had died before he had the chance to know love and have a family of his own. She would do her best to see that the same was not true for Simon.

Idly, trying to stifle the grief that lingered at the edges of her consciousness, she said, "If only Peter had lived long enough to marry and have a son, Simon would not have to scour the hillside for suitable heirs.''

The dowager's reaction was remarkable. Her eyes closed and her voice hushed to a whisper. "Sometimes I imagine that he did. He was far away in France then, and we did not hear from him. He could have married and been happy for at least a short while before his death. Sometimes I pray it was so.''

There was a tremor of sadness that could not be dismissed. For the first time, Miranda realized that the dowager duchess of Kerstone was still a fairly young woman. No more than forty-five at most.

The thought that Simon might have an unknown niece or nephew set fire to her imagination. "Did he investigate the possibility?''

"No. I don't suppose he ever thought of it.'' With an almost invisible struggle, the dowager regained the cold demeanor that Miranda suspected now was only a facade to hide a lonely and sad woman. "Certainly I didn't mention the possibility to him. It was merely a foolish fancy of mine.''

Unbearable sadness swept over Miranda. "I don't suppose it is very likely. Even if he were to have been married, how often does a short marriage produce a child?''

She was not thinking of his brother, though, but of herself. In this gallery of Watterlys, generation after generation, the ache for Simon's child was sharp.

She fancied, as she glanced from portrait to portrait, the eyes that judged her—women as well as men—seemed to have made up their minds as to her failure. And she was fearful that there was nothing she could do to avert that failure. She could not get close enough to Simon to do her wifely duty without causing him to become overwrought.

The dowager seemed to sense the conflict that per-colated through her. "Even a long union is no guaran-tee of children. Simon was my only child in twenty-five years of marriage."

Once again struck by the dowager's youth, Miranda had no time to puzzle the meaning of her statement, for at that moment the sound of childish sobbing, along with the rapid patter of feet along parquet, echoed in the hallway. Both women turned to see Betsy running toward them, tears flowing freely down her cheeks.

"Betsy!" **Miranda** bent to catch the child and raise her into her arms. Betsy's arms clung tight and warm around her neck as the sobs continued.

"What on earth is the matter, my sweet?" Miranda murmured soothingly.

Between sobs the distraught child managed eventu-ally to gasp out, "His Grace is going to turn me and me mam out. He don't like Mam at all." Her wails took on a piercing quality as she finished.

Miranda forced herself to smile. "Nonsense. I have hired your mother, and you will both stay here."

Betsy did not seem convinced, although her wails lessened in volume. Children were often fearful when adults argued, Miranda had found. The best reassur-ance would be for her to swiftly relegate such fears into the rubbish bin.

However, in order to convince the child, she needed to suppress her own annoyance with Simon. She forced herself to continue smiling as she hugged the child to her. "I'm afraid some of this might be my fault, sweet. You see, I had neglected to inform him that you and your mother would be joining our establishment, so His Grace was merely . . . sur-prised."

The child shook her head against the shoulder of

Miranda's gown, which was becoming increasingly damp. "He said he would not have her in his home."

"Did he indeed?" The dowager's question was tart. "I wonder why?"

Miranda ignored the pointed dig. "I promise, Betsy, you and your mother are staying here with me. I will explain everything to His Grace, and soon he will tell you so himself."

Betsy lifted her head from Miranda's shoulder. "For truth?"

"Of course." Miranda wondered how difficult it would be to convince Simon. She could not understand his reaction. He had affection for Betsy, that had been obvious when he had caught the child in his arms in the study. Even if Katherine was not experienced, she was intelligent and capable of learning quickly. But she hid her chagrin from the obviously frightened child.

The dowager's eyes were focused on Betsy's tear-stained cheeks and bright eyes. Her mouth was a thin line broken only when she asked, "Whose child is she?"

"My lady's maid, Katherine's." Miranda explained shortly, still stung by the dowager's assumption, in the study, that Betsy was Simon's own child.

The dowager nodded. "So you are certain the child is not his, then."

"I am quite certain." Miranda wondered if the dowager was aware that she asked the most outrageous questions as if she were inquiring over the weather. She suspected the older woman actually cultivated the practice, so she dealt with her accusations plainly.

She stopped in the hallway, forcing the dowager to turn and face her instead of walking imperiously forward. "And I must tell you that I would not think less of Simon if he did choose to take a child of his into his home to raise—legitimate or not. That he might do that would only raise him in my esteem.''

"Well, I am glad to see that you have a sensible attitude about such things. So many young women don't.'' There was a wistful look in her eye for a moment and to Miranda's amazement, the slim and elegant arm extended to allow the dowager to pat Betsy on the head.

The child's last lingering sobs stifled at once and she began to hiccup. "It must have been the blond hair that made me think . . . never mind. Come, I will show you both the line from which Simon has sprung.'' She looked pointedly at Miranda. "Perhaps you will understand him better, then.''

With that disheartening statement, she turned and walked briskly toward the end of the hallway in which hung the oldest portraits. As they moved back toward the more recent portraits, Miranda barely heard her pithy descriptions of each of the ancestors, male and female, so busy was she looking for Simon's portrait. It was puzzling to her, but apparently Simon had no portrait in the gallery. Perhaps it graced the mantel of another room? Somehow, though, that did not seem in keeping with what she knew of Simon.

The dowager's brisk recitation of history ended so abruptly that Miranda, Betsy still in her arms, nearly bumped into her before she, too, managed to stop. The dowager stood looking up at the portrait of one of the sternest of the men, which hung on the wall next to the one of Peter. There was a streak of white at his temples that seemed to emphasize the sharp jut of both his nose and chin.

"Was that his father?''

A flicker of distaste crossed the dowager's features. "My husband, God rot his soul.'' When Betsy's head once again came up from Miranda's shoulder, the older woman seemed to realize what she had said. "Forgive me. Children should not hear such talk. This gallery has always put me on edge. I think it best if we depart." She turned on her heel to leave and then paused to make one more comment, looking directly at the portrait of the old duke.

"Simon was a beautiful baby. I was happy to have him, despite the fact that his father was a wretched demon." She broke off, her expression indefinably, unbearably sad as she looked up into the stern eyes of the first duke. "It is sometimes hard to imagine any of these illustrious gentlemen as innocent babes in their mother's arms, is it not?"

Miranda tried in vain to see Simon as a babe in arms as he paced the room, anger setting his chin at such a sharp angle that he resembled his ancestors' portraits.

A vein at his temple visibly throbbed as he repeated, for the third time, "The woman is no lady's maid. I will not allow it."

"I hired her. I think I have that right. After all, you will not have to suffer any mistakes she might make in dressing my hair or tightening my laces." She truly could not fathom the reason for his upset. She had thought it was simple masculine dismay at not being consulted in the decision. But from his words, it was becoming increasingly clear that his objections were with Katherine herself.

He was adamant. "I could not bear it if she were to lay one finger on your hair, or even your clothing."

"Simon, don't be so harsh. I realize she is not your typical maid, but with proper training . . ." She felt slightly ridiculous, making a case for Katherine as a lady's maid when it was all a subterfuge to keep Simon from finding out that she would be trying to cure him.

"I would prefer to keep you sheltered. Please don't press me. Simply give the woman notice and send her home again."

"I know she made her living in a rather unorthodox manner—"

"Unorthodox?" He paused and glared at her. "Just exactly what do you know of how she made her living? Surely you did not discuss it with her?"

"Of course I did! She has much to teach me—"

"What?" He found this preposterous conversation was giving him a headache. "I shall be the one to teach you about such things."

"Well, I don't see how. You won't even consult a doctor about your health. I cannot understand why you are being unreasonable. I should be able to choose my lady's maid for myself."

"She is a wholly unacceptable person!"

Miranda rounded on him. "I had no idea you were so intolerant or I would never have married you. Katherine may have had a hard life, but she is a good person—too good to be a lady's maid. It is simply the best I could offer her."

"Too good?" He could not believe his ears.

"She has been living with her father, doing her best to keep her daughter fed and clothed with her healing talents. But her village is poor and they had little to offer. I will have her, and you will not stop me, Simon."

"A healer? What nonsense has she filled your head with, Miranda? The woman has been lying with men for money!"

Miranda blinked. For a moment she did not take

in his meaning. And then she did. "How dare you say that about Katherine!"

He shook his head. "You sound as if she were your most trusted friend."

It was true. She did consider Katherine a trusted friend. Miranda reflected that perhaps such was her nature. After all, she had bonded with Simon more quickly and fully than she had imagined possible in a lifetime of days together. "Perhaps that is because she has become one—because I took the time to get to know her."

He stilled, the muscle that twitched when he was overwrought pulsed in an alarming fashion. "What do you mean, you took the time to get to know her? Have you spent time with this woman?"

She nodded, understanding his dismay now that she knew the misapprehension under which he labored. "And Betsy—in fact it was Betsy I went to see, but Katherine's plight tore at my heart."

"And so you offered her a position here?"

"Yes."

"It will never work."

"We will see." She did not really care if Katherine was the worst lady's maid ever known. She wanted her husband cured and for that she needed Katherine here to help.

"I want her out of my home. You do not know what you are about in this matter. You must trust my judgment."

His harsh, unfeeling words echoed in her ears. He trusted her no more than her own father had. Worse, he had taken her for wife and did not treat her as a wife. "No. You must trust mine."

He looked at her seriously, then sighed. "She must go."

She felt herself inexplicably blinded by tears as she stood. "Very well, Simon. If you cannot be reasonable, then Katherine, Betsy, and I will be out of your home within the hour."

Chapter Fourteen

He watched as she retreated into a cold stranger who could stand there and calmly announce that she was leaving him—as if he did not know what he was doing in refusing Katherine. He thought briefly that she was simply being melodramatic. But a glance into her eyes convinced him otherwise.

She had no idea what she was asking of him, of course. Again, her innocence led her into trouble. Making a friend of a woman like Katherine. It was too absurd for words. And yet, he could still remember the difficulty he had had when his mother had accused him of fathering Betsy.

He wished he dared to throw in her face the simple fact that he would never deny a child of his—never keep a child from knowing the name of his or her true father, as his mother had done with him. But then the scandal would no longer be a family secret. He could not afford that. He had promised.

For a moment, he forced himself to consider letting

Miranda go. Just nodding, saying nothing as she walked out, her spine stiff, Betsy's tiny hand cradled in her own. She would do it, he had no doubt. She was not threatening him, she was laying down the battle lines and the terms of surrender in one clean shot.

Valentine would take her in. Her sisters would divert any lingering shame or misery with their demands upon her time. Miranda would go back to her old life as if she had never married. And he would be free of the torment of being married to her yet unable to make love with her.

But the thought of living the rest of his short life as the duke without her near enough to touch was unbearable. "Don't be ridiculous. You are my wife, you will go nowhere."

"Oh, Simon," she whispered. "I must."

"I will not allow it," he said, slowly and clearly. He wanted her to know it would be a waste of time to argue. In this matter, he knew better than she. Though he did not expect her to surrender easily.

She smiled, almost involuntarily, and his heart gave an extra jolt when he saw that there were tears in her eyes. "It seems that I am the pea to your Princess."

For a moment, he was nonplussed. And then he remembered the tale to which she referred, in which a princess was so delicate that a pea placed under twenty mattresses disturbed her sleep.

Fairy tales again. Would she never realize that they lived in a world that did not often see a happy ending? "Do not spout your fairy tales at me."

Anger, hurt, and distrust warred on her expressive face as she said softly, "It hardly seems a fairy tale to me, who must live it." Her eyes were liquid with pain, but she met his eyes without flinching.

Her pain echoed within him and intensified as he

realized that she was, for the first time, not convinced of a happy ending for them. He had wanted this, but the slow death of her innocence was horrifying for him to watch. As horrifying as the eager young faces of the men he had daily sent off to their deaths as a result of an indifferent ball of lead.

But what courage she had. Even with her assurance rocked, her voice was steady. "You have told me that to be your wife I must not try to stem the course of your illness." She clenched her fists convulsively as she spoke, he noticed, but otherwise she projected a calm front. "I must not sleep next to you at night— nor kiss you too passionately." A faint blush stained her cheeks and he felt ashamed of how badly he was hurting her. "Now you tell me that I am not capable enough to hire my own lady's maid." Her chin came up. "I *am* capable of running my own life. I don't *need* you." She paused and closed her eyes. "I just *want* you."

His throat closed as her quiet words cut through him.

She opened her eyes and made as if to step closer to him, but halted. Her gaze was clear and certain. "Don't you understand? If you do nothing to stop the course of your illness, you will die. And then I will need to do much more than hire a servant on my own."

The thought of her, alone, after his supposed death, was not a pleasant one. But then, neither was the thought of her being taken advantage of by people with the base kind of motives she was too good-hearted to comprehend. That was the battle, after all. Her autonomy. Not Katherine herself. "I will take you to London. You may hire anyone you choose there—"

She tried to interrupt, but he held up his hand and

finished forcefully. "But Katherine is unsuitable. To be plain, the woman lies with men for money and is no fit company for you." He knew her well enough by now not to be surprised that she did not react with shock or surprise to his bald statement.

"I see you have made up your mind." There was a touch of scorn in her voice that he could not credit.

"Some things must be done a certain way. It is not a matter of making up one's mind, but of knowing the difference between right and wrong."

"And Katherine is wrong?" she challenged, her voice taut with sudden fury.

"She does what she must, no doubt. But I will not have a person like that in my household."

"Your definition of right and wrong is too restrictive for me." She shook her head. "Perhaps for any frail mortal being, but especially for me. You were the one who insisted we marry and now that I am here, as your wife, I often feel as if you wished me anywhere but here."

The truth of her statement jolted through him, but he rejected it with his very soul as well as his words. "Of course I don't want you to want to be rid of me. You do not understand—"

"Oh, but I do, Simon." It was her turn to override him. She did so with an imperious military flare, sharply raising her arm high to halt his words.

"Katherine does not lie with men for money. She is a vicar's widow. From her mother, she has learned herbal healing. People come from London for her help, as Giles Grimthorpe did."

He was surprised at her naïveté. "She is no vicar's daughter—she would not be living as she is, threadbare, poor. You have been gulled in by a pretty story. But then, you are known to believe in fairy tales."

Indignation burned in her eyes. "So you would

think, Simon. But that is because you are a man."
She said man as if it were an epithet.

"When you are a woman and your husband dies,
you must fall back on the kindness of relatives." Her
eyes widened and he knew she was realizing that very
likely she would soon be in a similar position.

Certainly, he was realizing what that would mean
to her as he watched her argue her case for her friend.
Thankfully, she had Valentine to fight for her. But
it would no doubt set her pride on edge to be
beholden to her twin brother for a home.

Her voice was slightly unsteady as she continued.
"Katherine's father was a humble man before his
daughter married the vicar, but he gladly gave her
and her daughter room in his cottage when her husband died and she was turned out of the vicarage."

He saw the certainty in her eyes and realized
abruptly that he had been the fool, not Miranda. He
had come to a conclusion and forgotten to question
it. Such things got men killed in war. It only lost him
this one skirmish with Miranda.

He scrabbled for a place to make his stand. Surrender was not his way. He had been raised a duke, even
if he should not have been. If the woman was not a
slattern, then she was worse, a healer.

Miranda's true purpose in hiring Katherine became
clear to him. He felt the anger swell within him as
he realized how she had meant to manipulate him.
And he knew the weapon to use against her. "You
lied to me."

She did not deny it. But neither did she show signs
of remorse. "I intend to have her as my lady's maid,
but mostly, I want her so that she might help you.
She might discover something you or your doctors
have missed. Is that so wrong?"

"Yes. I will not be lied to." He had made it abundantly clear to her more than once that he did not wish to be subjected to a healer's scrutiny. If Katherine were any good, which was doubtful, she might uncover his secret—that he was healthy and illness-free.

He crossed his arms over his chest and fixed his features into the fierce officer's scowl he had used with his men. "This tendency of yours to think you know what is best for others, to try to force impossible happy endings upon situations and people who cannot have them is what gets you in trouble. You must stop at once before you hurt someone."

Or before you are hurt, he wanted to add, but those words would not sway her. For someone who cared so much about creating a happy ending for others, she didn't give a fig about her own happiness. One of many reasons he had taken the task over himself.

She flashed him a sad, but still triumphant smile. "Then you agree I must leave."

Again he found himself speechless. She had ambushed him with the skill of a professional. After a moment, he found himself able to utter a strangled, "No—"

Again she interrupted. "I cannot touch you, I cannot look for ways to cure you"—her voice cut with scorn—"I cannot even hire a lady's maid without causing you undue agitation. I believe, if I remain here, I shall shorten your already brief life, just as that fairy-tale pea shortened the princess's night's sleep."

"I am no princess."

That, he was relieved to see, provoked a smile from her, despite her agitation. "No, you are not. But I am definitely an irritation."

He crossed the distance between them before she could react. He closed his fingers on her shoulders and looked into her eyes. He wanted to make sure she understood him. This was not a fair battle, after all. She was his wife, not his enemy. "I crave the irritation you bring me. I'll never let you leave. Never."

She touched his chest and whitened. "Simon, your heart." She tried to push him toward his chair. "You must calm down, this disagreement isn't good for you."

He resisted the force of her hands easily. "Agree to stay." He knew he was using the lie of his health to coerce her, but he didn't care. Neither life, love, nor war was fair. If she left, his remaining days here would be unbearable.

She reached up and gently touched his cheek. Her fingers were cool and trembled lightly against his skin. "I want you to live, Simon. Is that so terrible?"

He shook his head. "Herbs will make no difference to my fate." He felt a bittersweet regret that there was no herb to cure bastardy. And no way he would win this battle without concessions. "If you wish her to attend you, she may."

He wagged his finger sternly, though, with a need to prove he was master in his own home. "But at the first sign that she is interfering in matters of my health, I shall send her packing."

Relief shone on her face and he felt a curious lightening of the heart to see it. He wondered if he had set a bad precedent, letting her threaten him this way. And then he realized that it would make no difference in a few months. He put his arms around her, determined to indulge her for the short time he could. She leaned her head against his chest, resting against him. He felt the smooth lump of the leather pouch between them. "Katherine will do well enough, you'll see."

"Just don't expect me to become an experiment for every obscure remedy she can concoct." He caressed the back of her neck. "I want to spend the time with you, like this. Can you understand that?"

She sighed. "I do understand, but——"

He quickly moved to cement his position and distract her from this matter before she had managed to persuade him to physic a body that had no need of it. She was formidable in battle and it would take all his wits to outflank her.

"If we are to introduce you and your sisters to society, we should do so immediately. So you had best see to ensuring that Katherine is adequate to the task of dressing you and putting up your hair. No one is so cruel as the ladies of the court."

He saw the shadow alight in her expression and cursed the thoughtlessness of his words. She, better than most, had cause to know exactly the measure of that cruelty. Her voice broke as she began, "Perhaps we should wait . . ."

"We cannot afford to wait. We will have a house party in mid-June."

She drew in her breath. "What?" The color drained completely from her skin. He watched in alarm as it rebloomed in her cheeks.

To calm her panic, he added soothingly, "Nothing large, Miranda, just thirty people or so." The thought seemed to distress her even more, so he added, "My mother can put herself to use in helping you plan the thing."

A memory came to him, unbidden, of the large summer parties his mother had hostessed for his father. She had seemed so beautiful as she drifted through the groups of guests in her flowing pastel gowns, cool, laughing, sneaking bits of pastry and sweetmeats for her son.

That was before he understood that the laughter wasn't real, it was rehearsed, calculated, cold. That after every weekend party his parents would argue bitterly, and his mother would retreat to her wing for days.

But there was no doubt that these parties had been successful affairs for all but the host and hostess. In fact, it was to her credit that no one realized how much she hated her husband. "She has a great deal of experience. I daresay she could impress Grimthorpe himself."

Her mouth quirked downward. "Shall we invite him also, then?"

"By all means. We have nothing to hide—or so we shall have them all believing before the weekend is through."

Her brow wrinkled and he longed to bend and brush it smooth with his lips. "Do you suppose he still has my boots?"

He knew what she feared—that Grimthorpe would somehow brew a new scandal. "It matters little, now. You are my wife."

"I suppose it is too late to cause trouble with a pair of old boots." The doubt did not entirely erase from her face.

"No doubt, if he hasn't already thrown them away, he's given them to one of his servants."

She nodded, but he could feel the worry radiating from her.

"The best way to ensure Grimthorpe's gossip is neutralized is to have you quickly accepted back into society." Knowing her weaknesses well, he urged, "We must be bold about introducing you. You do not want your sisters to suffer because of rumors and gossip, do you?"

"You are right. We will be bold." She turned her

lips up in a half smile. "Although, perhaps I shall temper my boldness with a touch of wisdom. Katherine, as a former vicar's wife, has much to teach me about patience."

She stretched up on the tip of her toes to press a kiss to his lips.

Fortunately, before he could move his arms to her waist and capture her against him, she slipped away. "I must tell Katherine and Betsy the good news."

"Curing someone who will not even admit the possibility for cure is difficult, Your Grace." Katherine's tone was grave, but her color was no longer pale. In fact, her cheeks had actually taken on color rather rapidly when she learned what Simon's objections had been. "I didn't realize . . . in our discussions he made it seem that he wanted someone with experience." Her mouth twisted with uncharacteristic bitterness. "I should have realized . . . everyone thinks such things."

"I don't," Miranda comforted her.

Katherine smiled in response. "Thank you for giving me a chance. Ever since my husband died and Betsy and I came back to live with my father, I have known what others suspect of me. I just don't know how to make them realize it isn't true. I've tried speaking the way they do, dressing the way they do, helping them. But nothing seems to work."

"What happened to you wasn't fair. You went out of your way to be kind to others, you deserve to be rewarded like the good kind sister in Mother Holle and be showered with gold. Instead you are showered with pitch, as if you were lazy and unkind."

Katherine laughed. "It is not so bad. I am paid for healing, and the money helped Da buy a cow and some chickens. We are better off than many. Perhaps that is why the lies persist.''

Miranda understood too well how that might happen. And it was a worry she must overcome before her house was overrun by those who would delight in her social downfall. ''Well, Simon now knows the truth. About you, and about my motives for bringing you to work for me. And he, as I had feared, has forbidden you to concoct any tonic for him.''

Katherine pressed her hand against Miranda's. ''I'm sorry.''

''Not that I will let his reluctance stay me—he will die if I do nothing. We shall just have to be cautious.''

''Perhaps we should simply tell him the truth?'' Katherine's voice was gentle, and her sojourn as a vicar's wife came through clearly. Miranda squirmed under the patient gaze, unwilling to give up any chance that Simon might have.

Betsy stirred and whimpered. The child, unaware of the reprieve she and her mother had been given, lay flushed and still upon a chair. It was perhaps for that reason that Katherine's hushed tone conveyed so much concern. ''Any patient, duke or no, must want to be well.''

Miranda sighed. ''I know. But for now, I shall have to do the wishing for Simon. He is beyond influence about his chances for survival.''

Katherine nodded. ''He is a lucky man, if only he knew it.'' She rose to her feet. ''It would help if I knew what ailed him.''

''He will tell me naught. But when we . . .'' Miranda broke off, blushing. ''When we are close, his heart beats impossibly fast, his breathing becomes labored, and his face becomes quite flushed.''

Katherine searched Miranda's face. ''More so than usual?''

Her face must have revealed her confusion, because when she did not answer, Katherine waved her hand dismissively. "Never mind. We shall both watch him from now on. Any unusual behavior, temperament, or daily habits shall be noted down so I may find out what is wrong with him."

With a tired smile, Katherine scooped her sleeping daughter up into her arms. "I had best get this little one tucked in for her nap."

"Yes." Miranda smoothed a stray lock of Betsy's hair, as she might have done to a sleeping Kate. "You and Betsy have a place here with us from now on."

Chapter Fifteen

"Less than a month to prepare a house party to reintroduce you to polite society? And I suppose it must be perfect? How very like Simon to set such an absurd standard." The dowager sat at a fragile cherry writing desk, a pile of invitations in front of her, her quill waving through the air for emphasis as she spoke.

Miranda wondered, not for the first time, if she would be better served to permanently alienate the dowager, rather than attempt a reconciliation between Simon and his mother. She smiled with strained patience. "We certainly have made a good start on it in these last weeks. I thank you for your help, despite the need to do so much so quickly. It's just that there are considerations . . ."

The dowager raised one elegant eyebrow, reminding Miranda uncannily of Simon. "Such as the haste of your marriage? The scandal you fear? Your five younger sisters, two of whom must be brought out quickly and well?"

Miranda thought she had hidden her anger—and astonishment—well, until the dowager continued. "My dear, don't look surprised. I am very well informed—even if not kept so by my son. And never fear. I am very organized. We shall be the talk of the season."

She couldn't help wondering if that would be a good thing or not, but she kept her reservations to herself and if she somehow let them show on her face, the dowager was mercifully tactful enough not to bring it to her attention again.

In the last few weeks they had planned a menu, entertainment and—most importantly—a guest list. Miranda found herself reluctant to make the decisions and deferred to the dowager on almost all things—where the dowager would allow the decision to be deferred, of course. All that was left to be done was pen the invitations.

"Are you certain you want to include him?" The dowager pointed to Giles Grimthorpe's neatly penned name.

"Simon thinks it best." Miranda was annoyed at her own timidity. She had agreed with him, why hadn't she said, *we* think it best? What was it about the dowager that made her feel as if she were back in the schoolroom?

"Yes, I can see his point. He is a relative, after all." The dowager brushed the feathered edge of the quill against the underside of her chin. "Still, it makes for an awkward weekend."

Miranda shrugged her shoulders. "I suspect the entire weekend will be unpleasant."

"I meant awkward in the sense of where to place his room, and who to seat him near at table, child."

She did not hide her amusement—or her condescension.

"I meant unpleasant in that he—and everyone else—shall be whispering and buzzing about the rumor that something untoward happened between us five years ago and hoping for a scandal. If they even deign to attend."

"Of course they will attend. The hint of past scandal as well as the curiosity about Simon's new duchess will ensure that." The dowager seemed to find that an encouraging fact.

She nodded miserably, trying to maintain the stiff upper lip the dowager so admired at the thought that she would be on exhibit like an ancient ruin for the pleasure of her guests.

The dowager said sharply, "And they will whisper, as well, but you will deal with that."

"I will do my best." Of course, her best had not been good enough five years ago. Had she learned enough cloistered at Anderlin, selling candlesticks and jewelry and raising her sisters, to handle London society again? Even with Simon's protection and in her own home?

She would feel safer back on the street where that awful man had relieved her of Anderlin's candlesticks and her mother's necklace. Those things were much less precious than the secrets that she had to guard now from the gossipmongers. How titillating they would find it that the Duke of Kerstone was ill—too ill to make love to his wife. Worse, would the rakes consider her sisters fair game?

As if sensing her concerns, the dowager commented with acerbity, "I trust that you have learned to control your own behavior. Have you spoken to your sisters? It would be unfortunate to have one of them repeat the lesson you have already learned."

"Yes, I have warned my sisters. But I would prefer to protect them by not exposing them to such potential for predation. I would not mind canceling these plans and never going into 'polite' society again."

The dowager's disapproval tinged her words with ice. "That is not the attitude of a duchess."

Miranda acknowledged the rebuke with a sigh. "It has been some time since I was in society, and that was only for a brief part of one season." And even then she had not coveted the position of duchess, which according to the dowager, required one to never allow any room for evil to be seen or spoken of in connection with oneself.

At times she felt very much like the miller's daughter, pretending to spin straw into gold and any moment waiting to be found out as a fraud. Only Miranda's Rumplestiltskin did not want her firstborn son—he wanted her husband's good name destroyed.

The dowager looked up at her. Her sharp eyes seemed to pick at the threads of Miranda's frayed nerves. "When do your sisters arrive? It is a wonderful tonic to have others to look after."

Miranda could not help but smile at the thought of the five females due to turn this sedate home into a beehive of activity. "They arrive tomorrow. Though perhaps you will wish them away the day after."

To Miranda's surprise, the dowager's expression grew distant and her lips curved upward slightly. "Five young girls running through these halls. Sinclair would never have countenanced it. He did not value girl children."

Miranda did not want to encourage the dowager to speak disrespectfully of her dead husband. She found herself all too easily picturing the man as a monster, and that could not be true. "Surely he would have loved a daughter, if you and he had been blessed with more children."

A brief flicker of pain crossed the dowager's face. "That would have been a miracle, indeed. More children. Sinclair did not need more children. He had Simon."

"Did you not ever wish for another child?"

The dowager's intensity surprised her. "Every day." Instantly, as if she regretted her revelation, she shuttered her features and gave a cold smile. "Children running through the house, the gardens, through the kitchens; they would have driven Sinclair to his grave much, much sooner."

The words shredded Miranda's anticipation of her sisters' visit. "Do you think they will have an ill effect on Simon?" She had not considered that the noise and flurry of activity that her sisters would bring might be detrimental to Simon's health.

The dowager knocked the pile of invitations askew with an awkward jerk of her hand, so very different from her normally elegant movements. "He always begged for brothers and sisters when he was small." She quickly rearranged the stack of invitations until the edges were even and straight. "Now he will have to cope. I'm certain he can."

"He seems to be looking forward to seeing them again."

The dowager touched the edge of one invitation. "Your sisters will need gowns and all the necessities. Simon has not overlooked that detail, has he?"

"No, indeed," Miranda laughed. "The girls arrive tomorrow and the modiste arrives the day after. Simon says she and her seamstresses are not to leave until my sisters are completely outfitted."

"It is a shame he will not be here to run Kerstone. He has a natural talent for the job."

Miranda sat silent, unsure how to respond to the unexpected emotion. When their eyes met, they held for a moment. Miranda felt compelled to reach out and pat the other woman's arm.

The dowager's eyes widened slightly and she regained her composure with a prim frown, but her hand came up to give Miranda's a quick squeeze. "He is even better at it than Sinclair was, and though I despised the man, he was a good overlord to his estates."

She was silent for a moment, as if contemplating the possibility. "Of course, he would never have thought of arranging for the outfitting of females." She sighed. "It is a pity that my son is depriving Kerstone of his leadership."

Miranda felt the wall rise up between them again, just when she had felt that she'd removed a stone or two. The dowager seemed to blame Simon for his illness. "He has no choice."

Haughty condescension was back in place, as if there had not been any vulnerable emotion moments ago. "You think not?"

"Perhaps he could make some attempts to treat his symptoms, but it is the mark of his care for his responsibilities that he tries to ensure everyone else will be taken care of when he is gone." Miranda blinked back tears at the thought. "That is why he is working hard to train Arthur—"

The dowager's eyebrows lifted quizzically. "Yes, he is working diligently at making a man of that meek mouse. You seem an intelligent girl. Isn't it obvious to you that he is wasting his efforts? He would be better served to train a manager to manage Arthur than to try to train Arthur to manage anything but his precious library."

Miranda was inclined to agree, but loyalty prevented her. "Arthur works very hard to learn what Simon must teach him about running the estates."

The dowager conceded the point. "It is only too unfortunate that he does not have more of the warrior and less of the chivalrous nature of his namesake about him. I suppose, though, that he is the best that Simon can do."

"What do you mean?"

"He scoured the country for any and all Watterly cousins." She crumpled an invitation on which she had evidently made a blot. "Of course, they do seem to be a feeble lot."

Miranda's curiosity was piqued. Simon had refused to talk about his difficult search for heirs. "Did you know any of the other heirs?"

"No. None actually arrived here. One died enroute in a carriage accident, and two succumbed to the grippe just before Simon's agent located them. He was quite put out." She looked at Miranda austerely.

"How odd that they should die so conveniently."

"I believe Simon hired an enquiry agent to make certain there was no sign of foul play."

Miranda wondered if she should confess to the dowager that not only had Simon set an enquiry agent to look into the deaths of his distant cousins, but she had sent an enquiry agent to find out whether Simon's brother Peter might actually have left an unknown wife and child behind.

She decided against it, after a moment's consideration. After all, it had been weeks with no word from the man. There was no point in getting anyone's hopes up for such an unlikely possibility.

But from every evidence she could see, Arthur himself was not thrilled with his own status of heir. His somewhat endearingly direct comments about children and the patter of little feet bordered on begging Miranda to give birth to a houseful of heirs for Simon.

She had found that he enjoyed collecting old manuscripts. She could imagine his relief if a son was born to Simon. He would be back to his books and his dusty library before the babe's first cry echoed in the portrait gallery. But babes were not conceived by husbands and wives who did not make love.

With a sigh, she crumpled the invitation she had just ruined with a careless blot of her pen. She closed her eyes and listened to the scratch of the dowager's pen against parchment.

Resolutely, she cleared her head of thoughts she could do nothing about and began writing again in a careful, flowing script her mother would have exclaimed with pride over. Duchess of Kerstone. Yes, her mother would have been pleased.

She thought of the life her sisters would bring to this austere home tomorrow. Swift upon the heels of that thought was the worry that Simon's health would be adversely affected. Well, then, Katherine and she would need to be even more observant than they had been. Not that there had been much to discover.

She wondered if Simon had tried the tea she had brought him this morning. The brew had smelled quite awful even with the lemon and sugar they had to add to make the odor more inviting, but Katherine thought it might help.

Try as she might to see Simon's point of view, she could not see the harm in drinking a cup of herbal tea. But his warning still rang in her ears—he did not want to be dosed.

When he had raised an eyebrow at the tea, she had forced herself to lie and say that Cook had overbrewed it. She wondered if he had believed her. At least, if he had not, he made no protest. She took comfort in that small victory.

"There is a gentleman to see you, Your Grace." Dome could not hide his disapproval—or, Miranda speculated, he chose not to hide it.

"May I see his card?" Miranda held out her hand.

"I'm afraid he has none, Your Grace." Dome paused, his face impassive except for the twitch of his nostrils. "He is an . . . American."

"Oh." Miranda smiled, intrigued. "I have never met an American. Send him in, then."

The man who followed Dome into the parlor stopped short at the sight of Miranda. He was tall and had a full head of gray hair. His manner of dress could only be called rustic and appeared to have suffered from a great deal of travel and little care. She supposed that Americans did not have valets.

His face called some recognition from deep within her, but she could not place it. Certainly, she had never met an American before today. The sight of his lined and sun-chapped skin seemed romantic to her. Americans were little more than ruffians and barbarians, but that had its own charm.

He stared in disbelief at her for a long moment— until she became uncomfortably aware of the danger of ruffians and barbarians, despite the romance of their hard lives. "How may I help you, sir?"

His voice was rough and his accent uncultivated when he grated out, "There must be some mistake. I want the Duchess of Kerstone."

Feeling like a schoolgirl caught in her mother's finery, Miranda protested with absurd formality. "I am Miranda Watterly, the Duchess of Kerstone."

He paled. For a moment she thought the big American barbarian would collapse to her carpet in a dead faint.

She hastened to add, "I am married to the present duke, Simon Watterly. Perhaps you were expecting his mother, the dowager duchess?"

His mouth twitched slightly as he regained his color. "Dowager? What an extraordinary thought. Don't expect it appeals to her."

That comment alone convinced Miranda that he was indeed an acquaintance of the dowager. "Would you like me to let her know you are here?"

"Please." He stood there, saying no more, a slight frown etching the lines deeper into his face.

She had to wonder if his extraordinary lack of certainty could be attributed to his being American, or was from some great emotion. "And your name, Mr.—?"

"Watson." He hesitated. "She might not remember me. Tell her that I have come to apologize for an injury I did her in her youth."

Hesitating a bit more, he added, "Perhaps I should give her a note, or she might refuse to see me."

Considering the injury had been done in her youth, and the lines on the American's face were deep, Miranda nodded. "That might be wise." She wondered if he had been a handsome young man, before time and trials had etched his face older than his years. Would the dowager even recognize him?

She settled the American in the parlor, rang for tea, and stepped into the hallway to dispatch a servant to bring the American's note to the dowager, who was taking her daily walk in the garden.

She hoped seeing the two together would explain the man's hesitation. An American! How had the dowager met him? Before she could spin a romantic tale for them, however, Simon touched her shoulder.

"A carriage is approaching." He was smiling at her, and his hand dropped to linger at her waist.

For a moment she was startled at his intimate gesture and then the import of his words hit her. Her sisters! All thoughts of the dowager and her American were pushed away. Her sisters were here. At last she would see Valentine and know if he had truly given up on Emily.

Chapter Sixteen

As they watched the carriage approach up the drive, her happy smile rebuked Simon, a silent testament to the loneliness he had forced her to suffer since he had selfishly cloistered her here with him and then done his best to spend no time with her—unless there was someone else about to ensure that he did not abandon his resolve not to make love with her.

Her eyes sparkled up at him like fine sherry as she danced impatiently at his side. Thinking of how small and forced her smiles had been of late, he realized just what he had wrought with his impatient need to possess her. He wanted desperately to lift her up and bury his face in her neck, where the scent of her was strong and sweet, and apologize for his unmeant cruelty.

He had not wanted to abandon her, he simply had no choice. He had not considered how full her life had been with family—or how empty of friends his home was. Katherine was somewhat of a confidante, but she was a servant. And he could not understand how Miranda tolerated his mother, never mind enjoyed her company.

Having her sisters underfoot would be a relief to both of them. She would have them to keep her giving nature from concentrating on his false illness, and he would have more than enough chaperones.

"Miranda! Your house is even nicer than Anderlin. I want to live here." Kate burst from the carriage before it had even rolled to a complete stop. He could not help his own smile as he hurried to catch the irrepresible elf in midflight and hand her to her happy sister.

"Kate! You could have injured yourself!" Miranda stood by the carriage, Kate clasped against her side to prevent her from darting into the path of the team as it came to a halt with a jingle of harnesses. The coachman opened the door formally for the remainder of her sisters to dismount more sedately, and Simon went to offer his hand.

The courtyard itself seemed electrified by the presence of the girls. Even the coachman, a thin-faced, normally somber man, was smiling broadly, albeit a little dazedly. He was not used to the constant high-pitched chatter of excited young persons of the female persuasion. Simon found himself overwhelmed with tales of the trip and the inns and food where they had stopped.

He watched Miranda, choked with emotion at her sisters tumbling from the carriage in bright flounces of skirts and even brighter smiles. She could not speak. He suspected she was close to breaking down into outright sobs. Her hands on Kate were tight, as if she might never let her go—until the little girl broke away to feed a carrot from her pocket to the lead horse.

He allowed his arm to encircle her waist as she, with tears in her eyes, embraced Hero. He saw similar tears in her sister's eyes and realized how much he had missed by never knowing his own brother.

The sisters hugged each other tightly. Miranda's voice was husky as she said, "It is so good to see you looking well."

"And you, as well." Hero smiled through her tears, blinking away the moisture until her gaze was focused on her sister. "I have missed you. How do you fare as Duchess of Kerstone?"

The question was pointed and Simon hurried to answer, fearing that Miranda would be too honest. "Your sister is the most gracious duchess we have ever known. I, for one, cannot think there is one more qualified for the position. And I would not change one thing about our last few weeks."

Miranda, on the verge of speaking, looked up at him in surprise. Her lips were turned up in a teasing smile as she asked, "Not one thing?" But her eyes were serious.

Fortunately, at that moment Juliet bubbled up to her. "Oh, Miranda, the duke's coach is just the thing. We traveled in the lap of luxury. You would not believe how comfortable the ride was, compared to our old carriage that father should have had resprung years ago."

She looked up at Simon with a flirtatious flip of her lashes that made him want to shout with laughter. But then, her eyes widened as she realized what she had said and the color left her face. "I did not mean . . ."

Miranda smiled. "Of course you didn't, Juliet. No doubt, if Papa and Mama had survived their carriage accident, Papa would have seen to the carriage. But that is neither here nor there. Are you well? How do things fare at Anderlin?'' She looked toward the abandoned carriage with a little frown line on her brow.

"Anderlin does well, as do we all.'' Hero smiled with a hint of pride and confidence. Simon was gratified to see it. He had not hurt the family by taking Miranda away, at least.

Noticing her sister's contemplation of the carriage, Juliet's hazel eyes sparkled as she added, "And Valentine sends his regrets that he was unable to accompany us, but his business ventures are doing so well that he must go into London first.''

"Oh. I'm glad to hear he's doing so well.'' Miranda could not hide her disappointment, though. Simon knew how much she had looked forward to seeing her brother again.

He pressed his palm firmly against the small of her back in sympathy, and she glanced at him, clearly aware for the first time that he was not behaving with his normal reticence. He addressed her sisters. "Your sister and I have a surprise for you. And your brother will be astonished when he arrives—he won't recognize any of you.''

Miranda smiled. With visible effort, she put aside her worries and addressed her sisters. "Yes, indeed. Are you ready to be poked, prodded, and pinned until you are veritable fashion plates?'' Halfway through her speech, he heard the excitement and pleasure return to her voice.

There was a cheerful chorus of assent. She turned to him with a worried frown, "They do add a bit of liveliness, don't they? If you think the uproar will be too much for you—''

For the hundredth time, Simon damned his "illness.'' "Not at all. The look on your face is worth every bit of inconsequential chatter and feminine foible. Perhaps they might even chase my mother away." He realized then, that his mother had not shown herself to greet the guests. "Where is she? Waiting to greet everyone formally like the dowager dragon she is?"

Miranda flashed him a guilty-innocent smile that made the hair stand up on the back of his neck. "I think she has an unexpected guest of her own."

"A guest?"

"An American."

That was interesting—and called for further investigation, without Miranda's involvement. "Well, I'm glad she's not here to put an ice to all this warm chatter."

"Perhaps it would be better for you if she did, though. I could not bear the thought of you becoming ill because—"

He bent to kiss her, once, quickly, just as they all began to ascend the stairs. "Don't worry about me. I'll enjoy being a brother for the first time." A little flicker of hope kindled in her startled eyes. And then Kate pulled on her arm, demanding to be shown her room.

He smiled. Her sisters were here and things were just a little bit more like they had been before he had come into her life with his proposal and turned it upside down. He hoped he could relax and enjoy her, now, in company. Once she had her sisters settled—which would likely take all day.

The one sour note in his perfect married life— besides the fact that he couldn't touch his wife—was his mother. He wondered if he could convince her to leave? It was worth a try. Especially now that she had brought a "guest" into his home.

He headed toward the gardens. He had no doubt that his mother's guest was a man. It infuriated him that she would bring her amoral ways to poison his home. He would not stand for it—especially now that he was the protector of innocent young women. He would not allow her corrupting influence to affect Miranda or her sisters.

He saw her then, among her lilacs. There was indeed a man beside her. A man with white hair. Unusual. He wondered, briefly, if the man was his father, and then shrugged his shoulders as he headed toward them. He doubted even his mother knew who his father truly was. Why else would she refuse to tell him, to give him the one thing he wanted from her?

They stopped walking when they saw him. For a moment he had the absurd impression that his mother was crying, but when he was close enough to see, her eyes were dry and her expression was, as usual, serene.

"Good day, Mother. Your garden looks lovely." He glanced curiously at the man beside her. Tall, craggy-faced, not her usual style in lovers. He would have expected young, leonine, a spoiled sneer, and a need for ready cash.

"Thank you, Simon. Has Miranda's family arrived?"

He nodded, still staring at the unintroduced companion.

With a glance at the dowager, apparently confirming that she had no intention of introducing him, the man startled Simon by sticking his hand out and beginning, "I'm—"

She interrupted, even as she raised her hand to pull on his outstretched arm. "We don't shake hands here, Mr. Watson." Her eyes bored into the American's, and he slowly, reluctantly, relaxed his arm to his side.

With a sigh, she smiled at him. "I'm so sorry. I

neglected to introduce you to my son. Simon is now the duke. Simon, this is Mr. Watson. He is from America.''

"I had not realized you knew any Americans, Mother.''

"I am not a snob. The colonies won their independence before I was born. I thought it quite romantic when I learned of it.'' She drew her mouth down, with a glance at the stranger. "As I said, I was just a child.''

"Your mother and I knew each other years ago, Your Grace.''

Simon was startled at the correct use of his title. Most Americans of his acquaintance called him My Lord, sir, or—with belligerence—Mr. Watterly.

To taunt his mother he asked, "How many years ago, Mr. Watson?'' He did not believe she had ever let this crude American touch her, so there was no question of his being the lover who fathered her bastard—no matter how young or how full of romantic idealism she had been. His mother had high standards when it came to the blood of her lovers; no stableboys, tradesmen, or Americans for her.

As if he understood the insulting nature of Simon's question, Mr. Watson said dryly, "I would say it was a lifetime ago, Your Grace. But how can I when your mother is still as young and beautiful as the last time I saw her?''

Simon felt a jolt of recognition as he watched the stranger. The man was infatuated with his mother. Still. After a lifetime apart. His stomach churned as he discarded all his former impressions. One glance at his mother's stricken face confirmed his fears. This man could be his father, after all.

Pasting a polite smile onto his face, he said exactly

the opposite of what he had intended to say. "I do hope you will stay with us for a few days. I look forward to getting to know you better, Mr. Watson."

His mother's face was white when he turned and walked away.

Chapter Seventeen

"May I really have two riding habits, Miranda?" Kate asked as she squirmed restlessly at the table.

"Do hush and finish your eggs, Kate," Hero reprimanded the child, patting the seat of Kate's chair as an indication that she should sit upon it. "You shall have what Simon provides you and count yourself lucky."

Miranda glanced nervously at the doorway, grateful that Simon had not yet come down to breakfast with them. After yesterday's swift changes in his attitude, she found her sisters' chatter distracting. He had touched her, kissed her—and then turned cold, practically snarling as he announced that his mother's guest would be staying.

What had changed his mood? Her sisters? The dowager's guest? And could she do anything to improve it? She certainly intended to try, if only she could be certain that she would not cause him harm.

She had confessed the truth of her virgin state to

Katherine this morning 'and had since been consumed by a single notion. The notion, which seemed to have taken root in her imagination, of deliberately seducing her own husband. Katherine didn't seem to think making love could do him physical harm. But she had warned her in no uncertain terms that a man's fear could be his worst enemy when it came to lovemaking. Seduction could make things worse. Or mend them and give Simon hope for the future.

She caught Hero's worried gaze and realized that some of her turmoil must be showing in her expression. No one else seemed to have noticed, though; they were all distracted by each other, the excitement of being in a new and different environment, and the thought of more clothes than they had ever had in their lives.

She smiled at her sister, and Hero smiled back, partially reassured, although Miranda knew she would be on the receiving end of Hero's questions as soon as they had some privacy. Thank goodness for her sister's discretion, she reflected with relief a few moments later when Simon entered the breakfast room.

"Good morning." His voice was calm and carrying, the voice of an officer, striving to gain the attention of his men. The chatter quieted at once, and a soft round of greetings met him as he helped himself to smoked salmon and buttered bread and sat down beside Miranda.

He seemed in a better mood this morning, but who knew when his mood might change for the worse. Worrying about him made her feel as if she were sitting on pins and needles. It was fortunate that there was no one else but Hero who might notice and question her distress. The dowager and her guest had breakfasted earlier and left for a ride about the estates.

Though she forced herself to smile at him as if nothing was amiss, she was not certain that her performance was flawless.

Before normal conversation could resume, Arthur entered the room. He stopped a moment upon the doorsill. There was a shocked expression on his face as he took in the very female, very youthful nature of the other occupants. He had been away until very late yesterday, in pursuit of an old book he had heard of in a neighboring town. Miranda could not help smiling at his expression.

"May I introduce you to my wife's sisters, Arthur?" Simon's voice held a hint of amusement. Miranda glanced at him obliquely, not wanting to catch his eye. There was no smile on his face, he seemed utterly earnest in his introductions.

As he took in the names of the five new faces, Arthur was his usual shy yet charming self. "How very fortunate I am, to be in the company of six such lovely ladies," he stammered, and then recovered. He smiled at Simon, as if making contact with the one person in the room he understood. "I had no idea how very lively a room could be made by so much feminine company."

Simon's brow rose. "Indeed. We must remedy that part of your education with a trip to London in the Season, then." His eyes roamed the room, lighting upon the twins, who were arguing over a pitcher of cream, and Kate, who had risen from her seat once more and was twirling about, in an ungraceful attempt at the waltz.

Juliet had brightened when Arthur had entered the room, and she tried to engage him in a flirtation. Arthur, however, as quickly as his plate was full, began a discussion with Hero about Plato and the works of the classical writers. Juliet pouted for a moment and then began to practice her charms on Simon.

He was patient, but with a smile at Miranda, he reached out to grasp her hand. "How is it to have your family back?"

"Wonderful." Turning from the spark of admiration that was in his eyes again, unable to bear the pain of hoping that her seduction might be a success, Miranda looked at both her sisters. They had grown up in the few months she had been away from them. Or had the separation only allowed her to see how very nearly grown they were?

Hero had a sparkle in her eye as she talked about long-dead authors with Arthur. The two seemed almost oblivious to the noisy chaos that had resumed around them.

The sound of a cream pitcher striking a water glass resounded clearly through the noisy room. Looking at the twins and Kate, Miranda realized the breakfast room was not the appropriate place for them. They, at least, had not grown out of childhood while she was not looking.

She turned to Simon, interrupting Juliet's flirtation. "I'm sorry for the disorder. I had not realized how great a disruption they would cause." She smiled. "It never seemed so obvious at home."

"You had a nursery set up at home," Simon observed dryly, but she did not sense that he was unduly upset.

Arthur and Hero looked up from their conversation and laughed together. Arthur teased, "Well it is only a matter of time, Simon. Soon the nursery will be open again."

Simon's hand tensed on hers, then withdrew. But if she did not know how the subject distressed him, she would not have guessed when he laughed along with Arthur. "Perhaps we might as well put it to good use now? I see what you mean."

The topic resonated with discomfort for her. Nurseries, babies, making love. She could barely look into his eyes. She hoped he could not read her mind.

As quickly as she thought of setting up a nursery, the need for a governess fixed one problem that Miranda had not known how to deal with—the fact that Katherine was not an adequate lady's maid. She would, however, make an excellent governess. "Shall I set the nursery up here? For my sisters?"

"An excellent idea," he concurred, just as Kate's glass of milk spilled onto the damask tablecloth. The servants leaped to clean the mess, but not one touched Kate when she began to wail.

Juliet scolded, "Kate, you clumsy thing, if you had been sitting still like a true lady, that would not have happened."

Miranda sighed and rose, feeling the familiar status of oldest sister falling back onto her shoulders. It was a sweet pleasure. She took Kate into her arms and lifted her up. The child was getting too big for such comforts, but Miranda needed the feel of her sister in her arms.

She glanced at Simon, but could not make herself smile. She would have to make up the nursery, look at the toys, at the cradle waiting for a baby that would never come. The thought made her want to cry, so she gave the command to see to the freshening of the nursery to Dome, ignoring his disapproval as she sailed out of the breakfast room.

"Miranda." Simon's voice halted her in the doorway. She turned reluctantly to look at him. "Shall we hire a governess?"

She smiled, and answered as coolly as possible with

Kate a squirming weight in her arms. "Katherine will make a better governess than a lady's maid. Unless you object?" She raised a brow, daring him.

"As you wish." He added, one hand on the honey pot and an odd expression that made Miranda suspect the pot was sticky under his fingers, "There is no reason, is there, why Betsy might not join your sisters?"

"None that I know of." She tried to remain impassive, but she could not help a tiny smile. His mother was right, he was excellent at running things. "I'm opening the nursery for my sisters. But if Katherine acts as their governess, it would work very well if Betsy remains there, with them."

"Perhaps then we might begin to have decent coddled eggs again," he said, turning to his morning papers.

Embarrassment shook her that he knew of the problems in the kitchen. After all, it was not as if Betsy had been a bad child. Simply a bit impulsive around the biscuits. Why had the servants seen fit to tell Simon their problems?

Running the house should be her worry, not his. One less burden. And she had failed in her duty yet again. Not wanting Simon to think that Betsy alone was responsible for the trouble, she said, "Cook threatened to quit yesterday. I don't know why the woman doesn't like children, but I certainly don't want Betsy around her any longer."

He looked up from his papers, then glanced back at his plate of inedible eggs. "No, we certainly don't want Betsy anywhere near the kitchens. Perhaps we might prevail upon the modiste to provide her with a dress or two, to convince her to stay in the nursery."

She wanted to strangle him—or kiss him insensible.

How could he be so concerned about others and so unconcerned about his own illness?

Belatedly, she realized just what Katherine's new position entailed—and curtailed. With her attention on four young ladies, the healer would have little time for brewing teas, or searching through her dusty notes for remedies for whatever ills Simon might possess. Had Simon foreseen that when he agreed to her solution?

Inexorably, the house party moved closer, as the dowager took every opportunity to remind her.

"Will you have a carved swan or a goose?"

"For what?" Miranda was puzzled. The food had been selected and preparations begun already.

"Ice sculptures, of course."

"Whichever you feel works best." She gave a standard answer to almost all these questions that the dowager put to her. She could not take interest in the upcoming weekend, the thought of it filled her with dread.

"I do wish you would take more interest, my dear." The dowager's irritation showed and Miranda felt contrite.

"I cannot help but dread this event, as you well know. But even if I did not, I would be content to allow you to make all the decisions. Simon himself told me how skilled you are at such things."

"Did he?" The unexpected compliment from her son seemed to quiet her objections to Miranda's disinterest. For a moment. And then she sighed and reached out to pull a cobweb from the shoulder of Miranda's dress. "I suppose you did not forget to have a suitable gown made for dancing in?"

"Of course not." Miranda had endured half a day

of fitting, pinning, and poking, much to her sisters'
amusement. "My gown is quite suitable." She remembered the warm flare of interest in Simon's eyes as
he kept her amused during the tedious fitting. "Even
Simon approved." Not enough to come to her bed,
unfortunately.

"Well enough, then." The dowager seemed satisfied by that confirmation of Miranda's wardrobe.
"And what jewels will you wear with your new gown?"

Miranda's heart sank. "Jewels?" She had nothing
at all.

"Yes. I know that you were a young girl for your
first Season, and that your parents were not wealthy.
But that should not matter to the Duchess of Kerstone. Have you asked Simon about the Watterly jewels? There must be something suitable there." The
dowager's hand had strayed to her neck, her fingers
played with the plain locket that hung there.

"I do not know. I had not thought . . ." Miranda
remembered her mother's beautiful swan necklace,
the one she would have pawned if that wretched beast
of a thief hadn't stolen it from her, along with the
candlesticks. That necklace would have been perfect
for her new gown, which was a beautiful scarlet hue.
But it was forever lost. She hoped whoever had bought
it appreciated the fine workmanship as much as her
mother had.

The dowager nodded briskly. "Well, then, see to
asking Simon about it. We cannot have you starting
rumors that the Watterlys are not well-set. Not with
five girls to bring out in the next ten years."

A light masculine harrumph of laughter made both
women look toward the doorway. The American stood
there, smiling. "Five girls to bring out. I pity the
duke."

"He needs no pity, Mr. Watson. He is an excellent

duke." The dowager seemed unnecessarily sharp to Miranda's ears.

Mr. Watson merely nodded. "Don't mean anything bad by my words. Indeed, I envy him his family." His gaze swept over the the papers on the dowager's writing desk and flickered to her face briefly. "I'm sorry to have bothered you ladies. I thought I'd find a little company for my walk."

Miranda smiled to herself. The man was obviously enamored of the dowager, although Simon's mother seemed completely unaware of his feelings. She grasped the excuse to leave the dowager's company with alacrity. "Indeed, we were just finishing for the day, Mr. Watson."

With a nod to the stiff-backed dowager, she added, "I shall ask Simon about the jewels immediately." Not, of course, that she cared about jewels or ice sculptures. She simply wanted to see her husband.

She headed toward Simon's study with a legitimate reason to interrupt him, finally, and visions of ice sculptures soon became replaced by notions of seduction.

Without so much as a knock, Miranda burst in on him in his study, startling him so that he would have made a blot if he had not quickly lifted the pen from the paper. He looked up at her. "Yes? Is something amiss?"

"No." She stood indecisively in the doorway for a moment. He was puzzled by the hesitation in her manner, given her brusque entry.

"Have your sisters broken a Meissen vase? Driven Cook from the kitchen? Chosen inappropriate gowns?" He could not imagine what matter might have brought her here. Especially since she had no cup of medicinal tea or bowl of noxious soup in her hands.

She came in quietly, closing the door. "Your mother reminded me that I should consult you about a piece of jewelry to wear with my new gown." Her apprehension was all too visible to him. She would not look him full in the face, but glanced from the fire to him to the settee perched under the window.

He steepled his hands in front of him. Jewels. "What kind of piece did you have in mind?" *And why are you so apprehensive?* But that question remained unvoiced. He did not want her to retreat before he had the answer to that particular question.

She seemed to have difficulty pulling her gaze from the settee to meet his. Her cheeks flushed from something other than her simple answer. "Something plain would do. Pearls, perhaps." He was intensely curious to know what she was thinking, but he was too wise to ask.

"Pearls are for young unmarried girls." He dismissed her request. It would be a pleasure to find the necklace that would enhance her beauty. "I have in mind something more elaborate. I will get the family jewels from the safe and allow you to choose whatever piece strikes your fancy." And even more of a pleasure, for him, to fasten it around her neck and feel her skin beneath his fingers. Perhaps he would allow himself to kiss her nape.

"Thank you." Her words seemed less than final, and she showed no signs of leaving.

"Was there anything else?"

Yes, her eyes told him.

"No." But she did not leave. And her nervousness heightened with every moment she spent in the room with him. Standing before him in the simple jonquil-yellow gown that he had chosen for her, she radiated tension from the set of her shoulders to the tips of her clasped fingers. And her gaze, for some reason, went frequently to the settee.

He had the absurd impulse to lock the study door and carry her to that same piece of furniture. But even a few kisses would be dangerous. No one would dare interrupt him at his business for anything less than a catastrophe. Knowing that, he could not trust himself to stop at only kisses. He forced himself to say a bland, "Good day, then."

She stood without moving, her eyes a dark, drugging brandy and he read her expressive face with a sudden jolt of dread. "Simon," she whispered. "I feel odd. As if I were like Sleeping Beauty. As if one kiss might awaken me."

He said nothing. He could not speak.

"What should I do?" She wanted what he did. But it was more than he could give. She wanted to find a way to touch his heart the way she had done in the past. The truth was written in her parted lips, in the way her eyes seemed unfocused and yet hypnotizingly drawn to him, in the way her breathing had become shallow and rapid.

Striving to maintain his sanity, Simon hit upon the perfect way to ensure that she maintained the distance between them. He would make her angry. Perhaps even angrier than she had ever been at him. She would most likely be hurt, as well, but it could not be helped.

"So you do not want to wait, then?" He laughed as if he were amused, not aroused, although the effort made sweat break out on his brow.

The dark want in her eyes deepened and he added quickly, lest she realize that he shared the fire of her desire, "Women do have an affinity for jewels, I suppose."

The palpable need she radiated abated somewhat, he noted with relief. "Let me get them now. That will give you time to change your mind a dozen times or more before the weekend."

He moved to the safe with heavy limbs, took his time opening it, struggling to batter down the urge to do as she suggested and wake the Sleeping Beauty within her. Even with his back to her, he could feel the heat of her want calling to him.

He put the box in front of her, knowing what she would say. Her eyes were on him as he flipped up the leather box lid to reveal the jewels, nested in black velvet. The velvet made him think of her skin and how it felt beneath his fingers. Soft. So soft.

With one last glance at the settee, she looked through the box distractedly. He wondered if she thought of his skin when she touched velvet—and drove the thought away. Impatience caught him as she looked through the box with little interest. He had buried her necklace at the bottom, under all else.

She did not find it before picking up a strand of pearls. "These will do."

"Of course they won't do." He took them from her hands and held them critically against her throat. Her pulse beat under his fingers. "You need something more striking to complement your gown. Something with more elaborate goldwork."

"These will be fine." Her hands covered his as he held the necklace, pressing his knuckles against the smooth skin that stretched over her collarbone. He forgot for a moment why he was holding the necklace as his heart matched the beat of the pulse in her throat.

After the silence had drawn tight between them and he could think of nothing but kissing her, he remembered his resolve and broke free of her hold. He dropped the pearl necklace into his pocket. "Look for something else, Miranda. You are a duchess, now."

With a sigh that disturbed the tendrils of hair that had managed to escape her pins and wisped at her cheek, she went back to looking through the box.

He knew the moment she found the necklace because she grew absolutely still. She did not even breathe.

"What is this?" Her voice was sharp, and yet it trembled.

He hoped he had not just made the worst mistake of his misbegotten life as she lifted her eyes to his, wide with shock.

Chapter Eighteen

"What is what?" he asked, pretending to innocence, though he was braced for the anger that he expected any moment, once she realized what he had done. He hoped her anger would burn cleanly through the fog of desire and passion that they shared.

Her hand reached in and came up with the necklace he had stolen from her. "This." She held it up between them, looking at him. No anger yet, only puzzlement. But her breathing had slowed and he could see the pulse at her neck beating more normally. He strove to control his own response to her nearness, her scent.

"That is something I picked up in London." He was not lying. He had indeed picked it up in London. He just happened to be dressed like a common thief and blessed with breath that would kill a dead man.

"Where in London?" Her voice was urgent. He could well imagine her hurrying there to find the thief and chastise him for stealing from her. Fortunately, she would not have to travel so far.

"On the street, actually."

She was still puzzled. He could see it, but had no idea what would be best, merely to let her have the piece and think he had bought it from a dishonest man, or to tell her the truth of how he had acquired it.

Telling the truth would encourage her anger, and keep her away from him, as he had been so successful in doing these past few weeks. It would also serve, he hoped, to teach her how dangerous it was for her to take matters into her own hands. But she would trust him no longer.

"It is the most beautiful thing I have ever seen," she whispered. The reverence in the tight planes of her face as her fingers traced the lines of the swans made him glad that he had chosen to return the necklace. Most probably, it was her last tangible link with her mother.

If he'd realized how much the piece meant to her, he could never have kept it from her for so long. He had foolishly assumed that if she meant to sell it, she could not hold it dear. But he had been thinking of it as a piece of jewelry, not a connection to her mother. How he could have misjudged so badly he could not imagine. He knew how much she was willing to sacrifice for her family. They meant everything to her.

It was blind luck that made his delay suit his purposes. Initially, he'd planned to give the necklace to Valentine to dispose of as he would. But any lesson to Miranda would have been muted, as she would not have known the disposition of the piece.

With it here, there was no choice for her but to acknowledge that it had found its way back in a quite unorthodox fashion. He wondered if she would confess her part in the loss of the necklace were he to press her. So he pressed her.

He closed the box, hiding away the rest of the jewelry. "You seem to be partial to that trinket. Why don't you wear it?"

"I will." She still could not take her eyes from the swans.

When she said nothing more, he prodded further. "You are quite enamored of the piece, I see."

He was rewarded by her singular admission. "It was my mother's."

"What!" He pretended astonishment. "Then how did it come to be on a London street."

He saw the war between expedience and innate honesty within her; the slim column of her throat worked as he stood watching her try to shape a response. "It was stolen from me."

Of course she would tell the truth. He was the one caught in a web of lies. "Stolen from you! How?" He pretended to be outraged, which he found to his surprise was not difficult. The desire to bed her was still strong in him and that passion, along with a healthy dose of self-loathing for what he was doing, rekindled his anger at the danger she had put herself in by going to London alone.

She pursed her lips and blew out, as if her admission cost her exertion. "I went to London hoping to sell a few things, including that necklace, and I was set upon by the rudest thief you might imagine."

"Do you imagine that thieves are known for their courtesy? You are lucky you escaped with only the loss of your silver candlesticks and your necklace." He had not consciously chosen to tell her then. But his slip of the tongue had hastened her understanding.

Her eyebrows lifted as one and a cloud of anger began to brew in her eyes. "What do you mean, my silver candlesticks?"

"Didn't the thief also get a fine set of candlesticks?" He struggled with the smile that seemed to want to break out on his face. He knew she would not appreciate it, but he was rather proud of his effort to teach her not to pawn goods in London again. The little fool, not knowing what might have happened to her. He shuddered, as the possibilities rolled graphically through his mind.

He could see the realization dawn upon her as a thundercloud upon the horizon speeds to bring rain. She was so quick-witted, his anger turned into admiration as her anger rose, erasing the last traces of desire from her gaze. "I thought those candlesticks on the mantel during our wedding reception looked familiar. What do you know of my thief?"

"I put them back the morning of the wedding. I didn't want them, and I didn't think you'd notice another pair of candlesticks on your wedding day."

"How dare you!" Her body grew rigid. The skirts of the yellow gown gave not a whisper of movement. "You hired someone to steal them from me and replaced them on the mantel without telling me." Her brow knit in puzzlement. "But how could you have known what I was about and hired someone so quickly?"

He could not resist. She was angry at him and he could risk touching her. He bent, shambled the few steps toward her, and pressed her back against the wall. "What's under your skirts, lass?"

It was a mistake. He knew exactly what was under her skirts and he could barely prevent himself from lifting away the layers of silk and cotton to find the heat of her beneath them.

Fortunately for him, she was distracted by the revelation of how he had tricked her. Her eyes narrowed with suspicion. "You didn't!"

He allowed one hand to rest on her hip, feeling the warm curve beneath the cloth, as he answered her in a way calculated to fan her anger to full flame. "I did. You needed a lesson badly. For dressing like a fishwife and walking the London streets alone."

She pulled his hand away. "But you were at Anderlin . . ."

He put it back, caressing the curve and stroking downward, to the swell of her bottom. What perversity in him made him cause himself such torment? He would be better served to stand away from her and fan the flames of her anger.

But he did not. "I was there to make certain Valentine was informed of our engagement, remember? I followed you out, saw you board the coach, and followed. And I traveled faster on horseback than you could in the coach."

Her eyes were fixed on his face, and he realized that her anger was not as unaffected by his touch as he had thought. It had dimmed dangerously in her eyes. "How could you?" Her words were soft, the accusation faint.

"You needed a lesson. I provided it." He pressed his palm against the rounded underside of her breast and felt the rapid beat of her heart beneath his fingertips. He kissed her. It was not wise, but he was beyond caring. When he realized that she would not push him away, he brushed her forehead with one last kiss and stepped back. "I must finish my correspondence. I will have little time this weekend for business matters."

For a broken moment, it seemed she would not heed him. She took a step toward him as if she might be the one to kiss him. A kiss he knew without doubt he could not resist, could not recover from.

But then she blinked, and held up her hand to gaze at the necklace she still clutched in her fist. Anger rekindled in her eyes. He told himself fiercely to be relieved.

He did not look at her as he resumed his seat behind his desk and lifted his pen to paper, wondering why he had chosen this particular torment for himself, as if it might expiate his sin of bastardy.

It was long after the door had closed sharply behind her that he noticed he had written several pages of nonsense. He crushed the papers with undue savagery before throwing them into the fireplace, and watched them catch flame and burn into ash in an instant.

Her bedroom was too hot, even with the curtains billowing in the breeze from the wide-open window. So he thought to teach her a lesson, did he? Well, perhaps it was time for her to teach him one. He thought he knew best. But he didn't always. And not making love to his wife was a mistake. It was time for her to prove it to him.

He was abed, she knew. She had heard the muffled sounds of undressing near midnight. She longed to put her plan in action tonight, while she was still angry enough not to worry so much over his health. But she did not want to wake him if he slept. He needed his rest.

Unable to restrain herself, she crept to the door and pressed her ear tight against the cool wood. There was no sound. Thinking that perhaps he was not even in the room, she turned to go downstairs and see if he might still be working in his study, when she heard him call out.

Without considering how he might feel at her intrusion, she opened the door a crack and slipped through. Simon was calling out a man's name as he tossed and turned restlessly. His voice was harsh with horror, and she realized he was reliving the man's death, yet again.

As she listened to the unintelligible words that came in fitful murmurs from the restless figure, she wondered if there was any possibility that his experiences might have contributed to his apathy over his own death. After all, facing death day after day and avoiding it while others didn't might have made him feel that he didn't really deserve to live.

Perhaps that was why he refused all her attempts to help him find a cure. Valentine might have told her, if only he were here. The murmurs stopped, plunging the room into a silence that felt like the heavy weight of a mantle around her.

If only he could share his thoughts with her, she knew she could ease his fears. The illness must be a terrible drain on his energy, and yet he refused to talk about it with her. He refused to share the burden with his own wife. But he needed her comfort, and she had every intention of providing it.

Even though she knew he would disapprove, she slipped into his bed and when he shifted restlessly, she took him into her arms, stroking his arm, his back, his neck with gentle care.

He settled against her with a groan of satisfaction and his restlessness faded as his breathing grew even once again. The feeling of closeness and warmth was exquisitely pleasurable.

Miranda could not bring herself to move away, though she knew he would not be happy to find her here if he awoke. His mouth rested against her neck, his hands were warm on her hips. She lay very still, so that she would not wake him, as she had the first time, when he had sent her so decidedly back to her own bed.

Having her sisters in the house had somehow intensified her desire to be closer to Simon, for some unexplainable reason. But now, with Simon's warmth and heat surrounding her, she recognized from where her desire stemmed. She had always thought that a husband and family were an unattainable dream. To marry, to give up one shred of her autonomy had filled her with fear. But it was not so hard to lose a battle to Simon now and again.

If they only had a long enough time together, she was certain that he would cease to question her judgment and learn to trust her. Certainly, she could manage to accomplish that. He was a reasonable man.

About most things.

For example, now that she had the husband, she found it impossible not to wish for the family. If only she knew how to accomplish that without risking Simon's life. She was certain that having a son would be enough to make him want to fight to live. How could it not be? Look how tender he was toward Betsy, and he had thought her mother unworthy to be in his home.

Snuggled against him, she was tempted to kiss him. That had always roused his passion before. Asleep, he would not fight her, would not pull away. And when he woke, he would have bedded her and would have nothing else to fear.

Or was it possible that he must wake to accomplish the deed? She wished she had consulted Katherine on exactly what manner of seduction would be the least upsetting to a dying man. Perhaps the shock of waking to find her in his bed would be more than he could bear?

"Coward," she whispered to herself, deciding she would stay for only a little while, and then quietly go back to her own bed. She would lie as quiet as Briar Rose in her hundred-year sleep. Her anger with him had fled when she had understood what caused his bad dreams. She could wait for a better time to seduce him. But she wanted the feel of him in her arms, and soon the comfortable warmth of his body lulled her to sleep.

Simon's dream was as always since he married her. She was in his arms. She felt right, her curves against his skin as if made to fit only his body . . . the warmth of her, the silk of her skin under his fingers. He brushed his lips against the softness and heard a sigh like the spring breeze through budding branches. Under his palm, he could feel the curve of her hip and the warmth spread through him until he felt as if he were dissolving, his flesh melting into her flesh not as men and women joined, but as two beings who become one.

His fingertips traveled along the curve from her hip to her rib cage and she moved in to him so that they were one from head to toe, their arms entwined so tightly that he knew he would never let her go. Never.

She was soft and warm and seemed to come alive at his touch. He felt a flare of possession as a rush of quickened breath warmed his cheek and earlobe. He reached for the heat of her and found it, was rewarded with a moan like the low wild sound of the wind just as the storm approaches. He released his own groan to entwine and mingle with the moan until there was nothing left of the sound but a fierce vibration in his very core.

He bent his head and filled his mouth with softness, roundness, heat. A rough, pleasurable pressure built in him as their one flesh began to undulate in a primitive rhythm and he held to the dream further than he ever had before, unable to give in to the need to wake and learn that there was no one next to him, no heat, no flesh melded with his.

And he touched her with his hands, his mouth; there was no part of him that did not touch her, that did not feel her swell with passion and know that passion himself. He did not want the dream to end, even when their body, her body, began to quiver and she whispered his name in his ear. "Simon," she said.

"Simon," she screamed, softly and their bodies shattered apart as he woke to the feel of her beneath him and knew that he was not dreaming.

She protested his retreat, wrapping her arms and legs around him. He hesitated, his body not yet his to control. And then he felt the tide of pleasure take her, her arms clutched him tight against her and she murmured against his ear. "I love you, Simon."

His body went cold in an instant and he raised his head to look into her eyes. They were open. Somehow, her words had given him the strength he needed to halt himself on the edge of a pleasurable abyss. He felt an absurd sense of panic as he pleaded, even as he knew it was futile, even as he mastered himself and his own need, "Tell me you are a dream, Miranda."

Her hands drifted up his side, deepening the feeling that he was on the verge of going mad. "I'm not a dream. I promise to be still, Simon. As still as you need me to be. I will not be too wild. I promise."

She tried to pull him back down to her, with gentle pressure on his shoulders. To his distress, he found he had barely enough strength to fight the insistent press of her fingers. A hoarse cry escaped him as he twisted away and left the bed.

He felt like a fool, standing nude and shivering in the cool breeze, afraid to come any nearer the bed where she lay. Even the distance between them gave him no sense of safety. He knew how easy it would be for him to slip back between the covers and finish what he had started.

She sat up in the bed. He guessed her expression to be puzzled, although, mercifully, he could not see her face from so far away in the night-shadowed room. "Simon, what's wrong? Are you ill?" He could hear her voice shedding the thickness of her passion, her pleasure. He felt a fierce flow of pride that he had given her release, even if he had achieved none of his own.

"Go back to your room." He did not trust himself to say more.

She made a movement, as if she might rise off the bed and come toward him. "But why—"

"Now!" He supposed the savagery he felt had been in the tone of his words for she ceased her arguments and rose from the bed.

He held his breath as the moonlight caught her in the instant it took for the hem of her nightshift to fall to her feet. The shift itself did nothing to hide the outline of her body. And then she was gone through the door. He heard it close gently and wondered what she must think of him.

Chapter Nineteen

She no longer knew what to think.

The stone of the garden bench was cool beneath her in the dawn's pale light. But the quiet of the morning had not calmed her churning fears. He had almost made love to her. He had reached for her in the dark, entwined himself around her body and her heart, loved her as she wished to be loved.

She closed her eyes against the tears that came despite her battle to remain dry-eyed and rational. His touch had been so tender and fierce at the same time—she had shattered beneath him only to find a surprising peace. And then that peace had been torn away in an instant by his harsh withdrawal. How could he have made her feel as if she had truly joined with him into one soul and not felt it himself?

Was it fear? And if so, why was he afraid to make love to her if he was convinced he would die shortly, anyway? He was no coward, she knew it deep inside her with a certainty that was absolute. Could his pride be the barrier between them?

Katherine said that a man could be afraid of failing at lovemaking. But if he roused her to such fever with only the touch of his lips and hands, how could he ever fail her?

Could it be that he was afraid he would fail himself?

Voices startled her out of her seat like a frightened hare. She could not be found here, not now. No doubt her eyes and nose were red and swollen from her tears. Questions would be unbearable, and gossip only a further insult to her own wounded pride.

As the intruders neared, she hid herself behind a box hedge and wished them away. It was only as she recognized the dowager and her American approaching that Miranda tore her thoughts away from her own misery to wonder what had brought these two out to the gardens at dawn.

Their voices were lowered, but it was clear the two were in the midst of a heated argument when the dowager ground out, "You are mad."

"Listen to me. You don't understand."

"I don't understand? I've lived with them, father and son for most of my life!" The dowager's eyes glittered with anger as she stood rigid and brittle, facing down her American, right in front of the box hedge where Miranda hid. "Proud. Stubborn. Fools. As are you."

"Not this time. I will not make the same mistake twice."

Her voice was flat, brooking no argument. "You already have, by insisting on returning to America."

"That is where our future is." There was an urgency to his voice, as if he needed her to agree with him.

"My future is here, with my son and his bride."

She added in a whisper, "And Arthur if Simon truly goes."

He laughed, a short, harsh bark. "You never belonged here. I should have freed you then, but I was too much a coward."

She shook her head. "You were not a coward." Her voice sharpened. "Not then."

He hissed with impatience. "Your husband is long dead, and Simon is a man now, capable of choosing his own path. I promise you if you come to America with me—"

She turned away from him and Miranda could not see her face any longer, only the proud set of her shoulders. "I cannot throw my hands up at my responsibilities to run away with you. I am not made that way. You, of all people should know that."

His voice was harsh with anger and grief. "Then why did you let me think you cared? Did you think I would stay and be your plaything?"

The dowager said nothing.

"You know that is all I could be if I stayed here."

She turned back toward him, a challenge in her eyes. "That is hardly true."

"Maybe you can't see that it is." He sighed, and Miranda knew sadly that he had finally given in and recognized her mind would not change. "Or maybe you think a title and position are more important than being married to me."

When she said nothing further, he spun around on his heel and left her standing in the garden alone. Except for Miranda, still trapped behind the box hedge.

Afraid to move a muscle lest the dowager discover that her most private discussion had had an audience, Miranda stifled the urge to gasp when the dowager whispered bitterly, "You and your family motto haunt me from the grave, Sinclair. *Honor and Truth in All.* Like father, like son.''

Her legs stiff and cramped, Miranda could feel only relief when the dowager wandered deeper into the garden and she was free to slip back to her room. There was no solace in the thought that the dowager's private life was as tangled up in pride and honor as her own. It had obviously been so for a very long time without resolution.

For once she did not have a solution for any of them. She had to hope that Valentine, as a fellow man, would offer a key to the puzzle of Simon's pride. At the very least, she needed her brother's encouragement to lift her spirits and allow her to believe there was hope for her future. Thank goodness he was due to arrive within the week.

> *Sister,*
>
> *I am fully aware that I am behaving in a cowardly manner and deserve whatever chastisement you choose to give me next we meet. But I find I cannot be in residence at the same location as Emily. Not now that I have read the news of her recent engagement.*
>
> *Please, forgive me. I am certain that Simon, Juliet, and Hero will be your support. And I trust that you will prove yourself to be the courageous sister I have known all my life, even without my presence.*
>
> *V.*

Miranda, perched on the bottom stair of the wide main staircase in the entry hall, stared down at the paper in her hand, and strove to quell the panic that Valentine's note raised inside her. He was not coming. Her husband would not make love to her and might possibly even hate her. In hours her house would be full of people armed with razor-sharp wit and keen eyes, and he was not coming. How could he do this to her?

She knew she wanted his advice, had counted on his level head to guide her. Until she opened the note, delivered by a towheaded boy in a grimy uniform, however, and read his words three times in order to make sense of them—believe them—she had not realized how much she relied on his arrival to bring sense to the chaos that her life had become.

How could he do this to her? She needed his male perspective in order to divine some answer as to what to do about Simon. And now, with Simon avoiding her, Katherine too busy with the children to practice her healing arts, and Grimthorpe arriving as a guest within hours, he had sent a note to say he was not going to be here for the weekend.

Coward! Not that she could blame him. He had ceased talking about Emily after those first few awful days. But she knew that he had not ceased loving her.

Miranda had hoped for a reconciliation between them. But she recognized as well as Valentine had that Emily's engagement made such a dream impossible. Perhaps it was just as well that he had not come. For him, at least.

She sighed. The first guests were due any moment, the grooms, stableboys and footmen standing at the ready with their uniforms ironed and their boots polished. The dowager, Hero, and Juliet waited in the largest receiving parlor. Where she should be now, instead of sitting like an errant child on the stair, reading over again this message that she most definitely did not want to read.

"Have you decided to greet our guests from here?" Simon came up behind her so softly she was unprepared. The sound of his voice set her heart to beating rapidly. But she was uneasy in his presence. He had been avoiding her since the night he had thrown her out of his bed. It was humiliating even to think about it. She hesitated to look up at him.

"No." Miranda glanced up and nearly lost her breath. He was so handsome he made her heart ache.

Katherine, Hero, and Juliet had to be wrong when they assured her that his love for her shone from his eyes. If he loved her, he could not look so calmly at her, as if he had not stolen her mother's necklace, not given it back to her and then kissed her, as if he had not almost made love to her. If he loved her, his heart would beat as wildly as hers and surely she would hear it. She held out the note to him.

He took it without touching her hand. He glanced at it and frowned. "I'm sorry. I know how much Valentine's support meant to you." There was sympathy in his eyes, but relief, too.

She knew he had been worried about having Valentine and Emily under the same roof. But he had stood firm when Emily's father had objected. Valentine was family, he had said.

His sympathy brought tears to her eyes. It was sheer irony that she would not have needed Valentine's support if things were well between her and Simon. "He would be here, if only Emily were not."

He sat on the step next to her. For a moment she thought he intended to put his arm around her, but he did not. "I think he is showing wisdom. Emily's betrothed will be here, as well as Emily and her parents."

How could he be so understanding and so very distant while she could barely resist her impulse to climb into his lap and bury her face in his neck? All at once it occurred to her that this feeling of tension, this not knowing what to say to make things right, was why Valentine had not come.

He was helpless in the united face of Emily, her family, and her betrothed. So he had chosen not to put himself in that position. If only she had the freedom to make such a choice. But where could she run? Anderlin was no longer her home.

She whispered. "I don't know how he can bear it. There is nothing worse than not being able to show the one you love how much you love them." Even when one was married to him.

The sympathy in his expression receded, even as she watched. He stood up. "Your brother survived army discipline and the heat and rain of India, he most certainly will survive the loss of one matrimonial possibility. With his fortunes looking up, there will be many Mamas and Papas interested in an alliance with him for their daughters, dowries and all."

"You don't understand." How could he love her and say something like that? Katherine was blind to think Simon felt anything for her at all. And then, she wasn't certain, but she thought she saw a flicker of pain cross his features.

He held out his hand. "Yes. I understand very well what he has lost." His fingers grasped hers as her hand met his, and he pulled her to a standing position. He let go of her hand as soon as she had her balance. "But we bear what we must."

His voice sounded so cold and distant she could almost have thought she was talking to the dowager. She stared at him, suddenly angry at his withdrawal. "Do we?"

He didn't respond, would have turned away if she hadn't reached out to put a hand on his arm. "I don't know if I can bear this distance between us, Simon. Must I?"

The sound of carriage wheels on the drive became clear in the silence between them. Then voices and a flurry of activity as the footmen began to carry boxes into the hall.

Without acknowledging her question, Simon turned toward the door. "We must go out to greet our guests."

Miranda did not stir. "Must we?"

He turned back to her and his coldness faded as he smiled ruefully and touched her cheek gently. "Better to face the enemy than to run and hide."

She pulled away, afraid that his touch would make the tears that threatened spill forth. "Easy for you to say. They are not your enemies." They were hers. And tears and tension would just add spice to the gossip.

There were two carriages in the drive. Grimthorpe, naturally would be among the first arrivals, and the other carriage contained Emily and her parents. The passengers had alit from their coaches and were brushing off their clothing in preparation for entering when Simon and Miranda went to greet them. Arthur joined them as they began to greet the tired travelers.

The last time Miranda had seen Emily, the girl had been laughing and waving as she headed off to the border with Valentine. Her brother's love, looking paler and more sober than that last time, greeted her politely, but did not meet her eyes.

Her mother, the countess, was a thin, forbidding woman. To Miranda's discomfort, she displayed an open curiosity over how Simon and Miranda had met. Her questions began immediately after her greeting and did not seem to have an end.

"Did you meet at a country dance at one of the local squire's homes?"

"Had you known Simon long?"

"Did you expect to be pulled from the shelf at this late date?"

Emily gave her one quick, sympathetic glance, but then seemed to find herself entranced by the sight of her slippers peeping from under her skirts as she walked. Miranda looked toward Simon.

There was no rescue from that quarter, however. Emily's father had left the chattering to the women and pulled Simon to the side. Before Miranda could blink, before the countess could finish her latest question, the two men were instantly deep in a discussion of business matters.

Seeing Grimthorpe's approach, Miranda braced herself.

To her surprise, she heard Arthur's firm greeting from behind her and was glad to find him there, as if he knew that she needed support.

Grimthorpe drew near, a wolfish half smile on his face as he quickly surveyed—and dismissed—Emily, to turn his attention to Arthur. "You're looking well, I see."

Arthur merely nodded and returned the compliment. "As are you."

"Thought for sure you'd have popped off by now, old man. Any bees around this weekend?"

"Certainly not." Arthur stiffened and gave Grimthorpe a stern look. To her surprise, there appeared to be animosity between the two men. Miranda had never before seen Arthur appear anything more than mildly chagrined. But his attitude toward Grimthorpe bordered on anger. She wondered from whence it stemmed.

Seeing Emily's mother preparing for yet another round of questions, and dreading lest Grimthorpe hear them, Miranda hastily led the other women inside to where her sisters and the dowager awaited.

She would let Simon handle the man. They deserved each other.

As they walked, Miranda tried to reassure Emily, without actually using words, that she did not need to fear any embarrassing disclosures about her this weekend. Or any anger. If Emily no longer wanted to marry Valentine, then so be it. Miranda would not interfere.

But what if Emily still loved him? What if she loathed her husband-to-be? *Don't ask for trouble,* she told herself, already knowing that she would not be able to rest until she was certain that Emily had truly put all hopes of marrying Valentine behind her with a glad heart. After all, her love life—and the dowager's—both seemed so hopeless she must look elsewhere for a happy ending.

"I hear the dowager and Simon have been reconciled. Is that so?" There was no ignoring the way that Emily's mother insinuated herself between them, even as she spewed her questions, as if she were afraid that Miranda might contaminate her daughter.

Or incite her to another elopement. Miranda smiled politely and murmured a vague answer to yet another of the countess's questions. She could not avoid the knowledge that the weekend was likely to be the longest of her life.

The guests continued to arrive, keeping the footmen and maids busy scurrying to see to the needs of the new arrivals and keeping Miranda so busy greeting people and making sure of their comfort that she barely noticed how Simon always seemed to glide away from wherever she moved. Even as the guests gathered in the ballroom, dressed in their finest and prepared to dance the night away, Simon stayed a room length away.

Not that she was overly eager to see the distant look

in his eye. Or to hear his detached comments about the number of guests and the scheduling of entertainments for tomorrow. Even worse would be his dry compliments on how beautifully the ballroom had been decorated. They both knew it was all his mother's work.

"May I have this dance?" She turned to find one of the eligible young bachelors had detached himself from Hero. He was tall and dark and the only feature which kept him from handsomeness was a petulant set to his lips and a thinness to his nostrils that suggested he did not like to breathe common air.

"Thank you," she accepted. She would have preferred to decline, but the dowager was staring at her from across the dance floor, and she had already been reminded three times that she was a duchess now. Miranda presumed that duchesses did not refuse dances from perfectly decent, if callow, young guests.

He was an adequate, if not perfect, dancer, and she was just beginning to enjoy herself when Simon cut in and swept her away from the young man. With a flare of his nostrils, the partnerless dancer headed quickly back toward Hero's vicinity, leaving Miranda to deal with Simon on her own. Her heart dropped as she looked up into his eyes.

He scowled. "I am not amused."

Chapter Twenty

His scowl did not lessen as they danced. But she seemed to have no idea to what he referred. And evidently his behavior that night he had found her in his bed had left her in no mood to coddle him. "By what are you not amused?" she asked, impatience stamped into the tight set of her mouth. "The decorations? The musicians? They seem more than adequate to me."

"You know what I mean." He said it forcefully, as if he meant it, just to make sure she had not simply learned to hide the truth in the time she had lived with him. God only knew how many lessons he had forced on her.

She stared at him in such puzzlement that his scowl relaxed and he found himself feeling groundlessly grim. Purposefully, he began directing their dance to carry them toward the entryway. With barely a pause, he led her into the dining room, its tables laden with food and guarded by huge blocks of sculpted ice. "Look at this."

Her glance at the tables was not cursory, and no glint of recognition shone in her eyes. He had just decided to explain when he felt her start of surprise. She went nearer, on tiptoe, as if she were afraid, and began to peer at the sculptures: Cinder Ella, her prince at her feet; Rapunzel in her tower, her hair let down; Sleeping Beauty; Little Redcape; Snow White, Beauty and the Beast.

Fairy-tale characters captured in ice. And that was not the worst—every woman had Miranda's face and every man was Simon—except that for the tale of Redcape he had been rendered with angular, wolfish features.

She put her hand out to the familiar features caught in ice and rested her fingers on the icy wolfen brow. "I had no idea."

His lips tightened, then twitched. "My mother, of course. Her idea of amusement." He gestured for a footman. "Take these away immediately."

"No." Miranda shook her head, and the footman halted, looking at Simon for further instruction. She touched his arm. He could not hide his anger, but she met his gaze full on. "Leave them. They are beautiful."

"We will be the laughingstock of society for this folly," he muttered.

Miranda shook her head, a shuttered look of sad certainty on her face. "Your mother would not do that. Your family name is too important to her."

He jerked his arm away from her. So his mother had even convinced her of the Watterly honor. How ironic.

She reached for his arm again, touching him lightly.

"Please. Leave them, Simon. No one will laugh. They are too beautiful for that."

Her eyes rested wistfully on the Sleeping Beauty sculpture, the handsome, princely Simon bent so that his lips met and melded with the lips of the icy Sleeping Beauty, carved in the likeness of Miranda. "Leave them for my sake."

He watched her, hoping his inner war was not obvious in the taut lines of his face. Why did he continue to torture them both like this? He should send her back to her family before she was ruined forever— not her reputation, but her heart. He remembered then that his mother had warned him of that very thing. Damn her.

"They're only ice, Simon. They won't last."

Just like your dreams, he thought, but did not say.

Of course, as he knew she would, she persevered. "By the end of the evening they'll be puddles on the floor. Can I not have them for this little while?"

He did not answer her, but turned his attention to the footman, who had watched their exchange wide-eyed. "Leave them. My wife wishes it."

He would have left her then, if she had not slipped her hand in his. "Dance with me again, Simon. The room is so full of strangers watching my every move. I would like to dance once more with you."

He sighed, about to refuse and she stopped him. "It is not much to ask, for a husband to dance one full dance with his wife."

His eyes raked hers, wondering if she would take his agreement as reason to slip into his bed once more. He could not say with any certainty what she thought a dance would mean as he gazed into the dark depths of her eyes.

But he nodded, realizing that it meant some slight relief from the gossiping guests. It was the least she deserved from him, since he could not give her what she truly desired. "It is not much to ask at all." He led her from the dining room and out into the crush of dancers.

To his surprise, the tension seemed to drain from him as they maneuvered the intricate pattern of the dance. He was smiling faintly at her, his face relaxed in lines of enjoyment and pleasure in an unguarded manner he had not dared since they had driven home on their wedding day. The thought was a sharp pain and he immediately sought to distract himself.

"Your sisters are doing well," he said when the dance step brought them together. "Even the shy one seems to be gathering the beaux."

Miranda whirled away from him in dance, her gaze searching for her sisters. He hoped she approved of the glow in both Hero's and Juliet's eyes as they were plied with food and drink by the eligible bachelors carefully selected by Simon and his mother as worthy candidates for the girls' affections.

As Miranda watched Juliet flirt outrageously with her fan with four men at once, she smiled. "Yes," she commented lightly when the dance brought them together once again. "They are both ready for a Season. 'Tis fortunate that Hero is not jealous that Juliet is coming out at the same time as she."

The dance ended, and they stood for a moment catching their breath. Simon smiled. "Hero does not seem the jealous kind."

The musicians struck up a waltz, and before Miranda could protest, he had led her into the dance and she was caught in the whirl of dancers. He noticed his mother, her American lover conspicuously absent, watching them dance with an avid eye. He wondered if she were simply ashamed of the man, or if she had sent him away to prevent him from speaking with Simon.

Miranda tilted her head up toward him, her eyes shining, and he worried that he had indeed raised her expectations. "Sometimes I think Hero was born without the capacity for envy. If the situation were reversed, I doubt that Juliet would be so kindhearted. Although I cannot think it is a bad thing that, with them both coming out, Juliet has fewer gentlemen upon whom to practice her flirtation."

His hand pressed her side gently. "Do you worry about Juliet being too bold?"

She answered defensively, "Juliet is not like me."

His hand tightened, and he brought her close enough for the dowager to frown as they swept past her. "No one is like you."

His compliment warmed Miranda, but she knew better than to believe he meant it in a favorable way. No doubt he was thinking of the unorthodox manner in which they had come to be married. "Juliet is so easily smitten."

He said nothing, but she did not think it coincidence that, even as she spoke, the path of their steps led them past Juliet and Hero.

Both girls seemed singularly untouched by the ardor of their suitors. Juliet gave them a small, gay wave as they spun past. Seeing that Grimthorpe was among those in Juliet's court, Miranda was not certain if she meant more to reassure Simon, or herself, when she added, "I have warned her well of my folly."

"I hope you have made it clear that you were not a careless flirt."

"Of course I did. My foolishness was in going anywhere out of sight of everyone else, and I have made that abundantly clear to both Hero and Juliet."

Miranda remembered the conversation uneasily.

Hero had nodded gravely and promised never to leave the crowd, unless accompanied by Miranda or Juliet. Juliet had laughed and claimed she would not want to stop dancing or being adored by many men simply to be alone with one of them. "Juliet seems to think being adored by one man would be somewhat dull."

"Let us hope she continues to feel that way."

Miranda thought silently, *Let us hope that she meets no one who affects her senses, as well as her common sense, the way that Simon affects mine.* Aloud, she admitted to only part of her doubt. "My only fear is that she will form an alliance with someone unsuitable. Someone who might break her heart."

His voice was hoarse, and ragged, as if it were difficult for him to speak. "It is better not to have the heart involved in marriage, but young girls don't always understand that."

"No." Miranda agreed. "They don't." And neither do some young married women who were old enough to have gathered dust on the shelf. They kept believing, despite everything, that their prince would arrive to wake them with a kiss.

Again they swept by the girls. Juliet was laughing at a joke, her eyes bright as jewels against her pale skin. Simon said calmly, "I do not think it would be wise for us to let her choose her suitors. But put those fears to rest. I'm certain I can choose her an excellent husband." His voice sounded with confidence and his hands held her with an arrogant sureness that piqued her.

Miranda resisted the pull of his arms. "I don't want to have her husband chosen for her. How cold, how—"

His steps grew more powerful, sweeping her inexorably into his rhythm. "What is it you would have her do? Find herself in some loveless marriage with a man who is not worthy of her? Or worse yet, have her reputation damaged beyond repair by some scoundrel like Grimthorpe?''

The waltz ended and he released her. She felt dizzy and yet clearheaded at the same time as she looked into his familiar face. "I want her to love her husband as much as I love you." His mouth, so quick to smile, was now set in a thin line of displeasure.

"I want her to be willing to follow her husband around the earth to prove her love." His hawk's nose, with nostrils flared when he was disturbed, as now.

"I wish her the devotion to pick up feathers, or look for cures, or whatever is necessary, as I would do for you." The lines around his eyes, drawn in by the worries of his position, and the weighty memory of the young men who had died when he had not.

The moment she spoke, the noises of the ballroom faded to silence for her. His throat worked soundlessly for a moment and then he sighed. "Miranda . . ." His voice became inaudible as the musicians struck up another dance.

She leaned close to whisper, "Can you not bear to hear it? That makes it no less true."

The lines around his eyes deepened as his gaze narrowed, his irises the dark green of emeralds at dusk. "But you will only be hurt."

"Yes." She wanted to ask him why, but she could feel the pain and knew it would only be worse if she pressed him. He would not tell her the truth. He did not love her. He had packed his heart away in the leather pouch and he kept the contents firmly guarded against even her. She held out her hand. "Shall we dance while we are still able? We might as well take the opportunity to set the tongues wagging at how well we dance together.''

He hesitated, and then swept her onto the floor, his touch firm but light. ''By all means.''

The moment was still a fading tingle down her spine when Hero began to scream. ''He's turning purple. He can't breathe!''

The room dissolved into chaos. Miranda tried to turn toward the sound of her sister's voice, but found herself wrapped tightly in Simon's arms, unable to see anything but the lapel of his waistcoat. After a moment, when the dance floor was emptied, he left her. Abruptly alone, she could see nothing but a knot of people surrounding the area where Hero and Juliet had been holding court.

As Simon forced a path through to the center of the tight knot of guests, Miranda followed. To her horror, Arthur lay on the floor.

His face was indeed purple. As Simon knelt beside him, Miranda turned and fled toward the nursery— and Katherine.

''He'll be fine, Your Grace,'' Katherine said calmly.

Miranda could see that Simon was, however, in no mood to be soothed. ''How can you be certain?'' He paced in the hallway outside Arthur's bedroom door.

The healer answered wryly, ''I gave him something that helped him vomit up most of the poison. And also something to absorb whatever was left in his body. His color is good. He is breathing well and has no fever.''

Miranda said sharply, ''Katherine knows what she is doing, Simon.'' She had not meant to sound so sharp, but her voice carried her own tension. He had sprinted the steps carrying Arthur, meeting them on the landing. Even now, his breathing remained ragged. She was afraid he had overexerted himself. "You need to rest or you will be joining him in the sickroom."

He shook his head. "I need to see him."

"Tomorrow—" Katherine began.

"I don't intend to wait for tomorrow to make sure my heir is not going to die!" His breathing, rather than slowing, had grown more rapid, and Miranda watched him with alarm.

"Please, Katherine," she added her appeal. "Just for a moment? To ease Simon's distress."

Katherine looked at him with doubt in her eyes for a moment. Then she nodded. "But see him only. He is resting after an understandable shock to his system and he needs no more difficulty tonight."

Simon nodded brusquely. "I understand. I will save my questions for tomorrow. Tonight I just want to assure myself that he will be well."

Before he passed through the doorway, he turned back to Katherine. "What manner of poison was it?"

She tensed and her brows drew together. "Toadstools. I very much fear they were some I had discarded from my basket this morning."

"Your basket."

"When I take the girls for their stroll, I collect leaves, bark, medicinal herbs—"

"And poisonous toadstools."

She flushed, and Miranda gasped at the slight to the healer held in his accusatory expression. "She discarded them when she realized that, Simon. You heard her say so."

"So she did." He turned his head toward her, and his eyes imprisoned hers. They were sharp as green glass. "Katherine and I will get to the bottom of this, Miranda. You must go back to our guests."

Miranda went downstairs reluctantly, leaving Simon to check on Arthur and question Katherine alone. She worried that he would be too hard on the healer, as tense and angry as he was. But he was a just man, and would listen fairly to her story, perhaps finding a clue as to what—or who—was causing all of Arthur's "accidents." It had become more than obvious to her—and she was sure that Simon felt the same—that someone was deliberately trying to kill Arthur. But who?

Downstairs, everyone seemed subdued. Although the musicians still played, there were few dancers on the floor. Many people had apparently chosen to retire, and had already been led away by footmen to their guest chambers. She checked anxiously for Hero and Juliet, relieved to find them still surrounded, though sparsely so, by admirers.

Though, she reflected, seeing her sisters still holding court in the ballroom, that meant they had not found anyone to lure them out to enjoy the fragrant gardens. She smiled, thinking that there might have been young men in the group disappointed that neither girl had agreed to a walk in the garden, or a turn about the balconies for fresh air. But she could only be glad. Perhaps her sisters did have more sense that she had had at their age.

A sinking feeling began in her stomach when she heard a familiar oily voice addressing her from behind. "The duke's heir seems likely to predecease him. Have you and my dear cousin been making a concerted effort to produce a less accident-prone male?"

Chapter Twenty One

Miranda turned toward the sound of Grimthorpe's chilling voice.

His smug demeanor so irritated her that she wanted to tweak him where it hurt. But this was her home, every nook and cranny filled with guests this weekend, and conversation with Grimthorpe in society tended to end with trouble for her. She did not want to embarrass Simon in that manner. No matter how angry she was at him this very moment.

"Arthur is recovering nicely. It was only a minor accident."

"If accident is the correct word for poisonous mushrooms being served to him and him alone."

He was fishing, Miranda knew. But she was beginning to become desperately afraid that he was right, as distressful as she found agreeing with Grimthorpe on any subject at all.

Arthur's accidents were stretching the line of credibility to the thinness of gossamer. It was no surprise that Grimthorpe had realized that someone intended harm to Simon's heir. No doubt he would be pleased to spread the gossip as thickly as he could.

She sighed. He would get no help from her on that score. "We are all fortunate he is well. After all, he is Simon's heir."

"Then there is to be no little Simon Watterly running about anytime soon?"

Miranda was shocked speechless by his audacity.

Taking her silence as a sign of consent to the subject of conversation, he moved closer. "Perhaps you would like me to hasten matters?" Suddenly she caught the scent of him, the same scent he had worn five years ago. Her fists curled of their own accord.

She stepped back, "You forget yourself, sir." She turned on her heel, and would have departed except that his hand had somehow fastened tightly to her elbow, preventing her from moving away into the safety of the group of remaining guests.

"Don't hurry away, my sweet. You have not heard the ways in which I'd please you." His face was slightly flushed. Perhaps he was foxed? "I am known among the ladies for my prowess. Surely you would enjoy a taste of spice now that you have had your fill of the dull attentions of the saintly Simon."

"I will assume that you have enjoyed the spirits a bit too freely this evening," Miranda said frostily, doing her best to imitate the dowager in her most quelling mood. "And I will not tell my husband of this incident, nor ask you to leave, if you release my arm at once."

Instead, his hand tightened, and he leaned forward until she could smell the brandy upon his breath. "Just one kiss for a pair of boots? Doesn't that seem like a reasonable request?"

She went cold with panic. Not now, not another

disaster upon the heels of Arthur's poisoning. "Take your hand from my arm immediately." He did so, with haste, when he felt the muscles in her upper arm clench. Obviously, he well remembered their last encounter.

"You will regret spurning my attention, one day, Your Grace." There was vicious emphasis on her title.

Wondering if he intended to display her boots to the remaining guests, Miranda found that she did not care. Arthur's accident had made such a trifling matter seem completely beneath her notice tonight. "I already regret having this conversation. I should have walked away immediately."

She half turned to leave, adding, "But that is something I can rectify immediately. I hope the rest of your weekend is pleasant, but I am certain that you understand my reluctance to spend time in your company."

He did not seem to understand her words. The smile was still fixed upon his lips. But he did not look at her, rather beyond her.

She understood why when Simon's voice, deep with anger, sounded from close behind her. "My wife has bid you good evening, Grimthorpe. Did you not understand her clearly?"

She twisted to glance up at him, and Simon enjoyed the feel of her soft curves pressed against his torso as he looked down upon her serious face. With her bottom lip caught between her teeth, she turned back to see Grimthorpe walk stiffly away from them.

He felt the tension drain from her, leaving her weight resting against him. "Simon, why is it that some men want women so very much that they make fools of themselves?"

He wondered that very same thing. "Lust is a strong emotion in most men, Miranda. I have seen it turn the most reasonable person into a gibbering idiot, and yet I cannot tell you why."

Smiling, she turned, bringing herself into his arms. She laid her cheek against his chest. He could not resist encircling her with his arms, despite the ache of need that filled him immediately.

"I am so glad that you are not like other men, Simon. I cannot imagine you behaving so foolishly." There was a touch of wistfulness in her voice. It called to the spreading need that he felt almost all the time nowadays.

He buried his face in her elegantly coiffed hair, enjoying the faint scent of roses there. "Nor can I," he lied, knowing how close he was to taking her upstairs to his bed then and there, be damned with their guests, be damned with begetting a child. Be damned with dying.

He released her and stepped away. It was becoming harder and harder to resist the urge to bed her, to make her his true wife. To make love to her. He groaned softly. If only there were some way to bring her with him. But he could not ask her to exile herself from her sisters, her brother. Nor could he ask her never to hold a child of her own in her arms. He knew what it felt like to lose a family.

He forced the sorrow away again, though he found it more difficult each time. Still, there were serious matters that needed his attention. He could not waste any time cursing fate. "Katherine discarded the toadstools in the dustbin. We checked. There are several missing."

Her eyes darkened to amber. He knew she would not miss the meaning of such a thing. "But who would have known that they were poison? If only we could find out, we'd have some answers from him."

He sighed. "Or her." Nothing about this matter

would be easy. "There were several guests around who might have overheard Katherine's lecture to the girls about the danger of those particular toadstools. She spent several minutes going over the dangers, and the way to recognize those toadstools from non-poisonous mushrooms."

"She did not know who, then? She gave you no names?"

"At the time, her concern was with ensuring that the girls understood the danger fully, her attention was given over completely to them."

Miranda shivered, her eyes huge in her pale face. "Oh Simon, what does this mean? There is no doubt now that someone is trying to do away with Arthur. But why?"

He embraced her tightly, wishing that he could reassure her. "It seems that someone does not want Arthur to succeed me to the title."

She nodded. "How long have you suspected?"

"Since I learned that the heirs who came before Arthur on my list all died unexpectedly before my agent found them."

"Is there nothing we can do?"

"I may send you to stay with your family for your own safety." He had just thought of it as he held her in his arms and realized how vulnerable she was. The murderer, if this was the work of one fiend, had no way of knowing that his bride was—and would remain—a virgin and in no danger of giving birth to a ducal heir.

"I won't leave you. I'm no coward."

He smiled. "You are indeed no coward, my fairy-tale warrior. Still, I would rest easier if I knew you were out of harm's way."

"I'll consider it." Her voice was cool, and he looked down to see her watching the deserted ruins of the decorated dance floor. "As soon as our last guest has left."

He would have felt a bit more comfort if the hairs on the back of his neck did not prickle when she spoke. He had no doubt he needed to find his answers swiftly, or risk having her launch herself into the effort beside him.

He wished once again, as he held her tight, that he had never been struck with moon madness and married her. He had brought her nothing but heartache, and he would never be able to bring her anything else.

Katherine's patient recovered quickly from his poisoning, and the next morning Miranda found him in the library with Hero. Her sister was reading in a clear and steady voice. Arthur sat with his eyes closed, an expression of bliss on his narrow features.

Miranda waited for Hero to come to the end of a line. "Good morning. How are you feeling?" She shot a troubled look at her sister. Did she not realize that Arthur was included in the category of men she should be careful not to allow herself to be alone with? Or had she so quickly come to think of him as family, though he was not?

Hero flushed guiltily as she hastily marked her place in the book and sat it on the table next to her chair. Arthur himself sat ramrod stiff upon the sofa, his color higher than that on Hero's cheeks.

"Good morning, Miranda. I was just keeping Arthur company. He did not feel like taking breakfast this morning." Her eyes did not meet Miranda's—a clear indication that she knew of her own forwardness. At least, thankfully, she had not sat beside him on the sofa.

"That was thoughtful of you, Hero." With her eyes, Miranda conveyed that no matter how thoughtful the gesture, it made it no less unwise for a young unmarried girl. "Why don't you go in to breakfast now. I wish to speak with Arthur alone."

Panic flared in Hero's eyes, a quiet mortification that expressed itself only in a slight gasp of protest.

Miranda, realizing that her sister was afraid that Arthur would be chided for her own transgression, put her fears to rest quickly. "I just want to see to his health. Katherine said he could easily have died last night. I must find out what happened so that I can prevent it happening again."

Hero paled and swallowed convulsively. Tears made her eyes bright as stars. Without further comment, she hurried out of the room. Miranda doubted she would be indulging in much breakfast, however. It was difficult to eat with a bruised heart.

Arthur hurried to say, "Your sister and I share a love of literature, that is all. Please be assured that I would not think to hurt her reputation in any way."

Miranda wondered if she had been too hasty in her judgment. She sighed. It was a sin she had committed before. She would do her best to try not to commit it now. "Exactly how many accidents have you had since coming here, Arthur?"

Miranda tried to keep her question casual. She knew that Simon would know the answer. Of course, he would refuse to tell her and be forewarned that she was asking questions. She did not want Arthur to let slip that she had winnowed the details from him. But she need not have worried. Arthur apparently had not a suspicious bone in his body.

"Let me see—" He closed his eyes to concentrate.

"When I was but a few miles from arriving here, my carriage broke a wheel and I was thrown a distance—fortunately I landed in a boggy spot and wasn't hurt. Not that Laddensby was any too pleased about the state of my clothing, I can tell you."

He was silent for a moment, whether in sympathy for his valet's annoyance or in thought, Miranda could not be certain. But she watched him closely, and saw the exact moment that suspicion leapt into his face.

"I say." His voice was pitched higher than normal, as if his mind might be racing. "It's quite extraordinary, really. Counting that incident, which actually happened before I arrived, I have fallen down the stairs, my room has been afire once, the girth of my saddle broke twice."

He sat forward, his voice sharp with excitement. "Oh, and I was set upon by a mad swarm of bees—the doctors have told me that if I am so set upon again, several stings at once might kill me!" He settled back against the sofa, obviously drained of energy.

Quietly, he added, "And, of course, that unfortunate substitution of poisonous mushrooms. Indeed, I have been quite unlucky of late."

Miranda smiled and nodded. Indeed. Or could it be that Arthur had actually been quite fortunate?

Fortunate enough to make someone quite desperate. But who?

Miranda could not help the frisson of guilt that assailed her at her intrusion into the dowager's privacy as she confronted Simon's mother as she rested with a piece of sewing in the garden gazebo.

The older woman had worked tirelessly these past weeks to ensure a successful party and deserved whatever moments of rest she might steal in between seeing to the needs of the guests and the duties of the servants.

However, of all those involved, the dowager had motive. She had been vocal about the fact that she counted Arthur a worthless heir apparent. Though the thought was absurd on the surface, Miranda could not dismiss it. Arthur had nearly been killed. Who knew if his luck would hold him safe if there were to be another attempt? The question must be asked.

And so she asked it boldly, without pretense. "Why do you object to Arthur as Simon's heir?"

A sniff of disdain met this bluntness. "The sniveling ninny has lucked into being a duke's heir, and he hasn't got the sense to appreciate his fortune. Not to mention his lack of ability in running the affairs of his own wardrobe, never mind an estate the size he will inherit."

Again, Miranda chose to meet the dowager's acidity with a blunt question. "Do you find his accidents suspicious?"

The dowager paused in her stitching. "Odd, yes, but not suspicious. He is simply clumsy—carriage accidents, riding accidents, bees ..." Her voice trailed off and she met Miranda's eyes sharply.

"I find them suspicious." Miranda did not elaborate.

As the needle flew, the older woman dismissed the possibility. "Who could possibly benefit from his untimely death—especially now that Simon is married? You, perhaps?"

The dowager shook her head, answering her own

question. "But not unless you had a male child to be Simon's heir. Otherwise, you have naught but a few coins and baubles to pawn in your later years."

The needle slowed. "Is that a possibility?" Her voice, uncharacteristically tentative, whispered across the distance between them.

Inside, Miranda quivered, but she did not allow that to show in her curt answer. "I am not expecting a child."

"I didn't think so." Her smile was bitter. "I do know my son after all these years." There was an infinite weariness borne of sadness in her words.

Miranda abandoned any suspicion that the dowager might have poisoned Arthur. She couldn't believe it of her. For as much as Simon and his mother hurt each other, there was love beneath it. The dowager had never tried to physically force Simon to her will. She had fought her battles with words.

Nerves raw, Miranda could not stop her own sharp words. "And yet, you don't know him well enough to know what he wants most from you."

"Perhaps I do know. And, perhaps, in hard-won wisdom derived from all my years, I know that it would only make him hate me more."

"What is it that divides you?" Miranda leaned forward, wondering if she might find the key to unlock Simon's heart in the dowager's answer. If she answered.

"The truth."

"How can truth divide you? I have always found it to be a healing thing." Except when she tried to tell Simon she loved him. Then it seemed to be razor sharp.

"The truth is a regrettable thing in this case. And it would hurt Simon more if I were to tell it to him."

"The truth can never be regretted, only dealt with,"

Miranda said with a practicality born of dealing with her own odd differences that had caused so much dissension for her with her parents. "Simon seems to be able to face truth. Why don't you try to patch up whatever rift has split you?"

"If only circumstances had been different. For a moment, I had hoped . . . but no, I cannot tell him."

Angrily, Miranda turned to leave. "Of course you won't. Instead, you will poke and prod until his control hangs by a thread. Sometimes it seems you mean to provoke him to murder!"

The dowager's mouth tightened so that her lips turned white at the edges. But then, to Miranda's astonishment, she merely nodded. "Perhaps. I can see what you say. Although I can't appreciate how horrible you make me sound."

"What I think of you is not important. It is Simon's desire to understand, to heal the hurt between you that you must concern yourself with."

"And if it is not in my power to heal him? If I hold the power to hurt him immeasurably more?"

"It seems impossible to me that either of you could hurt the other more. Especially if you tell the truth." Miranda felt the tears rising in her eyes, and added, "You might regret not having tried when he is gone." As she would. She knew she would.

"And he will be going soon, will he not?"

The dowager paled at the reminder of her son's pending death. "I suppose there is only one way left to break through to him. I shall tell him what he demands to know."

Miranda felt as if a burden had been taken from her. "You will not regret it." She hoped this would be the beginning of peace between them. And then she looked into the dowager's face.

"I will tell him." She looked grim. "But it will not make him happy."

Miranda felt a chill of fear shiver through her, but she had no time to ask why.

"What will not make him happy?"

Chapter Twenty Two

Simon's voice cut into their conversation, and Miranda noted that the dowager jumped as perceptibly as she herself did at the sound of his voice. He had come as if called—by angel or devil she could not say.

The dowager craned her neck to look up at the towering figure of her son. Each determined gaze met and clashed together—and neither gave quarter as she answered him. "I have decided to answer the question you have been demanding answered since the day your father died."

So she had meant what she said. Miranda grew numb, knowing what was coming and yet not knowing at the same time. Would the dowager's confidences heal the rift, or split them apart forever?

"Your tongue could not shape the truth, Mother." Simon lashed out at her as he reached a hand toward Miranda. "Come, Miranda, we have guests to see to."

She did not move.

Simon's jaw flexed in anger. "Miranda?" He had not raised his voice, but that did not mean he was not angry. He was. Very angry. She did not move.

The dowager picked up her sewing and resumed stitching, the needle flashing in the sunlight. "Are you so foolishly spiteful that you would walk away from me now, when you are only moments away from the truth you hold so dear?"

Simon glared at her, but did not move toward the house. Miranda could see his desire to have the truth from his mother etched upon his face. There was dread etched there, too. She could not help but wonder what awful secret lay between them to be exposed.

A dreadful thought made her catch her breath. Was his mother somehow the cause of his fatal illness? She pressed her hands together. Oh, please, let that not be the case.

Simon's mother sighed and indicated the bench next to her. "Sit please, Simon. I have a tale to tell you, and I do not like to crook my neck to look up at you."

He did not move. "It cannot take you long to say one name."

One name. Miranda tried to puzzle out his statement. Whose name? How could one name cause such a rift between mother and son? What infamy could one name hold?

The dowager's needle paused for a moment and then resumed. "I will tell the story in my own way, and you shall be patient. After all, you will have your answer—not, I expect, that it will make you any happier."

Her glance caught Miranda, held her, pulling her into the whirlpool of emotions. "But your wife seems to feel that I shall never overcome this rift between us if I am not honest with you."

His breath caught and his voice was harsh as he asked, "Have you told her? You have no right—"

"I have told her nothing." She pursed her lips thoughtfully. "Although she has guessed some things, she does not know what ails you, of that I am certain. Should we send her away before we have this conversation?"

Miranda could see that he was considering it, and she was torn between wanting to know what had hurt them so very much and running away from the painful purging she sensed would soon take place.

"No." His voice was crisp, decisive. "She might as well know."

"You trust her, do you?"

"With my life." His answer made Miranda's heart ache with a tightly controlled joy. She wondered if he would still feel the same way once his mother had spit out her awful truth.

He sat on the ground, heedless of the grass stains that might mar his clothing and, after a brief glance at Miranda, stared in challenge at his mother. "Tell me your story, Mother. But do not expect me to be swayed by touching pleas or sad tales."

"Never, Simon. You are much too much like me." The dowager composed herself, suddenly seeming to be at a loss for words. And then she began, softly. "Your father . . ."

"The duke," Simon interrupted.

"Sinclair Watterly took me to wife for one reason and one reason only—his older son, your brother Peter, desired a commission in the Navy. At first, your . . . Sinclair forbade it and refused to pay for a commission."

The sharpness in her face erased for a moment, as if she had been drawn back in time. "I heard from the servants that it was quite a battle."

Simon interrupted impatiently. "I know his temper well, Mother. But that happened well before I was born and is not of importance to me and what I want from you."

Her eyes focused on Simon. "Sinclair won the battle, of course. He was the father, and he held the purse strings tight to himself. Still, he knew it was only a matter of time before Peter attained his majority and received an income that could not be controlled.

"Since he did not want the dukedom to revert to another branch of the family if anything were to happen to his son, the duke decided that the solution would be to marry again and have another son of his own."

Simon stirred restlessly. "I know all this, Mother. The duke was fond of telling me the story, as you well know. He felt he was lucky to have taken the precaution, since my brother died. I'm sure he was horrified the day he learned I was a bastard."

Miranda gasped. A bastard? Simon? How could that be? He did not look at her, but she could see that her reaction had increased the tension that surged through him. She pressed her hands against her mouth so that she could make no more sounds, no matter what else was said.

"You are no bastard." His mother's eyebrow rose in an eloquent rebuke. "Sinclair knew that he was incapable of siring a child before he married me. He arranged for your conception."

"You mean, don't you, that he condoned your taking a lover?"

"Condoned? That is not the term I would use, but the truth is the truth. Sinclair was your father in all but deed, and there is no one to dispute that fact but you."

"What about Mr. Watson? He knew you when you

were young. Perhaps I should ask him if he knew my father—if he is my father. Or have you sent him away so that I cannot ask him for the truth? Is that why you are now willing to tell me? To keep him from it?"

"Do you think Sinclair would share such a secret with a stranger? An American?" Her laughter was harsh, and yet there was a glint of fear in her eye. "No one would father his son but a man of his choice."

Simon's anger burned at that. Miranda could see his jaw tighten and his fists clench, pulling up clumps of grass without even knowing he was doing so. "Are you implying that he put you out for stud service Mother? I know how proud he was of the direct descent of our family line. I will not believe that he would deliberately allow the Watterly blood to be drained from the line."

"No. You are right. He would not. That is why he . . ." There was actually a tinge of color in her cheeks, Miranda saw, wondering whether it boded well or ill. ". . . he commanded his son to sire a child upon me before he would provide the commission fee."

Silence lay like a blanket of heavy wool over the three. He had not expected this. A lover. An affair. But not this twisted . . . no. His mother was many things, but he had never known her to create elaborate fictions to hide her own crimes.

He could not bear to look at Miranda. He had expected her to be shocked. But she had done nothing but give a small gasp. He had not believed that she would turn against him. But he did not want to see her eyes. Not yet.

"And you agreed to this?" His accusation came sharply, cutting through the silent pall. He had no use for expedient truths. His mother had lain with his father's son to conceive him. Could it be true? "How much were you paid for your compliance?"

His mother's smile infuriated him. Of course, she was the duchess. What other payment could she expect? The thought made him ill.

"The duke thought it best if I were to remain unaware of his plans." Even now, her voice was cool and mocking. Even now, when the truth was no longer their secret, but Miranda's as well. "Your father came to me in the dark and left before daybreak."

He watched Miranda, not his mother. Her eyes were wide with shock. What did she think of him now that she knew? Would she repudiate him?

He asked mockingly, "And you didn't know the difference between a man of fifty and an eighteen-year-old-boy?" Had she not always known when he was into some mischief as a boy, even when he thought himself safe from her eyes at school? How could she have been so blind?

"I'm certain you cannot credit it, Simon, but at the time I was young and innocent." His mother's answer was so dry, the voice he hated when she'd used it to argue with his father. That voice she used when she knew she could not win. Not against Sinclair Watterly, Duke of Kerstone. "I had no reason to suspect that my husband was not the one exercising a husband's right. But now that I have told you what you wanted to know, I hope you see that you are the true-blooded duke and no bastard."

Simon stared at her in bitterness for a moment and then suddenly stood. "Thank you for telling me the name of my father. I believe you are not lying about that. But this absurd fabrication about the duke condoning—ordering—it, that I cannot accept. Our indisputably direct descent was a source of pride for him. I cannot believe that he would sully it with a bastard."

"He never considered you a bastard, Simon. You were of his blood and his making—his son would never have bedded me without your father's command."

"Perhaps it is well that my true father died, then, for he could not have been a man of great character. The duke always hinted that he was not cut out for running the estates."

"I did not realize that Sinclair ever spoke of Peter to you." She seemed surprised, even somewhat alarmed.

For the first time, he wondered why the duke might have been so insistent that Simon was a better man than the duke's older son. "He said little, only that Peter was cut out to be a warrior and didn't understand loyalty."

A spark of anger lit in her eye, surprising him. "Your father had a different dream, Simon. That does not make him lacking in character. You have no idea what the sacrifice cost him. He left before he knew that we had conceived you."

Simon remembered her cryptic comment that he might not have been born if . . . it was too painful to consider.

"He confronted Sinclair, refused to continue the charade, forced him to pay the commission fee, and left that very night. We never heard from him again."

"What if you had?" The horror struck through him. "What if you had to live here with him? All of you knowing—"

"Do you not recall Sinclair clearly enough? Do you think that would have perturbed him? If Peter had come home, to become duke and leave you as second son, Sinclair would have been overjoyed."

"And my father?"

"Who can say?" The dowager looked away, her eyes closed, her face shut in tight lines of pain. "The duke did not realize what harm he had caused, of course."

She sighed. "Not even to his dying day. He sent news of your birth to Peter." She put down the stitching she had been gripping in her hands. "It was shortly after that when we received the news of his death. He never even knew he had a son."

His gaze sought Miranda, sitting silently through the news of his disgrace and humiliation. Her glance was one of sympathy, as she rose in one graceful move and came toward him, her arms held out. He remembered the time long ago, the night of her scandal, that he had known even then she would not hold his birth against him. If only . . .

"Thank you for this information, Mother." Simon's eyes did not focus when he glanced toward his mother. He had to get away. Away from Miranda, away from his mother, away from this ill-fated life. His bow was brief, and then he was gone. Gone as far away as he was able, to ride away from this house of guests who all thought him the Duke of Kerstone. To ride away from his pain, his shame.

His brother his father, his father his grandfather. His mother—could she have told him the truth? Could the old duke and his son really have acted so callously? Creating him as a spare against the possibility that Peter might not return?

Miranda had never seen the dowager more shaken than she was now. There were tears running down her cheeks, although she made no sounds of sobbing as she watched her son's retreat.

She asked calmly, "Why did you lie to him?"

The dowager looked shocked. "I did not lie to him."

"I heard you in the garden. I heard you with the American. He is Simon's father, isn't he? Not Peter."

The sewing fell from her fingers to the ground unnoticed. "I can hold on to none of my vile, hurtful secrets, can I?" Her fury was intense when she raised her eyes. "Peter. Mr. Watson. They are one and the same." Her anger faded. "And yet not. Mr. Watson has taken America as his land and will not give her up."

"Find Simon," she whispered. "Go to him. You are his last hope. My last hope. I do not want to lose my son, but I have no power to sway him, only to hurt him. Perhaps you will believe me now that you have seen for yourself."

Nodding, Miranda wondered where he might have gone.

As if she read her mind, the dowager said softly, "He will ride. Perhaps he will fish at the pond. It is what he did when he was troubled as a boy."

"He is a man now," Miranda reminded her.

"Yes. He is a man. And I fear that I have been wrong in believing I knew him. I knew the boy, but perhaps I do not know the man."

She gazed at Miranda, her eyes awash with tears. "I can but tell you to try the pond, for perhaps he is acting with the wounded nature of the boy he used to be, before he learned the truth."

Miranda did not even excuse herself before fleeing the garden for the stables.

She tied Celestina several hundred yards away from the pond and picked a path through the high grass until she heard the sounds of rhythmic splashing.

Had the dowager been right? Was Simon fishing with such fury that the water splashed?

Within moments she could see him swimming, pumping his arms furiously in the air as he raced toward the edge of the pond where she stood. She watched for a moment, knowing that he was coping with the battle within him, worried that he would kill himself from the exertion.

Water cascaded from his body and yet still the silence grew loud as he stood up in the waist-deep water and shook himself. His gaze met hers and she burned from the anger in his eyes.

"Go away, Miranda. I am not in the mood for company."

"You will kill yourself with all this exertion. Come and ride with me."

His laughter was bitter. "I would like nothing better. But it is far safer for both of us if I stay in the water and you ride home alone."

Miranda blushed, understanding the hidden meaning in her words now that she had been privy to the talk of the married women this weekend. In the heat of his passionate anger he was too easily roused. It was amazing the difference in the conversation between the married women and the conversations she remembered from her partial Season as an unmarried virgin. Some of the women seemed to relish inciting their husband's anger just to get them into their beds.

The idea appealed to her. He could expend his frantic energy upon her, and she could offer him the comfort a wife offered a husband.

Certainly the risk was worth it, if only for the fact that he would begin swimming again were she to leave. No wonder he did not want to find a cure for himself. He thought himself a bastard, unworthy of his title and position. And yet he had been created to be duke with more forethought than most children could claim. Three people had chosen to create him, although two had apparently been destroyed in the process.

I will not let him be destroyed as were his mother and father, she vowed to herself. I will show him that I am proud to call him my husband. "I would prefer riding, Simon. Surely that is a more satisfying exertion than swimming?"

Slowly, she began unbuttoning her bodice. She had unbuttoned it completely before he closed his gaping mouth and said sternly, "Go home, Miranda." His gaze, however, was trained upon the skin that she was slowly revealing.

She stood nude for only a moment upon the bank before modestly plunging into the water and wading toward him. The pond was surprisingly cold and the moment after she began regretting her impulse, she began worrying that the cold water could not be good for him.

"If you insist upon exerting yourself, then do so by making me your wife in truth. At least then I can put my arms around you and hold you as I wish to. I can offer comfort—and I will not be too wild, Simon. I promise you have nothing to worry about from me."

Absurdly, as she approached him, he backed toward the opposite bank. She stopped two feet away from him. "Simon, I know we have been worried about your health, but this time, even if I am not perfectly calm, I can do you no more harm than this frantic swimming of yours."

Miranda's attention was pulled away for a second, and she started quickly when something bumped her hip. She looked down to see a silver fish nibbling at her, apparently in the mistaken opinion that she was dinner. She cupped her hands to capture the fish and with a gentle push, released it in the opposite direction.

"I thought you would be fishing. That, at least would be a peaceful sport."

"My health is my concern, Miranda. I have told you that before."

She stepped closer to him, and this time he didn't move away. Frustratingly, he did not seem any closer to taking her in his arms, either—though his gaze slipped from hers to rove lower more and more often.

"Simon, I know the idea of the duke deceiving your mother as he did is intolerable to an honest man like you, but you must not let such worries affect your health."

"My health is the last thing you should be concerned with." The anger in his eyes was so fierce she actually trembled at the sight of it. Or from the chill of the water. She could not be certain.

"These things happened in the past. They do not have to affect the present."

"Miranda, you do not understand—"

She opened her arms and stepped toward him. "Let me hold you, soothe you. I am your wife . . ." Another fish bumped at her hip and she reached for it. "Oh!"

Her fingers tightened on the "fish," and it pulsed heatedly in her hand. Shocked she stared into Simon's face. His eyes were closed and he was holding perfectly still.

"Miranda, please release me at once," he said, his jaw barely moving.

She began to loosen her grip instantly, and then changed her mind, tightening again. "Not until you agree to let me be your wife in all ways, Simon."

He said nothing at all, moved not a muscle. Curious,

Miranda looked down into the murky water, but she could not see what her fingers encircled.

With her thumb, she explored the rounded tip of him, to find a valley at the very center that made her feel a dizzying rush of warmth throughout her limbs. For a moment, she thought she might faint, she felt so very strange.

Simon did not allow himself to move when her fingers curled over him. He could not. "Release me."

She looked down into the water. And then she swayed toward him, her fingers tightening with delicious results. He crushed her to him with a groan, and she had to grab his shoulders for balance.

He buried his face in her neck and she released him at last. But it was too late. Far too late. "Miranda you have no idea what you're asking of me. This is impossible."

"You're wrong, Simon." She smiled as she rubbed her silken belly against him, pressing closer.

He groaned again and tightened his arms around her. "Miranda, Miranda, Miranda . . ." His control broke as he stared down into her eyes. There was a triumph in her eyes that she had affected him. And no sign that she thought him one whit less desirable now that she knew the truth.

The flash of triumph fled however, when he bent to claim her mouth. He knew his passion was too much for her. It was too much for him. But he could not stop.

He had wanted her five years ago, he had wanted her that night in the hunter's cottage, and he wanted her still.

She pushed against his chest with her hands as if to slow his sensual assault, but he did not release her mouth, and in a moment he felt her relax against him once again. He lifted her easily, and carried her to the bank.

He touched her breasts, her throat, her belly; he parted her thighs with his knee and rubbed himself against her. He knew he was moving too quickly and tried to slow himself. But when she brought her hips up to meet his, he was consumed with the need to be one with her.

He did not pause, knowing and yet not able to know, that he would regret this haste as he pushed into her, entering her, stopping only for the briefest of times before he groaned into her mouth, deepened his kiss, and pushed past the flimsy barrier that was no barrier at all against his need.

It was only once he was deep inside her, when she lay stiff and still under him that he remembered that he should have been cautious. He took his mouth from hers and buried his head in her neck, as still as he had been when she first touched him, thinking he was a fish. He laughed raggedly against the dampness of her skin. Certainly she would never make that mistake again.

She bucked her hips under him. "Simon, you're hurting me. Stop."

He wanted to. He tried to. But the urge to make her his was a burning need that overrode everything. His arms tightened around her as he began to shake in a silent battle with his body's need to stroke into her until he made her forget the pain and cry out with the wonder of joining.

"Simon!" She tightened her arms around him then and tried to roll him beneath her.

"Stay still, Miranda," he gritted out between his teeth. "Stay very still, and I think I may manage to remove myself before I—" He did not finish his sentence, but rolled away from her and lay still for another moment. She reached out to touch his hip and he jerked away from her as he began to shake. "Don't touch me Miranda. For God's sake—and my own—don't touch me."

She leaned over him, ever eager to ignore what he told her. He looked into her beautiful eyes and wished with all his heart that he could forget his burdens for a moment longer. He had hurt her. Worst of all, if he had not hurt her, he would never have had the strength to pull out of her before he achieved his own release. And then he'd be worrying about babies.

"I'm sorry Miranda. That should never have happened."

"Why not?" He could see she was hurt. But she was trying to make sense of things, as always. "You seem to have survived it, Simon." She smiled. "And I am your wife in truth, now, am I not?"

He knew, suddenly, the words that would send her away from him for good. "Of course I survived it. I am perfectly capable of making love to you. I am not really dying Miranda. I lied to you."

"You are not dying?" He could see her confusion, but terribly, there was joy there. He needed to puncture the hope that might even now be burgeoning in her fairy-tale heart.

"No. But the bastard Duke of Kerstone is."

"What riddle is this, Simon?" she asked impatiently.

"No riddle. Just the truth, Miranda. The truth I dared not give you before." He paused, to make sure that she was heeding him closely. "In little over three months, the bastard Duke of Kerstone will die. The dukedom and all its responsibilities will be handed over to Arthur, the rightful heir."

She stared at him with incomprehension and suddenly he knew a way to convince her. He rummaged through the clothing piled upon the bank and pulled out the leather pouch she had eyed so curiously for so long. Without a word, he tossed it to her.

She held it as she stared at him. And then she opened it and. hands trembling, began to read the first of two folded pages. When she was done with the two pages, she hefted the envelope marked *For the eyes of the Duke of Kerstone only* and looked up. "This is sealed, should I open it?"

"It will be opened by Arthur when he inherits. Until then, I will keep it safe with me, to remind me of what I am—and am not."

She quietly put the two pages and the sealed envelope back into the leather pouch and fastened it closed before she handed it to him.

He wondered if she had truly taken all the implications in when she asked merely, "Where will you go?"

"To America. To a city called Charleston. I have acquired a modest property there."

She watched him, saying nothing, but he could see the narrowing of her eyes as she pondered his answer. And then her breath caught and her eyes locked with his. "Oh." Her eyes filled with tears. "And you were going to leave me behind."

He did not want to see her pain, her growing distrust. For a moment he wished that she would refuse to believe it of him. But then, why would she not believe it of him? Had he not married her, tantalized her with kisses and caresses, yet refused to make love with her? He said grudgingly, "You would have been an honorable widow."

"I would have been a virgin widow!" She colored brightly, the flush descending to the tops of her breasts, and he wanted to laugh, to groan, to listen to his mother and let everyone believe he deserved to be the Duke of Kerstone.

But he did not. "I'm sorry. I didn't mean to make love to you. I should never have touched you." He had the blood of a cowardly Watterly in him. A man who would bed his own father's wife. That alone tainted him beyond redemption.

Unconscious of her nudity, she bent toward him. Her face was taut with grief for his betrayal. "Then why did you marry me?"

"Because I wanted you." It was the wrong answer and yet he could give no other. It was time for the truth. She had heard the worst and not flinched from him. Surely she could understand how important it was to him that the Watterly name not be soiled by a bastard duke. "I wanted just a taste of what could have been mine if I were not a bastard. I wanted you as my wife."

Incomprehension narrowed her eyes as she struggled to understand his motives. "But you refuse to make love to me."

"I cannot leave an heir behind." He realized how foolish his words sounded to his own ears, they must be doubly so to hers. She had argued against the marriage; he had been the one to insist. He had thought he could control events, control his own desires. But today had proved that near Miranda he had not nearly enough strength to deny himself.

She wrapped her arms around her knees and rocked back and forth, caught in her own misery. She whispered, almost to herself, as if no answer he might give would satisfy, "How can you do this? I can't bear the thought of being without you. And to know that it isn't death, but you yourself who have separated us? How can you ask this of me?"

He reached out to touch her hair, but did not. "I have no other choice, Miranda, I will not breed a child to one day make false claim upon the dukedom."

She looked up at him, reached out her own hand to grasp his, still hovering near. "We can prevent that from happening . . . we did not consummate our marriage for months, Simon. We shall simply never do . . . that . . ." Her nose wrinkled and he had the absurd urge to laugh—or to cry. He didn't suppose this was the time to confess that even now his body was urgently requesting that he do . . . that . . . again.

"It is better if I go alone." He had never thought she would agree to go; that was why he had only dreamed it in his darkest nights, never spoken the thought aloud. But he could not consider it. It was too dangerous. And she had not counted the cost to herself.

"Of course it is not better that you go alone."

"Miranda, you do not understand what would be required. I have another identity in Charleston. I am not the duke there. I will have no contact with anyone here ever again."

"I love you, Simon. I want to be with you."

The blood roared in his ears at her confession. But he did not deserve her love and he could not accept it. "Can you imagine living your life without hearing another word, exchanging even a letter, never mind visits, with your sisters? With Valentine? I have seen the bond between you."

She did not answer, which was in itself an answer to his questions. Stung by the truth, however, she attacked. "Do you want to be alone your whole life? Haven't these last five years been enough for you?"

Yes, they had been. Perhaps that had been why he was so vulnerable when the woman full of fairy tales whirled back into his life. "I grew used to it. I will grow used to it again." He stood and began to dress. Presently, she did the same.

He noticed that she had not referenced one single fairy tale and knew in his heart that he would bear that symbol of her despair as a sadness deep in his heart for a very long time to come.

Chapter Twenty Three

There was a carriage in the drive when they arrived home, both sunk in silent misery. Trunks sat upon the steps, and for a moment Miranda thought that Valentine had sensed her distress and come to support her. The thought of facing him, of explaining the nightmare her life had become, filled her with dread. He had given up on happy endings for himself; could he help her accept her own unhappy tale?

To her horror her brother was not the one waiting in the hallway. Instead, the American, with three young girls of various ages surrounding him, stood speaking in hurried low tones to Simon's mother.

The dowager turned toward them, and Miranda wanted to sink into the cool marble floor and disappear, as the keen eyes missed nothing of her disarrangement.

Their eyes locked a moment before the question came. "Were you reconciled?" Evidently her unlocked secret had not softened the bluntness of her tongue. Indeed, she almost seemed more distant then she had been when Miranda met her.

"No." She could say no more. Her throat was swollen with the need to cry, to scream, to deny what she had learned.

The dowager's brief nod, without comment, surprised her—until she noticed that the older woman was unnaturally pale, and trembling ever so slightly as she addressed her son.

"We must find room for an unexpected guest. It seems your brother, Peter, has arrived. You are to be allowed to live, after all." Her smile was halfhearted. "At least, to live without the burden of the dukedom. Although I expect you will find your wife and her family a handful to manage."

Simon glared at her coldly. "I beg your pardon, Mother? What lies are you telling now?" Miranda, numb with despair, wondered how he could dredge up such anger.

"How dare you speak so disrespectfully to your mother." The American ... no, Peter ... said. Simon's father. Simon's brother? Miranda sighed in confusion as he continued. "She speaks the truth. I am Peter Watterly, the eldest son of Sinclair Watterly."

Simon snorted rudely. But Miranda, standing next to him, saw the trembling in his fingers that he sought to hide with clenched fists.

Peter's eyes flashed with sudden fire, and Miranda was painfully reminded of Simon. Her doubts dropped away as he finished. "Apparently you and I think alike. I did not want the burden of the dukedom and chose to allow the false notice of my death to go uncorrected. But I am back now, to relieve you of the burden you no longer wish to shoulder."

He looked over at the dowager in silence, and

added quietly, "You have your mother to thank for that. She persuaded me that there was no other course."

For a moment, the import of the words did not come clear to Miranda. It was simply too much for her exhausted mind. First the news that Simon had lied to her about dying, then the crushing truth that he intended to disappear—and leave her behind.

She stared in bemusement as the man she had known as Mr. Watson stepped forward and held his hand out to her. "I'm sorry to have caused you such trouble in your young marriage, my dear."

She stared at the long, calloused fingers uncomprehendingly as he said, "I want to thank you for making things clear to me, young lady."

"I beg your pardon?" Miranda forced her mind to focus. Something important had happened. She knew it. She just could not understand it yet.

Peter. Simon's father. Hadn't he said he wanted no part of England? She had heard him with her own ears. But then, she had not understood the full import of his words. He was not an American. He was the rightful duke.

Simon stirred beside her, interrupting whatever Peter had intended to say next. He met the older man's challenge directly. "I understood my brother to be dead, sir. And I had not heard that he was an American."

Peter shrugged his shoulders, his manner still American, and still as rough. "But as you can see, I am alive."

"And what is that to do with me?"

The older man looked torn. "Perhaps I misunderstood your mother." He flicked a glance at the dowager, but she did not speak or move to indicate she heard. Her attention was fixed on Simon.

Peter's eyes met Simon's again, direct and intent. "If you want me here, if you don't want to be duke, I'll do it. If you want me to go now and never come back, I'll do that."

Simon flinched at the curt words, but said nothing in return.

The dowager cut in with her usual acerbity. "My dear, why must you persist denying the obvious? Peter has returned from the dead to give you back your life. There was no other answer once he arrived." The dowager glanced at Peter. "It just took him a short time to recognize it. He is a Watterly, after all—and stubbornness is inherent in your line."

All that he had learned that day pressed in on Miranda's heart. She wondered how Simon could bear it in silence as he stood without speaking, his eyes traveling from his mother to his father and back again.

They might have stood there in a mute tableau for all time, if Betsy had not come running up to Simon at that moment, with a note clutched in her fingers. She put the missive in his limp hand and tugged at his arm impatiently. He looked down at her as if he did not truly see her, until her words registered clearly in the hallway. "The bad man said to give you this. I don't like him. I'm glad he's going away."

At that very moment, while Miranda's heart was still between beats, Valentine strode into the hall. She had no time to be glad as their glances met and she knew he had felt her distress and come despite his own heartache.

"You've arrived just in time." Simon spoke brusquely as he looked at the note, looked at Miranda, looked at Valentine. And she could not breathe. For he handed the note to a puzzled Valentine and her brother turned white.

Her brother's eyes met hers and she could not understand what could possibly be so awful about Grimthorpe having left the house party early.

Until he said softly, "The cad has eloped with Juliet."

Miranda raced upstairs to confirm that no one had seen Juliet since she left for a walk in the gardens with Grimthorpe several hours ago. Hero and the twins thoroughly searched the gardens and found only several weekend guests calmly enjoying themselves with no idea of their hosts' growing agitation. The truth could not be denied any longer. Juliet had run off with Grimthorpe. Plans were swiftly made to follow the eloping pair.

Miranda gave orders for a basket of food to be packed, and the servants, ashen-faced, had it prepared and ready before the two freshest, fastest horses had been saddled. Valentine and Simon, changed into fresh clothes, followed on Miranda's heels out into the drive. She turned to look at them in surprise at the sight of only two saddled horses. "Did you not know that I would go with you?"

Valentine, with a glance at Simon, walked to his horse and mounted, so as to give them privacy. Miranda, hurt by his blatant defection, turned her anger on Simon. "She is my sister, Simon, and I am the fool who sent the invitation to that malicious weasel and brought him into our home—"

He smiled and she broke off, astonished at the joy that radiated from him as he came toward her and crushed her into his arms. "My God, Miranda, he is malicious and he is a weasel, but I shall make sure he suffers for what he has done to us, just when we have been dealt the happy ending you believed in so fervently."

She stared at him, trying to understand what had

caused this change in him. He looked as if years had been dropped from him in a single stroke. "Happy ending?"

As if he understood at last her bemusement, he kissed her. "I know fairy-tale happy endings are possible, now. " His breath was warm as he moved his lips to whisper in her ear, "Peter is back, Miranda. I am not the duke."

The distance that had been between them for so long was there no longer. She wondered if she should tell him what she had overheard in the garden? She doubted he would be so joyful knowing what Peter had turned his back on when he agreed to return to England and confess his identity.

There was no time, however, she decided as he kissed her cheek. After Juliet was safely home would be time enough. Then, perhaps, they could find a way for Peter to be happy, too.

She kissed him back when he put his lips gently on hers again, and felt the barriers drop away as he responded with a passion that was held back only by this peril of Juliet's. Shivering, she felt his whisper as he said against her cheek, "I am free to be your husband."

She wanted to believe it, so she pushed aside the images of the miserable pair of star-crossed lovers she had witnessed in the garden.

He pulled away then and smiled at her, a smile such as she had not seen on his face since her long-ago Season. "So you can understand why I will ensure this business with Grimthorpe and your foolish sister is cleared away before the sun sets tonight."

Reluctantly, but unable to argue with his logic, Miranda nodded. "Be careful of him, Simon. He is a crafty devil." With one more fierce hug that made her believe all would turn out right, Simon mounted and the two men she loved most in the world rode off to face their common enemy and rescue the foolish and very young Juliet.

Leaving Miranda to face the dowager—and Peter, back from the dead after nearly thirty years.

Before she could do more than step into the hallway, though, Hero was upon her. "Why would she do such a foolish thing?" Hero was pale, her hands wrung bloodless. "She didn't even fancy him. She said she was simply giving him a taste of what he did to you when she flirted with him."

"What?" Miranda stopped, all thoughts of the dowager vanishing. "When did she say this?" She shook her head at the foolishness of her sister. "He is much too dangerous for a young girl to use as a toy."

"But she didn't like him." Hero protested once again. "She didn't like him at all. She said he made her feel as if there was a spider crawling down into her bosom. What could she be thinking?"

Miranda remembered the determined look in Simon's eye, and thought of Valentine tall upon his horse. "We shall ask her directly when Simon and Valentine bring her safely home."

"What if they are too late?"

Miranda smiled ruefully, though the thought shook her. "Don't you recall how quickly Simon rescued Emily? And we both know that she did not want to be rescued from Valentine's arms."

The words did not seem to ease Hero's anguish, Miranda noticed. Deliberately seeking something to distract her gentle sister from her worry, Miranda added, "Until then, I suggest you go help Katherine with the girls—we should not want the young ones worrying, and now with Peter's daughters about, there are too many for her to manage alone."

Hero took one deep sniff, before she nodded and

hurried away. Miranda hoped she had not imagined the flicker of relief in her sister's eyes—a relief to finally have something that could occupy her hands and mind while her heart lay heavy as a stone.

She wondered if Peter's daughters were as capable of mischief as her own sisters. If so, Hero and Katherine would not have much time to worry about Juliet. Perhaps she would join them, after she had settled with the dowager the matter of how to announce Peter's return to life.

"Worry deepens the blue of your eyes, my dear."

With a startled gasp, Miranda glanced up to face the man she thought had run away with her sister. Grimthorpe. Here. She looked beyond him for Juliet, but he was alone. "Where is Juliet? What have you done with her?"

"Juliet is in a carriage bound for her fate, my dear."

"But you eloped . . ." Miranda trailed off. Obviously, if he were here, he had not eloped.

"Certainly I told you I did. But I would not want that penniless chit of a sister of yours."

"Then who . . . ?" Miranda had intended to ask who had taken Juliet off, but that was not the question he answered.

"I want you, of course."

She went cold. He wanted her, not Juliet? Why? "I am already married."

"That would present a problem—did I want to marry you." He smiled and Miranda's stomach clenched. "But I merely want to ensure that you don't present my dear cousin with a little brat of an heir."

She gasped. "It was you, then? You poisoned Arthur?" She glanced toward the parlor door, gauging whether she could make a run for it and enlist help quietly. Damage to the Watterly reputation or not, perhaps it might be best to scream. Scandal was not the worst thing that could happen to a family, despite the dowager's convictions.

"I wouldn't, if I were you." he said softly. It was only then that Miranda noticed the pistol he held in his left hand. It was pointed directly at her. "At least, not if you wish your sister's life to be spared."

She had tensed for a scream, but released it when she realized that he was canny enough not to threaten her, but Juliet. "What do you mean?"

"If you and I don't follow quickly behind my dear cousin and your darling brother, then your sister's carriage will plunge off a cliff before dusk."

"They will kill you when we catch up to them." Silently, she wondered what would then happen to Juliet. Was there any way to keep Simon safe without sacrificing Juliet?

"Perhaps." He laughed, a squeaky-sounding hiss. She began to realize that his sanity was not all what it should be. "Or perhaps your husband will choose to strangle you when you tell him you are leaving him for a life of sin with me."

The evil of the man was unparalleled. "Run away with you?"

He gestured with the pistol. "We can better discuss this on the way, don't you agree?"

No, she thought silently. But she moved swiftly toward the stables anyway, her mind working furiously. She had just made love to her husband for the first time today. She had no intention of standing by helplessly while he died the same day.

Chapter Twenty Four

"How much of a head start do you think they have?" Valentine asked, when the horses had slowed to pass through a village.

Simon glanced up at the sun in the sky, impatience rippling through his muscles as he watched the wagons and pedestrians on the road ahead. "The groom said the carriage left a good hour before we took off. But a carriage is always slower. I hope to catch up with them very soon."

"I suppose you would know—having done this before quite recently."

Simon felt the potentially awkward moment slip away as he glanced in surprise at the younger man and saw his wry amusement at the situation. "Yes. But I was chasing too relatively sensible, if momentarily muddled people. Grimthorpe is a different matter altogether."

Valentine smiled grimly. "I now understand how you felt when you pursued me. If I had Juliet here with me, I don't know if I'd embrace her or berate her. What could he have said to convince her to elope with him?"

"Grimthorpe is no love-struck swain. Perhaps he told her some tale." He did not want to speculate on his darker fear—that the girl had been forced. It was entirely possible, but if her brother didn't think of it on his own, Simon had no intention of mentioning it aloud.

"Perhaps. Or perhaps Juliet told him some tale."

"Is she that like Miranda?" Simon smiled.

Valentine looked at him curiously. "That was said like a satisfied husband. May I be so forward as to ask if your health has taken a turn for the better?"

"Decidedly so." He laughed, thinking of the shocks he had suffered today. None of that mattered, though. He could leave both his father and mother behind him to start a new life with Miranda. "The rumors of my early demise are completely groundless, I am happy to say." Not to mention miraculous. But that was a secret for him and his wife to savor once they were well away from here.

"I am delighted to hear it."

Simon saw the shadow of hesitation that clouded Valentine's features. "Do you have some doubt about my ability as husband?"

Valentine looked at him in surprise, and then shook his head. "No, I am truly delighted for you and Miranda. But I have a favor to ask you and I am not certain of your reception."

"I will not help you elope."

"Of course not." Valentine's eyes shone with indignation.

"It had to be said." Simon offered the only apology he could and was relieved when Valentine nodded in acceptance.

"I suppose Miranda has been trying to convince you that is the proper way to mend things." He looked away, at a young carter with his arms around a woman who beamed at him like a new bride.

"You need to ask? Knowing your sister?" Simon turned his gaze away quickly, trying not to think of tonight, with Miranda. He could not allow himself to be distracted or he might find himself coming back to her as a corpse instead of a lover. He felt a flash of sympathy, understanding, at last, what Valentine had lost when he lost Emily. "I am sorry for the way things turned out. I hope that you find another like Emily."

Valentine sat up in his saddle. "Thank you, Your Grace. And I assure you that I will not attempt to see your cousin or influence her into a poor marriage with me. I have investigated her betrothed, and he is a good enough man."

Startled, Simon could not help a question, "You investigated him?"

He cleared his throat. "It is just that I could not bear to see her hurt by a brute. But this man seems decent enough."

"I understand." And he did, for hadn't he had a similar dilemma five years ago when, even knowing that he could not ask Miranda to marry him, he had not wanted her to become Grimthorpe's pawn?

Miranda clung to Grimthorpe's waist as if her life depended upon it. Probably because it did. The speed they traveled was for madmen and fools. Fitting, since he was a madman and she a fool. Unable to do anything else, she closed her eyes and prayed that Simon and Valentine would reach Juliet and Arthur soon enough to prevent the disaster that Grimthorpe had paid his men to ensure.

The irony was evil. Grimthorpe and his desperate willingness to commit murder to become duke, while Simon's honor prevented him from accepting the title because of an accident of birth.

The landscape blurred and her mind grew numb as her arms gripped her enemy fiercely. Try as she might, she found little hope that there would be a happy ending to this day. Grimthorpe was mad.

Only a madman would do what he had done. He had killed every man who stood between him and the dukedom—except Arthur. Now he meant to kill both Arthur and Simon. Juliet was simply a convenient means to an end, no matter to him that her young life would end before it had truly begun.

She shivered. Certainly he would not hesitate to add Valentine and Miranda to his murderous list.

She could see only one way to stop him. But he had given her no time to tell him about Peter.

He had gleefully explained his plans to her, allowing no words from her, as he held the gun to her ribs and walked her casually to where his horse stood saddled and ready—not a groom in sight. And then the ride had been too fast, too breathless.

She would have to take her chance when they stopped, as they must soon.

The story was so preposterous, though. Could she find the words to convey it quickly and convincingly?

As soon as they slowed enough that Miranda was certain they were stopping, she began to speak. "Simon is not the true duke. Peter, his older brother has been discovered in America."

He did not turn his head toward her, or make any indication that he heard her. Her mouth went suddenly dry.

She did not pause to swallow, or for breath, afraid that he would interrupt and her chance would be gone. "An enquiry agent brought him here." As the horse stopped at the top of a small rise, she pulled her arms from around his waist, surprised at the way they trembled from exhaustion and tension. She raised her voice, hoping to get through to him. "Stop this now. Killing Simon will not get you what you want. You will never be the Duke of Kerstone."

Her voice was high and shrill now, at the edge of control, but she sobbed out a breath and repeated herself. "Stop this now. You will not achieve what you—"

Her words broke off abruptly when Grimthorpe pulled at her trembling arm, toppling her from the horse to land solidly on the ground. She fought through the shock and pain, knowing that Simon's life depended on her.

For a moment she had no breath, but when she had gathered it again, she was not interested in speaking, only in scrambling to a stand so that she could see what had captured Grimthorpe's attention.

They stood at the rise of a small hill. There was a perfect view of the road from here. Simon and Valentine were toy figures on horseback, racing toward a toy carriage. The sun shone on the pretty picture, gilding Simon's golden hair, much as it had been when she'd waylaid him at the hunter's cottage.

Miranda ran forward, crying out for them. She tried to wave her arms to get their attention, but Grimthorpe had stopped too far away.

She turned back to her enemy, chilled to see the satisfied grin on his face. "I tell you, you will gain nothing from this. Tell your men to stop their murder, now."

"If you think I'd believe your pitiful story of a resurrected heir, you are mistaken. Peter is long dead and buried, and soon he will have company for tea," he snarled. Miranda turned back to the toy figures.

Simon and Valentine were gaining on the carriage, which had begun running full out, the horses eating up the roadway as the carriage bounced and jounced on the rutted surface at a speed that was much too fast.

At first she thought the carriage would shudder apart from the battering it was taking. As she surveyed the scene, however, her breath caught in a gasp. There was a sharp turn ahead and she realized in horror that the carriage would go over a small embankment if the horses did not change direction.

A small but fatal twenty-foot embankment.

Even as she watched, the horses drawing the carriage veered away from the edge of the embankment sharply, tipping the carriage over the side. It seemed to take hours for the carriage to unbalance, tip, and fall out of sight.

Miranda could not even find the breath to cry out her sister's name. Grimthorpe sighed contentedly when the traces separated and the horses hurried on, unhurt.

She could not tear her eyes away from the sight, as Simon and Valentine managed to stop their mounts and dismount to peer over the edge. With their attention on the fallen carriage, they did not notice the ruffians who were even now sneaking up on them.

Miranda strained forward, but could not see them well. Were they bigger and stronger than Simon and Valentine? She had no doubt they were well armed with weapons and cheerfully lacking in conscience. Unlike both her husband and her brother.

Unable to watch the carnage without acting any

longer, Miranda remembered what she had accomplished by slapping Simon's mount on the rear. Without thinking any further, she turned and advanced toward Grimthorpe.

He did not retreat. Instead, laughing softly, he said, "Give it up, my dear. They are dead men, now. You cannot help them."

Miranda let out an inarticulate cry as she lifted her hand and slapped his horse sharply.

A fierce satisfaction coursed through her when the horse responded by rearing and then, as Grimthorpe lost the reins and grabbed for the mane, the horse streaked toward the group of men confronting each other at the edge of the embankment

Miranda prayed for Simon or Valentine to see the runaway and realize that something was very wrong— besides the carriage that had held Arthur and Juliet having plunged over the embankment. She kept her mind from the thought of them, concentrating only on her husband and brother.

Let them see Grimthorpe.

Let them see the men who are intent on killing them.

Let them live.

Winded, Grimthorpe's horse ran for only a short distance, perhaps a quarter of the way toward the men. To Miranda's surprise, he uttered a hoarse cry and spurred the flagging horse on toward the men, instead of back toward her.

It was her chance to escape. Should she head toward the copse or toward Simon? She focused her gaze on the distant battle. Could she help them?

Chapter Twenty Five

As she scanned the distant tableau, her heart skipped a beat. There were only two men standing. The other two were dark lumps on the scuffed-up ground. For a moment she wasn't certain, and then she was. That shining blond head had to be Simon's.

He and Valentine had overpowered their attackers. And now they were standing, with pistols in hand, waiting for Grimthorpe. She sagged with relief, at the same time as a sunlight glinted from something in the mounted madman's hand. His pistol.

Before she could scream, uselessly or not, she saw Valentine's arm raise and buck. There was a sharp report. Grimthorpe fell from his still-running mount and lay still.

She bent over, burying her face in the cool grass and wept, for Juliet, for Arthur, for Simon and Valentine. For herself.

She could not stop when Simon reached her and took her into his arms. And he did not ask her to, holding her tight, rocking her against his chest as if she were a baby.

After a moment, she realized he was not just repeating soothing noises, but actual words. "Juliet's all right. Juliet's alive."

She broke away from his grip so that she could look into his eyes. "How could she be all right? I saw the carriage—"

He interrupted her with a kiss and a grim smile. "My cousin Arthur has more Watterly in him than I ever believed possible. He suspected something was wrong when the men who were to take him to see an interesting rare book seemed so disreputable."

"But what could they do?" Miranda thought of her wild ride with Grimthorpe. She had been unable to stop him. How had her sister and Arthur escaped a speeding carriage unharmed?

His lips tightened in suppressed amusement. "At the inn, when the carriage was forced to stop to change horses, they both recognized their chance to escape. As soon as the carriage started up, they jumped free without being observed by their abductors."

Miranda blanched. "They could have been killed." The absurdity of her statement struck her as soon as the words were uttered. They almost had been—all of them, by a cunning and devious madman who wanted the dukedom that was now Peter's. How ironic that both Peter and Simon would have gladly let it go.

She looked up then. The affection in Simon's eyes jolted her for a moment. And then she remembered that he had unbarricaded his heart. She laid her head against his heart, content to hear it beat, no longer afraid that the sound heralded coming death. "Where is Valentine?"

Simon looked down at her resting against him so trustingly and could not swallow for the sudden fearful realization that he had almost lost her just when he could claim her. He touched her cheek softly. "He has gone back to the inn, where we met up with Arthur, to notify the authorities about Grimthorpe. We should join them there." He turned her face to his so that he could reassure himself that she was alive and well. His fairy-tale bride.

Her tone was scolding, but her eyes brimmed with tears. "And so you and Valentine were prepared for a trap, then? I needn't have worried at all watching those two huge bullies trying to trounce you and toss you over after the carriage?"

"Of course not. You had nothing to fear. And you never will again. You're married to me." He kept his reply bland, but his arms tightened around her and he lowered his lips to hers for a long kiss.

He did not break apart from her until she began to shudder in his arms. No matter that she was enjoying the kiss, she had still been kidnapped and watched a runaway carriage dash off a cliff, believing her sister to be inside. He wrapped his cloak around her and drew her to her feet. "Let's get you to the inn and cleaned up."

She laughed, a trifle breathlessly he was pleased to note, as she looked down at her torn and dirty gown. "And you, as well."

His eyes lit with warmth. "A bath for two. I think that can be arranged."

With a sigh, he watched as Miranda surrendered to the feelings that were quickly replacing the grief, fear, and despair of minutes ago. She wrapped her arms around his neck and pressed her lips against his eyes, his cheek, his ear, his mouth. Soft, warm kisses of love and hope and desire.

As if murder and treachery and danger were an aphrodisiac, he realized that she had no wish to wait for their room at the inn to reaffirm their love and the simple joyous fact that they lived.

She did not even seem to realize that she was sobbing despite the smile that lit her face between kisses, until his lips caressed her cheeks and his tongue tasted her tears. He had been given a gift this morning, which he had refused. That she offered him this chance again was a blessing he did not have any intention of refusing.

He felt the crushing need and translated it into a lingering exploration of her body. The torture was no less than it had been when he found her in his bed and had had to drive her away. This time, however, there would be no worry about a child to keep him from completing their joining.

For all he cared, they could have a hundred, a thousand. He was no longer duke. He was only a man who wanted his wife. He lay her back, spreading his cloak on the grass and allowed his lips to play with her ear before moving to her mouth to swallow her sigh. She turned her head and met his lips with her own, impatiently. They kissed—not briefly, but possessively. Forever.

Miranda caught fire within as she undid the fastening of his shirt and rubbed her sensitized palms against his firmly muscled ribs. She surrendered thought, listening only to the demands of her body and the soft sounds of pleasure—hers or Simon's she could not tell and did not care.

His hands had found their way under her skirts, as if he sought to assure himself that she was whole and real, not a fairy ghost, by touching her, reaching for the heart of her passion and helping it to burst through the pain and sorrow that had held them apart for so very long.

Still sensitive from their encounter in the morning, Miranda was shocked at the wanton way her body burned for him. When he pressed into her, she welcomed him, waiting for the pain and finding only pleasure that washed away any last doubt that she and Simon were made for each other as perfectly as any couple in her fairy tales.

When he groaned against her skin and drove deeper, she wrapped her arms and legs around him, helping him closer, where he belonged, until there was no more two, only a long shuddering cry sounding the triumphant music of one shared soul.

"So he has killed before? And to think I flirted with him." For once, Miranda was pleased to see, Juliet was subdued. She had not bounced over to greet them when they entered the inn—although that could have been because of the state of their clothing or Simon's obviously besotted possessiveness as he ordered blankets and hot cider for his wife.

But the likelihood was more that her younger sister had finally realized how dangerous a man she had tangled with. Why, Miranda realized with a smile, she wasn't even flirting with Arthur. And flirting had come second nature to Juliet since she'd been a child. Instead, she sat pale and quiet, a blanket thrown over her shoulders and a warm cup of tea cupped in her hands. When she caught sight of Miranda examining her, she said softly, "I thought you were dead."

Miranda swallowed down her own sudden tears. "I

thought you had gone over in the carriage. Thank goodness the two of you were so quick-witted."

Arthur seemed somehow sturdier, and Miranda marveled at the transformation that a bit of confidence had made in the shy scholar. She was glad that her worried questions had alerted him to the danger. If not, from the ruins of the carriage, she did not doubt that she would have lost her sister today.

Simon, his arm tight around her waist, gave a quiet laugh. "I expect the quick-wittedness of all the Fensters helped us win the day against that monster. You are indeed a formidable family. Grimthorpe was a fool not to have learned his lesson five years ago."

Miranda blushed at the reminder of the black eye she had given the cad.

"Thank God my shot hit him in the heart." Valentine flashed her a quick reassuring smile; but then his expression turned grim. "He tried to destroy my sisters enough for one lifetime. I don't regret killing that wretch and I'll gladly hang if necessary."

Simon's hand tightened to prevent Miranda from leaping to her feet before he could quell her sudden panic by saying, "It is not. I spoke to the magistrate when he came to examine the madman's body. He is a sensible man and agrees that you acted as you had to in order to save our lives and those of your sisters. There will be no further inquiry. We are free to go."

Juliet stood. "Yes." Her eyes scanned the occupants of the inn. "I must get back to the house party and make sure that Hero is coping."

Miranda could not help smiling when she met Valentine's eyes. Their sister was returning to normal—she worried that Hero might be even now stealing her beaux.

When she would have followed the group as they

left the inn, Simon stopped her. "Valentine," he called. "Your sister and I have never had a proper wedding trip. I think we shall spend a few nights in this inn. Tell the new duke and my mother to manage without us."

Miranda's mouth fell open. "Have you told Valentine?"

"Everything." He seemed unperturbed, and even a bit surprised at her astonishment. "Don't you trust your own brother?"

"Well, yes. But I cannot believe you do, so suddenly."

"I have learned a great deal about your brother since you came back into my life, Miranda. I am certain that he can be trusted with our family secrets."

Valentine met her eyes and nodded. "I'm glad that you have your happy ending, Miranda. You both deserve it." He smiled crookedly at her. "And enjoy your privacy." His look was skeptical as he glanced around the sturdy old inn. "What little you'll have of it."

He turned to leave, and then turned back, addressing Simon directly. "I'll make certain that Juliet and Arthur arrive home safely. You take care of my sister."

She looked after the others, torn for a moment. "Perhaps we should go along, there are so many things to clear up."

He tipped her head up until she was looking directly into his eyes. "So far today I have taken you by the side of a pond and in a grassy field. I think it is only fair that the next time I give you the luxury of a bed." His eyes twinkled. "And it is a long ride home."

She looked up at her husband, who was as much the worse for wear as she was, and said with a thoughtful frown, "Do you think we can persuade the innkeeper to find a bath big enough for the both of us?"

His grin began slowly and then spread across his face. "I shall pay whatever he asks to ensure it."

Chapter Twenty Six

Peter asked for a month to accustom himself to his former home, to allow his daughters to adjust to the changed situation. Simon granted it. It did not please him, but he understood.

Just as he understood when his mother requested he not tell Peter that he knew he was his father. "He turned away from this life because of his shame, Simon. Don't add to it by making him face it every day when he sees the knowledge in your eyes. It will be hard enough for him as it is."

He had wanted to refuse her request. Miranda had persuaded him to abide by it instead. When he agreed, he had every expectation that the secret would make the month pass slowly and painfully. But he had not counted on coming to like the man who had cuckolded his own father and then faked death to avoid living with the results of his own perfidy.

Perhaps he had been a fool to trust such a man. He

hoped not. For today was the day that they officially disinterred him from the dead.

He hoped his troubles were over. He had dismissed Miranda's worries about Peter; if the man's decision made him miserable, it was only just. He had made so many others miserable for so long. Simon had felt free to make love to his wife with abandon at night even as he tutored his father in his duties as duke in the day. He was determined not to regret this idyll. And to that end, he was willing to do almost anything. Including forcing Peter to resume his responsibilities. And his title.

With a bold stroke he signed the necessary papers and gave them to the waiting servant. "Deliver these at once."

"Yes, Your Grace." The man nodded.

Not the proper title for much longer, Simon reflected. "You may tell my brother that I am ready to speak to him."

"Very good, Your Grace." The door closed quietly, opening again almost instantly.

"I have begun the paperwork. The agreed-upon month is over. Welcome home, Your Grace." Simon used the term determinedly as he stood away from the desk he had sat behind for five years.

He took the leather pouch from his pocket and removed the sealed envelope meant for the true Duke of Kerstone. He tossed the envelope, unbroken seal up, atop a pile of papers that would require the new duke's attention. He commanded, "Sit." Peter would not escape the truth of his destiny. He would not allow it.

The older man—his father, Simon acknowledged painfully as he looked into eyes the same color as his own—met his gaze steadily. "I don't believe you have considered all the ramifications of my becoming duke, Simon."

"Of course I have. A matter of a few formalities. I have just sent the papers on this minute. No doubt we must wait a few weeks, but Parliament will not refuse to recognize you. You are Peter Watterly, Duke of Kerstone."

"I am. I am also the father of three daughters. No sons." There was a flicker of shame in Peter's eyes for a moment. Simon was sure he saw it, even as the chill of his mother's long-kept secret coursed through him. "You, as my brother will be my heir."

Simon was prepared. "Then you must marry and father a son."

"I cannot."

He looked at Peter in surprise. "You are still a young man. You can marry and father enough sons to fill this house."

A sad smile lit Peter's face. "Indeed. But I will never marry again." He seemed to regret it, but there was no doubt he felt he would never change his mind.

Simon refused to accept that. "My mother has explained to you that I am a bastard. I thought you understood." He shook his head. "If you can't bring yourself to remarry, then I suggest you keep Arthur nearby."

"Simon—"

Simon interrupted. "I will leave you to the business of Kerstone, Your Grace. He tapped the envelope that had weighed down his life for so long. "I believe this deserves your attention." He continued, with his hand on the doorknob, "It has been waiting five years to be opened by the true heir to Sinclair Watterly and the new Duke of Kerstone."

As he fled the room, and the sad misery of the man

who had fathered him, he said quietly, "I will see you tonight, at the celebration of your rebirth."

Katherine offered the only advice she could, little that it might be. "You must take care of yourself, rest, eat well, and take the air frequently. At your age such things are dangerous."

The dowager sighed. "I shall have to leave, of course. I never should have stayed."

Of course not, Miranda agreed in silent yet sympathetic mockery. *You should have turned your back on the only man you ever loved simply because his father had the bad judgment to marry you.* "Where will you go?"

"Italy, I think. At least for . . . a time."

Seven months. Miranda understood all too well, although the thought of a forty-four-year-old woman with a grown son becoming a mother again was somewhat shocking. And thanks to the laws of consanguinity, this child, too, would be a bastard. It just wasn't fair that she and Simon should be so happy while Peter and Cassandra should be pulled apart.

But the dowager had made it very clear that this confidence was to go no further then the three women in this room. Even Peter had not been told. Miranda understood why, but she could not believe it for the best. "There must be some way—"

Katherine raised her eyebrows in unvoiced warning. "She must remain calm and careful in order to deliver herself safely of a healthy child. Italy will provide her a sunny confinement."

"But to be separated from Peter is not—" There was not a way to describe the distress of such heartbreak.

"A happy ending?" The dowager smiled. She had been pale and wan, tired and listless for weeks. Now they all knew why. "I will have Peter's child and a second chance to be a good mother. That is enough for me."

"You will not isolate yourself from your family," Miranda protested. "You must come to America with us. We can say that you are a widow. We do not have to say for how long."

The dowager raised one eyebrow and smiled. "I do not believe my son would think that wise."

"Simon will not be angry. You know how much he loves children."

The dowager glanced toward the door, ready to answer, and her skin drained of blood. "Simon."

Miranda watched, her heart in her throat as he came into the room. He glanced at her and smiled. She could see no anger in him, although he was wary. "What is it about the children I love that will not make me angry."

Miranda answered nervously, "Oh nothing. I was speaking hypothetically about children in our American home."

His eyes locked on hers with concern. "Are you pregnant?"

"No!" The denial came too quickly. Miranda realized that she would have been better to say she was not sure.

He glanced quickly at Katherine, who sat next to the dowager, holding her wrist in one hand. "You?"

Miranda was shocked. "Of course she is not, Simon." She chided him. "She is a vicar's widow."

He bowed slightly to Katherine. "I apologize." He smiled coldly at his mother. "At least breeding is a condition I cannot accuse you of, Mother."

The room grew silent as the dowager blushed pinkly. "What an imagination you have," she managed at last, her voice faint.

"No." Simon's voice was harsh as he sank to the seat beside Miranda. She reached for his hand, but he pulled it away. "I did not know such things were possible."

The dowager rejoined, "Nor did I."

He smiled grimly at his wife. "I suppose you mean to find her a happy ending? Well, I will not have it. Peter is duke. My mother cannot legally marry her own stepson." He glanced at his mother then. "I thought you hated scandal, Mother, and would do anything to avoid it." His voice was scornful.

The color drained from her face. "I will have this child without disgracing you, never fear."

"Simon, I must speak with you." Peter stepped into the room and Miranda felt Simon tense like a caged lion beside her.

"You are too late. I have already heard the news."

Peter stared at him in puzzlement. "How could you? I just found it out myself. I think it will change everything."

"It changes nothing." The intensity and anger in Simon's voice finally caught Peter's attention. He took a careful look at the shocked faces in the room. "What is it? What has happened?"

"How dare you and she bring another bastard into this world?"

Peter glanced at the dowager in confusion, his gaze hardening as he realized the import of Simon's words. "Is this true, Cassandra?"

"Yes, Peter. I'm afraid so." Cassandra. Miranda marvelled at the name of the austere dowager. It was a beautiful name, full of magic and mischief. So unlike the Dowager Duchess of Kerstone. But perhaps like the young woman who had captured and held Peter's heart through a thirty-year absence.

"*Another* bastard?" The shock on Peter's face

flashed into anger. "You told him I was his father? Are you mad?"

His words were harsh, but the dowager did not flinch. "I did not know he was at the door of the room, Peter, or I would not have spoken so freely to Sinclair. Some mistakes cannot be erased." Miranda's heart squeezed with pain as she watched the two tearing open the wounds of the past.

The dowager continued her explanation, her voice husky with emotion. "You said you would not come back and rescue him. I thought that knowing he was true-blooded might change his mind." It was when Peter softened and put his arms around the dowager's stiff frame, that Miranda thought of a tale of hope.

For all the two took notice of the others, they could have been alone. Peter sighed softly against the dowager's elegantly coiffed head resting full on his shoulder. "What a fine mess we have made, haven't we?" Miranda thought of Rapunzel, letting her hair down, and the prince taking hold, and climbing up to free her from her prison.

She looked at Simon, watching his parents, recognizing what she had already known. They loved each other as much as she and Simon. And their love was breaking their hearts. Gently, she tugged on his hand, pulling him from the room.

Miranda was gazing at him, her eyes full of sorrow. He knew some of her sorrow was for him when she asked softly, "What shall you do if Peter is not willing to be duke now?"

Her words struck fear in his heart. He could not allow it. "He understands his obligations."

"His obligation to his father? The man who embroiled him in this untenable situation."

"To his blood."

"And what about his obligation to your mother?

He cannot marry her unless he returns to America as Peter Watson."

"He has none. I will take care of her and her bastard. She is my mother."

"And what about her? Is she to have no say?"

He did not want to consider his mother. Wed to an older man, bedded by a young one. Falling in love with her husband's son. "Nothing can be done now." He stayed her lips with a gentle kiss. "Not even one of your fairy tales can save them. In the eyes of the law she is his mother—she married his father. They cannot ever marry."

"In England, yes." Miranda closed her eyes. "I wonder how she will bear it."

"She always manages."

"Simon—"

"No more fairy-tale endings, Miranda. They cannot have a happy ending together. They cannot marry."

"I owe your mother, and I owe you, so I'll stay." His father had been drinking. His American habits were more pronounced when he was foxed, Simon found. "Your mother is a stubborn woman."

Simon felt only relief as he glanced at Miranda and wondered if he should ask her to leave them alone. "I believe I know that well."

Peter watched him from his position slumped in a chair by the fire. "We've got a problem, Simon."

Simon tighted his arm around Miranda's waist and drew her closer. She smiled at him, but her expression was troubled. "I have none, Your Grace. You solved them all for me."

"Wrong." Simon found himself slightly uncomfortable with this new, hardheaded Peter. "You're still my little brother to the world. I don't plan to marry again, or outlive you. Not by a long shot. So you've got some time to sort yourself out and take your responsibilities like a man. I don't like it. But like I said, I owe you. And I owe your mother."

"Take her as a lover, then. She has had her share."

Miranda shot Simon a look filled with disappointment, and he warmed with shame. Why he said it he could not explain, even to himself.

Peter sat up, incensed. "Your bitterness is out of place, Simon. Your mother was blameless. Sinclair, our father, and I were the fools."

"Your father, not mine."

The older man met his gaze steadily. "I wanted to explain to you why you are truly Sinclair's son, and not my own, when I came in and got the news I was going to be a daddy again." He sighed. "But it's time for you to face the fact that you are a true heir as no future son of mine could ever be."

"I do not need to accept a lie as fact."

Peter lurched over to the desk and shuffled through the papers on the desk and tossed something to Simon. "Read this."

It was the envelope, seal broken. The one meant only for the eyes of the duke. "This is not for me to read. He told me you did not understand the Kerstone motto. I presume that is why he was so careful to drum it into my head."

"Honor and truth in all." Peter's lips twisted with distaste. "It is as much a part of me as the Watterly blood."

"It could not be."

"Read it. Until then, you do not know enough to judge."

"Who are you to tell me this?"

"His son." Peter looked away, his hands massaging wearily at his neck as he gazed out the windows and onto the lawn where Kate, Betsy, and Jeanne, Peter's youngest daughter, were playing blindman's bluff with the older girls. "His other son."

"No son would have done what you did. I don't want you to think I hold my mother blameless, but—"

Peter's eyes blazed with anger. "Your mother was completely innocent in this. She was the victim of a controlling old man and a young man with much too much self-conceit."

"I cannot excuse her for what she did, and you should not either."

Miranda intervened at last, with a gentle pull on his arm. "Look out there, Simon." She pointed to the window. "Look at those girls, laughing, playing games as children should."

Simon looked, reluctantly, just in time to see Juliet captured by a blindfolded Jeanne.

"Your mother was younger than Juliet when she married."

Simon had known her age—fifteen—at her marriage, but he had not stopped to imagine her as a girl, like Juliet. It was impossible even to imagine. "I doubt she ever stopped to play a game. She was never as young as those girls out there."

Peter's hushed tone disputed that contention. "Oh, yes, she was. So very young and so very serious about her new role as duchess. She had no idea what my father wanted of her. I doubt he knew, at that point, either. He had not thought beyond a child, to the years of marriage ahead."

"Why did he not have you marry her, then?"

"Control, Simon. Control. I was entering a dangerous profession, and he did not want to risk having to fight my widow for control of the fate of any child of mine."

That certainly meshed with what Simon knew of

Sinclair Watterly. He disliked defiance and used every weapon necessary to demolish it at the first sign.

Simon took the wrinkled, water-stained envelope that had remained sealed since he received it. Now broken, the Watterly seal sat above a strong bold hand declaring, *Honor and Truth in All.*

Another fairy tale, he thought bitterly. There were three pages enclosed, in three separate hands: Sinclair's, the Eighth Duke; Mortimer's, the Fifth Duke, and Geoffrey's, the Third Duke. Three generations. He read, Miranda's body warm next to his, lending him strength to face this last hurdle.

After a long silence he looked up to see Peter staring into the fire. He knew Sinclair's sin, and now he knew the reason for it. An unbroken line from father to son. It was a lie. Mortimer had been injured in a hunting accident, unable to father children, and had taken his dying sister's bastard to raise as his own son. Geoffrey had been afflicted with syphilis and had conspired with his younger brother to impregnate his unknowing wife.

"Do you expect me to be comforted by the fact that we both spring from a line of men who do not know the meaning of honor?"

"They made sure the blood was true, and that was what they honored most."

"I cannot be like them. I will not."

"I understand. I tried—and failed."

Looking into the pain-shrouded gaze of his father, Simon suddenly felt understanding flood through his heart. He knew why Peter had never come back. It had not been cowardice but honor. The same twisted Watterly honor that held him here against his will.

He stood watching his father. The man was willing to give up the woman he loved, the child he wanted.

For what? Not for the same reason the men in the letters had. Only to restore Simon's own sense of honor.

Peter rubbed a weary hand across his sun-weathered skin. "You're going to have to succeed me, Simon. I'm sorry. I hope you can reconcile it in the years to come. But I don't see any other way. We're both the true heirs to their tradition."

"No." Simon stood and went close to the fire. "We're not their heirs." He tossed the generations-old papers into the fire and watched them burn.

In the flare of light, his eyes met Peter's. "We're beginning a new tradition."

Peter eyed him warily, as if he was afraid to dare believe that Simon meant what he said. "And what tradition is that?"

Simon crossed to where Miranda still sat, watching him with hopeful eyes. "The tradition of the happy ending."

Peter allowed a small smile to soften the rough-hewn planes of his face. A thread of doubt crossed the older man's features. "Are you sure you can live with this? Because once I marry that woman and take her away, I'm never coming back."

"Honor and Truth in all. Our family thought to circumvent that motto to keep the bloodlines passing from father to son. We won't pass on that legacy. Instead, we'll begin a new generation who'll learn what's most important in life."

Miranda rose to face him and asked softly, "What's that?"

"A happy ending, of course—and no more lies."

"Except that Peter Watterly is dead." Peter's eyes darkened.

"Is that a lie?" Simon could not break his gaze from his wife's dawning joy.

He shook his head slowly. "No. Peter Watterly died a long time ago."

Simon looked away from Miranda's joyful gaze for a moment. "Yes, he is. And Peter Watson has a woman who loves him. I'd have to be a fool to stand in the way of his happy ending." He held his wife close. "Or my own."

Miranda whispered to him, softly. "To new traditions, and happy ever afters."

He replied in her ear, "To sons or daughters as they may come—no more will the Duke of Kerstone put a cuckoo in his nest to satisfy pride. Honor will out, now and forevermore."

"Not love?" she teased.

He held her against him, tightly, and yet without binding her so that she could not breathe. "Of course. How else can one have a happy ever after, if not with love?"

If you liked THE FAIRY TALE BRIDE, *be sure to look for Kelly McClymer's next release in the Once Upon A Wedding series,* THE STAR-CROSSED BRIDE, *available in March 2001 wherever books are sold.*

After an elopement with an earl's well-dowered daughter ends in disaster, Valentine, the only Fenster brother, decides love must wait. But his intended bride has no intention of letting her father marry her off to a nefarious marquis when Valentine has already captured her heart . . .

COMING IN NOVEMBER FROM
ZEBRA BALLAD ROMANCES

_EMILY'S WISH, Wishing Well #2
by Joy Reed   0-8217-6713-5 $5.50US/$7.50CAN

Intent upon escaping her troubled past, Miss Emily Pearce flees into the night, only to come upon Honeywell House. Rescued from uncertainty by celebrated author, Sir Terrence O'Reilly, Emily becomes the heroine of the greatest love story of all—their own.

_A KNIGHT'S PASSION, The Kinsmen #2
by Candice Kohl   0-8217-6714-3 $5.50US/$7.50CAN

Ordered by the King to wed two cousins from the borderlands of Wales, Raven and Peter met their match in Lady Pamela and Roxanne. Thrown into marriage by royal decree, the brothers soon find that what began as punishment can end in love.

_ADDIE AND THE LAIRD, Bogus Brides
by Linda Lea Castle   0-8217-6715-1 $5.50US/$7.50CAN

Seeking a fresh start in a virgin territory the Green sisters leave for the charter town of MacTavish. There is only one thing that stands between the sisters and a new life ... they have one month to wed if they are to remain in MacTavish. Will the necessity to leave lead to the discovery of love?

_ROSE, The Acadians #2
by Cherie Claire   0-8217-6716-X $5.50US/$7.50CAN

Warm, vibrant, and exceedingly lovely, Rose Gallant vowed to keep alive her family's dream of finding her long-lost father, but her heart dreams of finding true love. Amid the untamed forests and moss-strewn swamps of Louisiana Territory, Rose discovers the fulfillment of love.

Call toll free **1-888-345-BOOK** to order by phone or use this coupon to order by mail. ALL BOOKS AVAILABLE NOVEMBER 1, 2000.

Name _____

Address _____

City _____ State _____ Zip _____

Please send me the books I have checked above.

I am enclosing	$ _____
Plus postage and handling*	$ _____
Sales tax (in NY and TN)	$ _____
Total amount enclosed	$ _____

*Add $2.50 for the first book and $.50 for each additional book.

Send check or money order (no cash or CODS) to:

Kensington Publishing Corp., Dept. C.O., 850 Third Avenue, New York, NY 10022

Prices and numbers subject to change without notice. Valid only in the U.S. All orders subject to availablity. **NO ADVANCE ORDERS.**

Visit our website at **www.kensingtonbooks.com.**